ON THE BENCH

On the Bench

Elysia Nates

This book was written while I was pleading with my daughter to start her homework. While my dog repeatedly dropped his cactus on my foot for me to throw. While the washing piled up. Long after I had finished work for the day, or long before I had to start. While the house was asleep, in lunch breaks, in car rides.
This book was written around the life that I am so lucky to call mine.

Dedicated to my mum and dad; forever the biggest influence on who I am and who I aspire to be.
And to my sisters, Renee and Amanda, forever my best friends.
To Paul and Stanley, the boys of the family.
And to my daughter, Ruby. Being your mum is my most favourite thing ever. You make every day feel like a Saturday. Thank you for cheering for my books as loud as I cheer for your basketball.
And to a special person who saw me when I didn't feel worthy of being seen.

You can waste your life waiting for the wrong people to believe in you
or you can listen to the ones who think you are amazing.
Make your dreams come true. Publish the book yourself.

Sadie

His pungent breath warmly coats the side of my face. He hovers too close for comfort. I scrunch up my nose at the smell of beer polluting the already stuffy kitchen. You'd think I'd be used to it by now, but the scent of alcohol just makes me feel sick.

He wants to fight. A few tears fall without my consent or control.

"Tears don't work on me!" he slurs in his standard drunken stupor.

Stupid idiot, why are you crying in front of him? I steady my hands as I pick up my plate, desperate to retreat back to the safety of my room with my vegemite sandwiches.

"Sorry, I'll get out of your way," I utter into my chest.

He deliberately knocks into me, visibly enjoying the sight of me struggling not to drop my plate.

"You think you're better than me?"

"No." I don't say any more. He is angry and the sheer sound of my voice will only provoke him.

The smell of booze lingers in the air between us. The kitchen blinds sway from the breeze of the open window, forcing me to breathe in the stench of stale alcohol that permanently clings to his greying beard. I stand stiff next to the cupboard and pray that he is boring of this encounter so he'll go back to his room and stare at the wall. Or whatever else it is that he does in there.

"Pathetic, just like she was," he spits.

He sways over to the fridge and pulls out a six pack of beer. I cautiously lift my eyes in anticipation of the welcome sight of his rounded back returning to his room at the end of the perpetually dark hallway. The bottles clink as he stumbles down; a sound that instantly triggers an inherent feeling of unease.

His door slams shut and I bolt to the safety of my own room. The knot in the pit of my stomach slowly unravels.

"Asshole," I whisper warily, "why can't you just disappear already?"

It's boiling in here. Adelaide must be going for a record for the hottest summer ever. I can taste the sweat painting the top of my lips. It's 7 pm but it feels like it's the middle of the afternoon. It was 42 degrees today and the house is struggling to cool down but I dare not turn the fan on. I cost him too much as it is. He reminds me every day.

My bedroom is hotter than the rest of the house, but not by much. I strip my damp socks off and chuck them in my laundry basket, pull the blankets off the bed and sit with my top sheet loosely draped over my knees.

I take out my pen from my faded Looney Tunes pencil case and open my book back to the page I was on: complex fractions. I'm finding Year 12 maths pretty hard so far and the year has only just begun. Mrs Carrington is a good teacher though. I don't hate her. It's not her fault I'm stupid.

I smash out my homework in the silence and safety of my room. My little sanctuary. I admire the work on the pages before me, running my fingertips over the blotchy blue ink. It's a shame all the answers are probably wrong.

7.45pm. Thursday night.

I don't have a telly in my room and I've read my library books for the week. I'm paranoid about making even the slightest noise, so I can't turn on the radio, which means that I'm missing Ugly Phil's Hot 30. I have mastered being invisible when we are both home at the same time but when he's in this mood, being invisible is not enough. I need to not exist. It's safer if he forgets that I'm still *here*.

Solace comes as I delve into the TV Hits magazine resting on my bedside cupboard. I've already read it but I don't mind a second flip-through whilst I eat my vegemite sandwiches. I turn the pages in slow motion, conscious of drawing attention to the fact that I am still alive behind closed doors. Jonathan Brandis is on the cover yet again. I pry up the staples on the middle page and pull out the Silverchair poster, being careful not to rip it on the open staple. I'll get some Blu Tack from school tomorrow so I can add it to the collage of posters on my wardrobe.

He doesn't normally venture out of his room like to-night but he was itching for confrontation. I suspect he's put out by his pay going in a day late because of the Australia Day public holiday last week, which meant he couldn't go straight to the pub after work today.

He never comes in my room but the day is bound to come when I finally push him over the edge and he puts a bullet in my head.

I have basketball training tomorrow after school. The hour's practice means that my Friday nights don't drag as much as the weeknights do. It means that I don't get into bed at 8pm and stare at the ceiling until boredom finally forces me to close my eyes just for something to do.

It also means that he will be at the pub.

He normally staggers through the back door just before midnight on Fridays, long after I am safe in my own room. Like I said, he never comes in here.

The school holidays felt like they went on for years and I was lost without basketball. I reach under my bed and pull out a shoe box from the back corner. I don't have many photos from when I was younger but I cherish the few that I do have. Rummaging through the shoe box, I find my favourite and hold it tightly in both hands. I'm in my basketball uniform, ready for my first game. Mum is squeezing me tightly, visibly overwhelmed with emotion. Mum played basketball back when she was at school and she was so excited when I wanted to play, too.

I can still smell his breath, as if it has attached itself to the tiny hairs in my nostril. I return the photo to the box, delicately placing it on top of a 1989 clipping from The Advertiser: Christmas Day Tragedy, Fatal Car Accident.

Saturday is my favourite day because it's game day. I am out in the morning at basketball and he is still sleeping off his hangover when I leave. When I get home in the afternoon, he is gone and doesn't come home until after 11pm. Fridays and Saturdays give me the break I need to prepare myself for Sunday, when he is home all day and so am I. He doesn't like that part.

I pull the bed sheet up to my chin and roll onto my side. I hate myself for crying in front of him. The last time I cried in front of him, I was nearly 13. It was my first day of High School and I wanted Mum. *For fuck's sake, it's been 4 years, stop trying to make everyone feel sorry for you.*

I don't know why I let him get to me more than usual today. Why I couldn't hide it. I will never make that mistake again. There is nothing more humiliating than crying in front of the one who enjoys breaking you.

I fall asleep dreaming about the day he comes home to find I am gone. Or more favourably, when I come home to find him gone.

It's Friday tomorrow.

First basketball training for the year.

She's always with me at basketball.

Sloopy

"Don't forget your cheese sticks, darling! I left them in the fridge for you!" Mum calls out just as I am about to leave the house.

My hand is already grasping the door handle. I sigh as I release my grip and rush back through the lounge room to the kitchen, vigorously rubbing the nail of my thumb five times on each hand before I reach the fridge to retrieve the cheese sticks.

Mum sits at the kitchen table, sipping her morning coffee. The house already smells like Windex and her hair and make-up are immaculate. She's got one of her favourite summer dresses on; long and flowy with pink and purple flowers all over it. I never see her in her PJs or trackies, even though she stays home all day on her own. She is always dressed like she is presenting herself, like she's *expected* to be ready just in case someone happens to come over. She has to look her best.

"First practice tonight, darling?"

I stuff the cheese sticks through the partially opened zip of my school bag. "Yeah, and then Josh and Adam are coming back here, if that's okay?"

"Of course, I'll order pizza for you."

"Thanks, Mum." I bend down to kiss the top of her head. Her hair always smells like perfume. "You're the best."

Mum smiles into her cup as if she is waiting for the compliment to disappear.

I hesitate before asking, "Will Dad be home tonight?"

Mum takes a long sip of her coffee. "Not tonight. He has to do an extra rehearsal for Sunday's sermon, or something like that."

She smooths her hands over her hair, as if suddenly aware that maybe it's not as neat as it could be.

I nod, selfishly relieved but simultaneously disappointed for Mum. "Make sure you order enough pizza for you, too. You can pig out with us."

Mum gently holds onto my arm. "Love you, my Sloopy. I'd be lost without you."

"Love you too, Mum. See you tonight."

I sling my backpack over my shoulder and flick on the kitchen radio for Mum before I go. She snaps alive and starts singing along, suddenly content to sort through her new batch of Avon orders.

My bag is heavy but I leave it resting on one shoulder only. Kids who loop their backpacks through both arms get picked on.

The cheese sticks have made me a couple of minutes late. I run down the street and turn the corner, hoping to see everyone still waiting at the bus stop. Of course, just as my luck would ensure, the bus is already pulling away.

I run along the footpath, pleading with the driver to stop as I level up with the closing door.

"Guess you didn't say your prayers this morning!" he chuckles in animation, accelerating away.

An elderly passenger stares at me out the window, visibly judgemental. She must think my generation are all worthless layabouts who can't even get to the bus stop on time.

I stop running and resign myself to the fact that I am going to be late for school again, now that I have to walk. I wonder if I look as pathetic as I feel. I don't even like cheese sticks.

I finally make it to school, sweating and panting, twenty-three minutes tardy. I head into the office to fill out a late slip, my fourth one already this term thanks to that jerk bus driver, and it's only the second week of school.

I apologise to Mrs Barry behind the desk and tell her she looks nice today.

She smiles knowingly. "Don't worry, Noah; I won't tell your dad."

She reaches across the counter, takes my late slip from my hand, rips it up and chucks it into the bin next to her.

"Thank you, Mrs Barry," I say with relief and gratitude.

I hastily walk across the courtyard to my Homeroom, frantically checking my white shirt for pit stains along the way. My body odour is noticeable now. Thanks, bus driver. I slip past Mrs Carrington as she stands in front of the class passionately talking about complex fractions.

I sit in the back row, behind the quiet girl who always wears her hair in a low ponytail with various Looney Tunes scrunchies. Not sure why a sixteen-year-old girl would be into Bugs Bunny but it's impressive to me that she isn't afraid to have her own style. I'm fascinated by the notion that someone our age can already be so adamant about who they are when everyone else is trying so hard to look the same and fit in. My mum still makes me eat cheese sticks so I get enough calcium.

Back when I was at private school, we had to wear a uniform and even our backpacks were embroidered with the school's coat of arms. But there isn't really one here, more just like a uniform code. The boys have to wear grey, navy or black shorts or trousers and a white, collared top or button-up shirt. The girls can choose between a white polo top and dark culottes or a blue chequered dress. Most of the girls seem to wear the dress. At my old school, everyone looked exactly the same. I'm not sure if I preferred that or not. You weren't really expected to be an individual.

"Alright everyone! Let me see those homework books!"

We rummage through our desks and pull out our homework books. Mrs Carrington walks around collecting them. I place mine down at the top, adjusting it so it sits perfectly in the corner of the desk. It looks slightly crooked so I fiddle with it again but Mrs Carrington reaches out to grab it before I can adjust it four more times. I tug at my index finger five times to make it right in my head.

"Noah Blean." She rests my homework book on her forearm atop the pile she has already collected. She flips it open and smiles warmly at me. "Meticulously neat as always."

I return her smile before she steps towards the girl in front. She picks up Sadie's book and waits, I guess looking for recognition. Sadie doesn't lift her head or even acknowledge that Mrs Carrington is standing right next to her, now glancing over her homework questions. My mate Josh catches my attention from across the room. He makes some crude gesture with his hand and his mouth and I quickly look away.

"Meet me here at recess, Sadie." Mrs Carrington tries to sound more stern than usual.

Last Sunday, Dad instructed us to pray for anyone who we thought needed a secret prayer. I didn't tell God her name, but I prayed for her. I prayed for the girl with the low ponytail and the tattered Bugs Bunny scrunchie.

The bell sounds for recess soon enough. I put my maths book away and meet Josh and Adam at the front of the classroom.

"Late again, Sloopy," Josh pesters me. "Did your dad need a hand to carry his bible to work?"

"You're hilarious."

We head out of the classroom and I look back at Sadie. She still has her eyes firmly fixated on her desk. Mrs Carrington is heading towards her but the boys and I are already on our way out the door.

Sadie

Mrs Carrington taps her perfectly manicured fingernail on the chaotic scribbles in my homework book.

"Look here, you were so close! All the steps were right, you were heading for the correct answer! And then it's like you just made something up at the end. Like you just gave up on it."

I mentally tally up the pen marks etched on the top of the timber desk. Mrs Carrington sighs. She's annoyed with me. I instinctively clench my fists.

"Sadie," she speaks softly, leaning in from the chair she has pulled up alongside me, "we can work together, just you and I. Why don't you stay back Tuesdays after school? We can spend an hour going through everything from class, make sure you understand?" She moves her head to meet my lowered eyes. "What do you think about that?"

"Okay, whatever," I shrug.

She daintily claps her hands together. "Excellent! The sooner we start, the more I can help you."

Her hands look younger than mine. She must buy really expensive moisturiser.

She is a nice lady, really. I like her. Sort of. She's just a bit too perky. I reckon she would be in her mid-40s but there's something almost childish about her that ironically makes her come across as motherly. She has an underlying innocence and thinks the world is a wonderful place. I can't imagine her ever saying anything bad about anyone. She is demure and charming, like a lady from a book set in the 1800s.

"Get your uncle to sign this permission slip."

I nod and fold the note into quarters so it fits in the pocket of my tunic. I'll sign it myself tonight.

"Okay Sadie, go hang out with your friends now. You've still got fifteen minutes to enjoy the sunshine."

I leave the classroom and step out onto the gravel. Mya and Callie are waiting for me on our bench by the water taps.

Sloopy

I'm glad she has friends. Most kids in school think she's got an attitude problem but she's been sitting with Mya and Callie since high school began so they must be close, even though it doesn't really look like it. Sadie doesn't seem very involved with them. She just sits quietly, eating her vegemite sandwich while they do all the talking, quite animatedly.

Mya and Callie aren't in our Homeroom; I'm pretty sure they're both with Mr Benson this year.

They are the only girls I ever see Sadie hang out with. I hear the other girls in the school call their group names sometimes, like that horrible 's' word and other crass things. Mya likes attention, and she gets a lot of it. The hem of her blue chequered school dress barely covers her undies.

The three of them sit on the bench by the water taps, under the veranda which looks out onto the court. They perch themselves side by side like pigeons on a power line.

Sadie always sits in the middle. Even if she is the last one out, Mya quickly shuffles over so that Sadie has no choice but to sit in-between them. No one else even tries to sit there, it's just understood that that's their spot. People give Sadie space out of fear, and her friends by association. I try not to look in their direction too much though. I don't want to look like a pervert. Plus, the boys pay me out when I look at girls.

"I'm open, Sloopy!"

I bounce-pass the ball to Adam as he rushes up to the ring. He shoots and scores, catching his own rebound and slamming it victoriously onto the court.

"It sucks that you had to beg your dad to let you join the team," Adam pants, "but you're gonna kill it."

"It cost me an extra bible reading with the oldies," I admit, embarrassed with myself.

Josh slaps me on the butt. I'm not sure why he does that so I slap his butt, too but he looks at me like I'm a weirdo.

"The oldies are worth it if it means you can hang out with us and be normal," he laughs.

I tug five times on a loose thread inside my shorts pocket.

The office sent out the Expression of Interest form for Mixed Basketball last week. Dad refused at first, reminding me that it had nothing to do with my future, but eventually he begrudgingly agreed as long as it didn't impose on my school work or 'upstanding reputation as a promising member of the church community.' He told me that if I embarrassed him or our family, it would break Mum's heart. Got my first practice today after school and first game tomorrow.

I look over to the girls. Mya and Callie are talking and Sadie is staring into her lap. I lift the bottom of my school shirt and wipe the sweat from my forehead.

Sadie

"He's a bit scrawny, hey?" Callie giggles, nudging shoulders with me.

"I don't know, I wasn't looking at him," I snap.

"I wonder why they call him Sloopy?" Mya chimes in. "Noah's a hot name."

"I wasn't looking at him!" I bite hard into my apple, deliberately trying to drown out the sound of their voices.

"I'd totally go there!" Mya proudly declares.

She opens her packet of barbecue Samboys and holds out a chip, offering it to me. She shoves it in her mouth before I can shake my head *no* and then stuffs even more in while she keeps babbling on.

"Even though he's churchy, I could educate him. Or corrupt him." She does this obnoxious chuckle that makes me dislike her even more but I manage a fake smile. "Too bad he only ever checks you out," she winks.

Something happened over the Christmas holidays that I obviously missed out on. They changed. Callie grew out of her baby fat and Mya grew into a self-assured exhibitionist. All they talk about now is boys. I didn't like them before and now they annoy me even more.

Or maybe they just grew up more than I did.

Mya is probably the hottest girl in school and she knows it. She pins her chunky blonde bob back off her face with mini pastel coloured butterfly clips. All the girls bitch about her and all the boys ogle her. She is overtly confident, to the point of intimidating even some of the teachers. She is acutely aware of how attractive she is and is addicted to the attention it gives her.

Callie has long, mousey brown hair and a full fringe that rests bluntly on her eyebrows. She always wears it in a plat which stretches all the way down to her waist. Since school started, she has been the target of snide remarks and jokes about her weight. Last year Cassie Wingfield called her a beached whale. Callie cried in the toilets for the entire lunch break. Mya wrapped her arms around her and kept telling her that she was beautiful. I just stood there.

She must have lost a good 10 kilos in the Christmas break. She'd be about a size 10 now. I already thought she looked fine before and she still looks fine now. I don't know how to tell her that.

Callie slumps her shoulders. "You know what, that Matt guy never called me back last week. His *Mum* answered the phone! She said she'd get him to call me but he never did."

Mya scans her eyes across the court, no doubt on the hunt for fresh prey.

"That Matt guy's a wanker, no real loss there. You only had one date, at least you didn't waste too much time on him. Personally, I think I might try to get reacquainted with Josh this year. We had fun in the Christmas holidays."

This conversation is irritating me. My friends are irritating me.

"The bell's about to go. I'm going to the loo. See you at lunch."

I chuck my apple in the bin and head to the girls' toilet block.

Sloopy

Sadie was looking at me when I wiped off my sweat. I play the moment over and over again in my head, trying to calculate if the bottom of my shirt was still pulled up when she looked my way. My cheeks burn and I sweat even more, wondering if she had seen my torso.

I'm going to start doing sit-ups tonight.

The bell sounds and the boys and I head back to Homeroom. I grab my Chem books and head off to Room 18 for the lesson. Adam is off to History and Josh has Chemistry with me.

It's a double, and it drags. I check the clock constantly, annoyed that it's not lunch time yet.

"What's eating you?" Josh whispers as I ready the Bunsen Burner.

"Nothing, I just noticed that Sadie didn't come back to Homeroom after recess."

"Who? What are you going on about?"

"Sadie. She didn't come back after recess to pick up her history books."

"And you noticed this, why?" Josh smirks, hovering the test tube over the Bunsen Burner.

"I don't know, I just thought it was weird."

"Maybe she got back before you and had already taken her books?"

I try to sound nonchalant. "Yeah, maybe. She's normally one of the last ones back, though."

Josh drops the test tube and clear liquid spills on the counter. "Crap!"

The class laugh and Mr Flinch taps a ruler on the black-board, motioning everyone to be quiet. I tear off some paper towel and lay it over the spill. Kelly smiles shyly at Josh from the station next to us and he smirks confidently back at her. He is very sure of himself, more than ever it seems since the holidays. He swaggered back to school with a new-found bravado that all the girls evidently find irresistible. I think he's bordering on arrogant.

He runs a hand through his wavy, sandy blonde hair, no doubt for Kelly's viewing pleasure. I don't remember his shoulders being quite so broad last year.

"How do you even know she has History now? What did you memorise her timetable or something?"

I shake my head, laughing him off. "I only know she has History because Adam does. I just hope she didn't have to go home sick or something, that's all."

Josh rolls his eyes. "Good young Christian, always worrying about other people. Even the seriously weird ones."

Sadie

I sit on the closed toilet seat, tapping my heels together anxiously. I don't like my friends. They annoy me. I sit with them because I have to. High School is safer in numbers. Kids are less likely to pick on you if you have your own group.

I've never even seen them outside of school and I know they secretly hate me. We just sat together at the start of Year 8 because you had to sit with someone. It's not like we actively chose to be friends because we actually liked each other.

How so very typical of Mya to joke about 'educating' him. She talks about educating someone new almost every week. I hear the things the other girls say, the names they call her. Just because I don't say it to her face, doesn't mean I don't secretly agree with them.

She's got tickets on herself if she thinks someone like Noah would fall for her routine seduction. He's a perfectionist. He wipes his apple on his top before he bites into it. He's paranoid about someone else having touched his *apple*: as if he'll want a girl who's been touched by half the boys in school.

I check my watch.

I'm twenty minutes late for History.

Right on time then.

Sloopy

Mrs Carrington wipes down the blackboard, tapping the duster against the tray on the bottom. Adam and a girl called Nikki distribute copies of the class text to everyone; Of Mice and Men.

"Alright everyone, almost the end of yet another glorious week here in Room 4! No doubt you want to cherish these last few moments together but alas," she proclaims, theatrically bringing the back of her hand to her forehead, "we depart company in ten minutes. Adam and Nikki are handing out our first book for the term, Of Mice and Men. It's only a short one to start the year off, so I don't want to hear any whinging. Okay, clean up your desks, pack everything you need and do all of that with a smile on your face because it's nearly the weekend!"

The buzz of the classroom grows louder. I put my Maths and English books away in my bag and scoop up a few pencil shavings from my desk. I cradle them in my hand and walk up to the bin at the front of the classroom.

Heading back, I watch Sadie as she dives into Of Mice and Men already, oblivious to the ruckus around her. She must like reading. Her hair is messier than it was this morning; lots of fly-aways fall onto her face and don't seem to bother her. If it was me, I'd be frantically tucking them behind my ears. She lifts her eyes to meet mine: her daggers pierce right through me.

The bell sounds and we all rush to get to the door first. Sadie sits still at her desk. Looks like she has detention.

Basketball starts in half an hour.

Hope she won't be late.

Sadie

"So, apparently you owe twenty minutes on the clock," Mrs Carrington speaks in her usual excessively perky voice. "Mr Hans is a stickler for time, you know that. If you're twenty minutes late for his class, he'll make sure you make up for it."

"Yeah, I know," I mumble. "I just lost track of time. It won't happen again."

"Second week of first term and you're already in detention, Sadie. What's going on? Don't you like school?"

Can't she just let me sit here in peace? I suck on my bottom lip, mentally willing her to go away and start marking or something. I shift uncomfortably in my seat and tuck my hair behind my ear, feeling it brush against my cheek. I normally like it when it falls on my face; it's like my body senses that I need to hide from the world and covers me up. But Mrs Carrington makes me aware of how messy I must look, especially compared to her.

"Yeah, school is fine."

My response seems to fuel her with a burning desire to impress me with tales of her youth. She circles my desk, practically skipping around like a 6-year-old telling Mummy about her first day of school. She is such a nice person. I kind of feel bad that she irritates me so much.

"I liked school, too but I never really fit in. Sure, I had a couple of friends, but I never really clicked with anyone, you know what I mean?"

Her baby blue blouse catches the sun's rays shining through the window and I wonder if she knows that you can slightly see her bra through the sheer material. She strikes me as the sort of person who would wear a singlet underneath if she knew.

"And anyway," she rambles on, "finally in Year 12, a guy asked me out! Trent was his name. My parents were pretty strict. We weren't allowed to go out during the week, only on Saturdays. They wouldn't even let him call me if it was a school night!"

I try to swallow my smile. I'm not sure Mrs Carrington even realises that I am still sitting here. She gets carried away when she talks. She starts off with one topic and goes off on a tangent, babbling about five other things all at once. Her hands get more and more excited as she speaks.

"We went out three Saturdays in a row. He dumped me because he kept trying to kiss me but I wasn't ready yet. What a broomhead!"

I can't help but chuckle. I didn't know anyone outside of Degrassi Junior High used the term broomhead.

Mrs Carrington laughs along with me. Her laugh is just as feminine as she is but it's a laugh that would ordinarily come from a child. I can't think if I've ever heard Alvin laugh but it's how I imagine a chipmunk would sound.

"Anyway, I met my husband in church a few years later and he's a wonderful man. Very caring. We've been married 21 years this September."

I guess that means she'd be about my mum's age.

Mrs Carrington checks her watch.

"Alright, Sadie, you've done your twenty. I'll let Mr Hans know. You're free to go."

"Thank you." I notice she is letting me go five minutes early. I would prefer to stay for the twenty.

I leave the classroom and walk to the girls' toilets across the hallway. I change into my P.E. clothes in one of the cubicles, taking my time to accommodate the extra five minutes now, and stuff my uniform roughly into my backpack.

When I get to the court, everyone on the team is hanging out, like one big group. There's only half an hour between school and practice so they all hang around on the court together straight after they've changed.

I wish Mya or Callie would take up basketball.

No, I don't. I take that back. Stupid thought. I don't need them. I don't need anyone.

I drop my bag by the side-line. Coach brings the whistle to his lips and my favourite sound in the world announces it is basketball time.

Sloopy

Geez, I don't think I've ever seen her smile before. Her whole face lights up like magic. She is by far the prettiest girl in the school; her smile induces my own. I don't understand why none of the other guys seem to notice her. But she doesn't really strike me as the sort of girl who wants to be noticed.

I see her before she sees me, but I always do. She catches me looking at her and returns my gaze with daggers. Her second for the day.

To be honest, I haven't really got into girls all that much. Adam and Josh talk about girls all the time, non-stop actually, but it kind of bores me. Well, maybe bore is the wrong word. I guess I'm just a bit disinterested in all of it. Girls aren't exactly featured in Dad's step-by-step manual on being the perfect teenage son of a priest.

Today at lunch, Josh was bragging about he hooked up with Mya in the back of his mum's car in the Christmas holidays just gone. All I could think about was whether or not I remembered to flick on the radio for Mum this morning and if Dad was going to make me run the under 6s Sunday School class this week. It seems that every-one grew up in the holidays and I forgot to keep up. I'm behind.

But I find myself looking at Sadie. A lot. It's strange for me. I can't help it. I try not to but I always find myself looking at her. Looking for her.

Coach tells us to run five laps of the court and I die a little inside at the thought. This is the first voluntary exercise I have ever signed up for. My extra-curricular activities have always been dictated by Dad; bible study class, volunteering at the local aged care home, debate, the kiddies Sunday School class. All academic activities or for the greater good of the community. Impressive foundation for my expected future as a pastor, but not exactly fitness building.

We line up on the side of the court. Coach blows the whistle and we commence jogging in line to the first corner. I am behind a girl called Naylene. Her ponytail sways from left to right with each stride. Her P.E shorts are heaps short and I make a conscious effort to not look down at my sneakers for fear that someone will think I am checking out her bum. I anxiously keep my eyes fixated on the back of her head, counting how many times her ponytail bounces side to side.

Coach blows the whistle as we jog past our original starting point. I can't believe I have to do this four more times. I may honestly throw up. My lungs are aching and I'm sure I taste blood in my mouth.

Naylene's ponytail isn't swinging quite so fast now.

Sadie

The scrawny boy from my homeroom is really struggling to keep up with everyone. He may very well be Top of the Class, but evidently not in sport. I am one of the last in the line but I can hear him panting from here. The two guys he hangs out with are right behind him, encouraging him in a mocking sort of way. I wonder if he actually likes his friends.

He wasn't on the team last year. Him joining means we have ten players now. Seven boys, three girls: Noah, Josh, Adam, Sam, Craig, Lachy, Will, Naylene and Bec. And me. There was an odd person out last year so one of us, and by that, I mean me, had to partner with the coach for passing practice. I was never anyone's choice, so I feel bad that someone will be forced to choose me just because the numbers say they have to.

Coach usually puts two girls and three guys on in the games. He keeps me on the bench most of the time. All of the time.

The whistle blows as we pass the starting point again. Three more laps to go.

Scrawny boy will collapse by then.

Sloopy

I'm going to collapse any second. I had no idea I was this unfit. As we near the starting point for the third time, I am acutely aware of every single muscle in my body. My legs are in so much pain and the only reason I haven't let myself drop dead to the ground yet is because I know she is at the back of the line and would see me give up. I hope no one is noticing how much I am struggling.

Sadie

His strides are laboured, as if he is in the final stages of an actual marathon. He seems hypnotised by Naylene's ponytail; his eyes are glued to her head like he is literally counting her strands of hair. I'm surprised Coach hasn't told him to sit down. I can't help but laugh to myself when Coach blows the whistle for the fifth and final time.

Sloopy

That was the best sound I have ever heard: Coach blew the whistle for the fifth and final time and Sadie giggled. Whoever or whatever it was that made her laugh, bless them.

Naylene's ponytail bounced back and forth 387 times.

Sadie

"Alright kids, partner up!" Coach shouts across the court. "Two metres apart, alternate bounce and chest passes until the whistle blows. And go!"

There is a mad flurry as everyone frantically grabs hold of their desired partner. I stare at my feet awkwardly and my hands form fists at my sides. I frown and wait for someone to claim me like a toddler who's lost their mum in Target.

"Looks like it's you and me," Adam, the boy from my history class says.

I half-heartedly attempt a smile and take my place two metres opposite him.

He shoots a chest pass my way. "Your ball."

The leather feels nostalgic in my hand, evoking within me some sort of heartache over a life that no longer exists. I bounce-pass the ball back to him and he shoots me another chest pass, a bit more forceful this time. I send one back to him with matching oomph.

"Nice one!" he praises.

It feels atypically natural to smile in response to his friendliness. "Thanks," I utter quietly but I am not sure he even hears me.

His glasses slip down his nose slightly, no doubt due to the humidity. He self-consciously pushes them back up. "You're Sally, right?"

"Close, Sadie," I reply stoically, looking over to the school buildings to avoid looking directly at him. I sense that I'm making him nervous. Good.

He sends a bounce-pass my way. "I th-think we have History together."

I nod as I send a chest-pass back to him. I'm not sure if I was meant to actually answer him, but I didn't feel it was necessary to carry the conversation on any further. Plus, this is his second year on the team, my third. As if he doesn't know my name.

Sloopy

We practice shots before Coach blows the whistle again, signalling the end of the hour. My first basketball practice is finished.

I'm not sad about it.

The boys pat me on the back and I feel gross when my P.E. top sticks to my skin. I am sweating so much and desperate to take a shower. Sadie is crouched on the ground, fiddling with her school bag. I quickly fan out my top in case she looks up and sees it clinging to me, drawing attention to my scrawny frame.

We grab our backpacks and head off to find Josh's mum's car. She lets him drive it to school on Fridays. He's the first one in the whole school to get his full licence. Every other single car in the student car park is branded with P plates. Adam and I feel cool by association, even though Adam hasn't even gone for his learners permit yet and I'll be stuck on my Ls forever.

Josh's mum has a white Honda Civic. The windows are freshly tinted and we pile into it as if we are the kings of the school. Johnny Diesel blares out of the stereo as Josh revs the engine. I sit in the back seat. I tug three times on my seatbelt, click it in and then pull on the strap two more times. We take off in a cloud of smoke.

"How'd you go partnering up with that weird chick?" Josh teases Adam.

My ears prick up at the mention of her.

"I tried talking to her," he replies, "but she doesn't give you much to go on."

"She doesn't say much to anyone," Josh replies with attitude. "I wouldn't take it personally. I've never even noticed her before. I think this is the first year we've been in homeroom together."

"Dude!" Adam laughs, "she was on the team already when we started!"

"Oh yeah, you're right! It's not like she does much though. She used to partner with Coach in training and just sits on the bench in the games. She'd be pretty if she wasn't in such a bad mood all the time. Wait, what's her name again?"

"Sadie," I instantly reply without thinking.

Josh and Adam look at each other and smirk.

"Just drive!" I laugh, smacking the back of Josh's headrest.

Sadie

Practice ran late. I check my watch. 4:58pm. Bus leaves the stop at 5pm. I quicken my pace.

Sloopy

"Hey, speak of the devil!" Adam points ahead.

Sadie is walking with haste on the footpath ahead.

Josh moves his shoulders back and forth and bobs his head along, presumably trying to look like a runner. "Looks like she knows she's gonna miss the bus!"

"She doesn't catch the bus," I observe, "well not on any day I do."

Josh frowns at Adam but I ignore him. I catch the bus every day except Friday after school, when Josh has his mum's car. I've never seen her on the bus before. Typical, I think to myself: the only trip I don't take the bus, it looks like she does.

"Want me to offer her a ride?" Josh asks eagerly, smirking at me in the rear-view mirror.

"Um..." I tap my knees five times and fan out my P.E. top. I take a whiff of my arm pits: I could smell better. "Yeah, okay, offer her a ride."

"You got it, stud," Josh laughs.

Sadie

The air around me grows smoky as the volume of a Johnny Diesel song grows louder. I look back to the road at the bomb heading towards me. I can make out the song now; Never Miss Your Water. I love it. If I don't have it, I'm going to make it my mission to tape it over the weekend.

A normal person would probably panic if a suspicious looking car pulled up alongside them. We are meant to have a natural fight or flight response in traumatic situations. I face the car that may be seconds away from abducting me, and I stand still. No flight. I wonder if I'll even fight. A guy from school sticks his head out the window. It's scary to think I'm actually disappointed: he's hardly the serial killer type.

Josh attempts an American accent as if he's some big famous movie-star. "Need a ride?"

My arms instinctively cross on my tummy and I tense my face. "No."

He laughs right at me. "Come on, we'll give you a ride! You're probably pushing it a bit if you're heading for the bus stop."

He stretches out his arm and taps his neon green watch. I wonder if he is deliberately trying to come across like a jerk. I have a sudden urge to push his arm back so he slaps himself in the face.

"I said no," I say with unbridled annoyance, "like any girl with an ounce of intelligence would say to you."

Josh makes an exaggerated huff noise and speaks to someone in the back. "I tried!"

The bomb revs off, leaving me standing in the street engulfed in its smoke.

Thanks a lot, arseholes.

I really am going to miss the goddamn bus now.

Sloopy

I slump in the back seat and pick at the scab on my wrist. "You were a bit of a jerk, man. No wonder she didn't want to get in the car."

Josh laughs and slaps Adam on the shoulder with his free hand.

"Sloopy's got it bad! There are girls out there who aren't such total bitches though, mate. "

"And remember," Adam chimes in, "no sex before marriage, Sloops. I'm stuck in the same church you are. I don't want to be pegged as the friend of a sinner!"

"Yeah right! As if *you're* a virgin!" Josh chuckles. "You lost it before I did!"

"Yeah, but my father's not the local priest, is he?"

The boys look back at me and I'm not oblivious to their look of pity. Josh is lucky; his parents aren't religious. He's never even gone to church. I grew up in Sunday school with Adam. It's easier for him, though.

"Well, better hurry up and marry her then so you can join the club!" Josh brags.

I roll my eyes and flick a bit of scab off my wrist. I didn't realise they had both gone all the way. I really did fall behind in the Christmas break. I've never even kissed a girl. "I just think she's interesting, that's all. There's a lot to her."

"I don't think she goes to church on Sundays," Josh pipes up. "Good luck trying to get your dad's blessing on that one."

I nod knowingly. "Yep, I get that. But I don't even think of her like that. I just think of her."

Except I do: I do think of her like that. I think of it constantly.

Sadie

I'm nearly there. 5:07pm. My hurried strides send my backpack bouncing up and down. The bus stop is right on the next street. I've missed it, I just know it.

I sprint around the corner, expecting my heart to sink at the sight of the empty bus stop. But the bus is right there, waiting. Everyone is already on board and the bus is waiting for me. My face erupts into a relieved smile and I run even faster to get there. I practically jump up the two steps into the bus.

"Thank you! I was so worried I was going to miss you!"

"No worries, Sadie. I waited for you. You know I'll always wait for you," Cameron, the bus driver, kindly replies.

He always says that.

Sloopy

The boys dump their bags on my bedroom floor and we head downstairs to the kitchen. Mum is sitting at the table, just as she was this morning, as if no time has passed at all; sipping her coffee and organising all her Avon orders. Her whole face lights up when she sees me. It's like she lives on pause until I'm home and I'm the only one who knows how to press play.

"The boys!" she cheers, dropping her pen onto the table. "Pizza is already on its way! I ordered ten minutes ago."

Josh kisses Mum on her cheek and helps himself to a can of soft drink from the fridge. Adam sits down at the table, passing Mum a silver envelope as he does.

"It's from my mum, for her 40th next month. She's booked a band and everything."

Mum opens the envelope and delicately pulls out a fancy-looking invitation: silver paper with black calligraphy.

"Cocktail dress," she recites softly, but I'm not sure she meant to read it aloud.

An air of sadness floats by her before she seems to remember herself. She shakes it off and smiles.

"I'll ring Holly later tonight and let her know I'll be there. We'll be there, I mean."

Josh jumps up onto the kitchen counter, dangling his legs against the cupboard. "You'll be the most beautiful woman there, Mrs Blean."

Mum giggles sweetly and I catch myself thinking how right he is.

"I'll go shopping with you, Mum. I'll help you choose a real nice dress."

Mum cups her hands over her mouth, her hidden smile evident by the creases next to her eyes. "Okay, let's do it. Glam me up!"

Being a mother is Mum's favourite thing. She comes alive when someone needs her; me, my friends, even her Avon customers. It's like her cue to be *on*. Without it, she seems weighed down by something, something that seems to have an underlying hold on her. Something that she constantly tries to supress.

The doorbell rings and Josh leaps from the bench, grabbing Mum's purse from the table.

"Pizza! I'll get it."

Sadie

"See you Tuesday, Sadie!" Cameron calls out just as the doors of the bus close behind me.

I wave shyly as the bus drives away down my street. Cameron drops me off right outside my house, even though the actual stop on the route is another two streets back. There are only ever three or four other passengers on Friday afternoons, presumably on their way home from work, and none of them seem to mind the minute's detour. Not that Cameron gives them a choice.

I told him that I could do with a lift home Tuesdays now too because of the tutoring and he seemed oddly happy about it.

I turn the front door handle before I even bother to look for my keys. As expected, it's unlocked. I roll my eyes knowing he was the last to leave the house today, as always.

The house is dark and stuffy inside. He didn't even open the curtains. A stale odour mixed with the lingering presence of booze sticks to the rucked-up carpet.

I jerk the lounge room curtains open to let the last couple of hours of sunlight through. The curtains are orange, no joke. They are literally orange. I suspect back in 1972 this house was quite on trend, but considering nothing has been done to it since, it's just an ugly means of safety from the weather outside. A place to stay because I have nowhere else to go.

I straighten the cushions on the couch: faded brown corduroy also left-over from the Whitlam era. Dust puffs into the air and I cough at the musky smell. I'd sit, but I never know who else has sat on that couch, so I just don't.

Entering the kitchen, I slide my backpack off my shoulders and cook my tea in the microwave. Cameron never eats his lunch on Fridays. He says his wife packs too much food for him and he doesn't want to hurt her feelings by not eating it, so I help him out by having it for my dinner. When I return the Tupperware to him the Friday after, he's always got another one filled with food.

Cameron gave me vegetable frittata tonight. I eagerly watch it spin around in the microwave. My tummy rumbles in anticipation at the smell of real, proper food. I wipe down the countertops and aimlessly tidy the kitchen, just to be around the scent of cooking.

6 minutes later, the microwave pings. I gratefully take my dinner and eat it sitting cross-legged on my bedroom floor. I rest my back against my bed and listen to the magpies outside my window. They are so loud this evening. Or maybe they just seem that way because the house is so quiet.

Sloopy

Mum's laughter fills the whole kitchen, and it's contagious. Adam and Josh continue to mock my fitness abilities for her benefit.

"Make fun all you want," I play along, "but I was seriously this close to going into cardiac arrest! Do we have to run around like that every single week? I might actually die!"

Mum laughs from deep in her belly. I feel happy from the inside out at the sound, more so because I'm the one who caused it. I seldom hear her laugh. I scratch at the loose skin around my thumb, realising that's my fault. I make a mental note to make her laugh more.

Mum spared no expense and ordered five pizzas between the four of us. We eat as if we haven't eaten all day.

"Sloopy certainly worked up a sweat today, Mrs Blean," Josh teases. "Especially when he was checking out his new girlfriend!"

I bite into my pizza and sigh. "Here we go."

Mum excitedly straightens up her back. "What have I missed here? Girlfriend? Really? What's her name? Tell me everything!"

"She's not my girlfriend, don't get all excited. They're just being idiots."

Mum bites into her pizza, making an exaggerated sad face.

"Well, this is true," Adam chuckles, "she's not his girlfriend. But Sloopy definitely wants her to be!"

Mum beams. "My Sloopy. Your first crush is a big deal."

I roll my eyes as Adam and Josh make juvenile kissing noises.

"I just wouldn't mind getting to know her a bit, that's all. I don't think anybody actually does; know her, I mean. She's a bit of a loner."

"What's her name?"

"Sadie, she sits in front of me in homeroom. I've seen her in school heaps but I've never had a class with her before this year."

Josh leans across the table and puts his hand on Adam's cheek. Adam flutters his eyes. Mum presses her lips together, trying to suppress her laughter as it fights to escape.

I put too much pizza in my mouth. "I'm glad I amuse you all so much."

Sadie

I wash my dishes and his, left sitting on the sink. I put Cameron's container straight away in my school bag so that it's safe. I close the curtains in the lounge room and check the front door is locked. I leave the kitchen light on for him.

I stare at the back door that he will stumble in through in a few short hours. I always leave it unlocked for him, even though it is night and it scares me to. He gets angry when he has to fumble around for his keys. If someone breaks in, I hope they kill me quickly. As I think this, I notice the cornice is pulling away from the ceiling and I wonder if it might fall on his head one day and maybe kill him first.

I close my bedroom door and change into my black tracksuit pants and pink Sportsgirl top. I brush my hair, leaving it down and pull out a suitcase from underneath my bed. I tip the contents onto my rug; my entire CD collection lays before me. I rummage through it, reading the track lists on the back covers of the Smash Hits ones to check if I've got any Johnny Diesel.

Sloopy

"I'll do the dishes!" Mum jokes, collecting the pizza boxes and putting them in the recycling pile. "Done!"

Adam hugs her. "Thanks for dinner, Mumma Blean."

Josh lets out a belter of a burp and Mum taps him on the shoulder.

"Manners, young man!"

"We're heading upstairs to settle in, Mum." I feel like I'm abandoning her, leaving her on her own on a Friday night. "We're just gonna watch some New Releases if you want to join us?"

"That's okay, baby. I've got a few phone calls to make. I need to call your Aunty May about those bath salts she wants to order. Make sure you turn it down when your father gets home."

Adam and Josh roll their eyes and I forget myself for a second and emulate.

Sadie

I must have close to a hundred cassettes and CDs sprawled out around me. I find my How Do You Talk to an Angel single and excitedly put it in my player. I sing along while I lay out my basketball uniform for the morning.

This will be my third year playing on the team. I don't get a lot of court time. I'm not a great player like the ones Coach wants out on the court. But I'm still part of the team, even after everything that's happened. Coach didn't use it as an excuse to just get rid of me.

Sloopy

I lay out my brand-new basketball uniform in preparation for my first game tomorrow.

Josh and Adam are camped out on the floor of my bedroom; tucked up in their sleeping bags amidst a mountain of pillows. We're watching Indecent Proposal. It's pretty good. Dad would make me do a million extra bible study classes if he knew. We hired Dead Poet's Society too, just in case Dad was home.

I pull out a pair of rolled up white socks from my top drawer and unravel them to make sure they are the same length, then roll them back up and place them next to my guernsey.

Josh purses his lips lustfully as he ogles Demi Moore holding a black dress against her body. "You probably won't even get any time on court, being your first game and all."

I stretch the laces on my sneakers to check that they're equal. "It's okay. I won't mind if I just sit on the bench."

Sadie

I don't need the shower to wake me up: I was awake for a good hour before the standard morning chatter of the magpies commenced outside my window. The water feels heavenly on my skin and I allow myself the luxury of enjoying the sensation for a minute, before I catch myself daydreaming and hastily rinse the soap off my body before I rack up the water bill too high.

My basketball uniform lays waiting for me on the rim of the bath. 81. I'm 81. Even if I just sit on the bench, I'm 81.

My hair is damp but I don't have a hairdryer, not that I would use one even if I did. They haven't invented a silent one yet. My hair is a bit longer than I usually like it so I make a mental note to cut it soon. I squeeze the ends until the water stops dripping, roughly smooth all the strands together and wrap them up in my Road Runner scrunchie, loosening the ponytail so it rests at the base of my neck. I'm ready to put on my uniform.

I was worried because the top is sleeveless but I think the marks have faded enough now to not be so obvious. I dab a bit of concealer on my upper arms just to be safe.

Sloopy

I look ridiculous.

"You're all legs!" Josh teases.

Staring at the mirror in disgust, I agree. The basketball uniform is giant on me. I look like a twelve-year-old kid wearing his big brother's hand-me-down. I make a mental note to add push-ups to my upcoming routine. I loathe the sight of the scrawny child staring back at me in the mirror and fully intend to vanquish him.

"Be honest, am I embarrassing myself? Do I look pathetic?"

Adam pats me on the back. "Nah, you're alright, Josh is only teasing."

I push my hair off my face. It's pretty shaggy considering I only had it cut just before school started. I'll ask Mum for some money to get it cut soon.

The scab on my wrist is itchy and I scratch it vigorously.

Josh stands next to me, checking himself out in the mirror. "Stop picking at yourself all the time."

I flick the last bit of scab off and track its decent to the floor, wondering how many other pieces of scab it will join down there. I rub some cream over the dry, red patch left behind.

Sadie

The walk to school is really lovely today. I've left in plenty of time; more than an hour early actually. It's probably a good forty-minute walk to school. I walk there and back every day, except Fridays when Cameron takes me home in the bus, and soon on Tuesdays too, now that I'll be staying back with Mrs Carrington. He's a nice man. He wants to pick me up every day but he never lets me pay for a ticket and I don't want him getting into trouble. Besides, when I've got nothing on after school, there's plenty of time for me to be the first one home.

It is already quite warm. I take a big gulp from my water bottle, put my headphones on and press play on my discman. I turn up Jenny Morris, She Has Got to be Loved as loud as it will go and bounce my basketball in time with the beat.

Sloopy

"First big game today!" Dad jovially announces as he enters the kitchen.

Mum is at the sink washing Dad's dishes from last night's dinner. He got in late, again. She dries her hands on the tea towel and smooths out her hair before rushing up to him on her tip toes, kissing him on the cheek.

"Good morning, darling."

Dad frowns and gently pushes her back down off her toes. "I just brushed my teeth."

The boys and I are finishing our orange juices at the table. I watch Mum fiddle awkwardly with the waistband of her skirt as she heads back to the sink. Dad drops the newspaper down on the table and sits opposite me.

"Don't blow it, Noah. You've only got one term to prove to me that this silly basketball thing won't affect your grades or create more time away from your duties."

"I know, sir."

"What will everyone think if you start flunking at school? Don't bring our family's name down. Don't forget, I expect a one thousand word re-telling of Genesis 2-3 by tomorrow morning. They'll be looking at your knowledge of the very basics. I thought the seminary application would come this week. Guess I'll have to request another one if it doesn't come soon."

The application came on Wednesday. I ripped it up into tiny pieces and then ripped those tiny pieces into even tinier pieces.

His glare makes contact with my eyes and I nod obediently. I skull the rest of my orange juice and the boys take their cue. We give Mum our empty glasses and I kiss her on the cheek. She is washing the same dishes she just washed.

"Good luck, Sloopy. Tell me all about it tonight."

On top of the fridge sits a red, bulky ghetto blaster. It's been up there for as long as I can remember. I flick it on as we make our way out, hoping that a song comes on that Mum likes.

Josh's mum's car waits for us in the street where we parked it last night. I've lost my excitement about the game and reach for the back passenger door with my head hung low.

Josh chucks me the keys just as I am about to climb into the back seat. "Wanna drive, Sloopy?"

"Fuck, yes!" I almost squeal. "I'll go grab my Ls!"

"You know he's had enough when lets a swear word slip," I hear Adam say as I rush back inside.

Sadie

The new housing estate being built half way between home and school is nearing completion by the looks of it. A brick wall on each side of the road connects a sign high above the gated entry; *Greener Side Estate*, as if purposed to create a new community, separate from the aesthetically displeasing weatherboard housing trust homes which it neighbours. The sign has the feel of a 'Welcome Home' banner. It must be really nice to be welcomed home, even it is by an inanimate object.

I take off my head phones so I can better hear the sound of my basketball as I chest-pass it against the brick wall. It's a comforting sound.

I'm distracted by an abrupt honk. I look back towards the noise and my shoulders slump at the sight of the bogan white bomb from yesterday swerving towards me.

"Great. Please don't talk to me again."

Sloopy

"Jesus, dude! Pick a lane!" Josh laughs from the front passenger seat. "You just cut that old lady off!"

I thought I was driving pretty good today, but then I spied Sadie up ahead and lost my concentration. I tighten my grip on the wheel three times and ease my pressure on the accelerator, then quickly squeeze the wheel two more times. I flinch when Josh takes the Lord's name in vain, but not because it offends me like I know it is supposed to. I'm just paranoid that Dad will somehow hear from a whole suburb away.

Josh checks my speed. "Come on, Gramps, it's a 60 zone! You're barely even doing 40!"

Adam leans forwards. "Do you want to stop and say hello to my basketball partner?"

"No." I tense my lips together tightly. "She wouldn't like that."

I know she wouldn't. She just likes to be left alone, especially by obnoxious boys from school.

"Pull up next to her, we won't embarrass you. Promise."

The thought of Sadie seeing me drive does make me feel pretty cool, so I do as Josh suggests and pull the car into the curb next to her. She catches her ball and turns to face us. I picture a Bone Thugs-n-Harmony music clip in my mind, push my bottom forward so I slide down my seat a little, rest my arm on the open window like a gangster and nod my head at her.

"S'up, Sadie?"

Sadie

That car seems to make 17-year-old boys more obnoxious than they already are. I hold my basketball low against my tummy and give him my most disinterested scowl, hoping he will go away.

"We're getting Maccas before the game, do you want to come?" the annoying, albeit good-looking dude from yesterday says, leaning across the scrawny boy from homeroom.

I maintain my frown and the Noah guy sits up straight.

Adam pokes his head out the back window. "Our treat!"

Adam has a friendly face. I don't feel the urge to punch him. He has brown hair and freckles that I like the look of. It's a shame they're mostly covered up by the thick, black frame of his glasses. Waste of perfectly cool freckles. But his glasses are cool, too. He's like a funky, popular nerd.

"Come on, Sloopy here has his first game today, we need to give him a good feed!"

"I fail to see how that needs to involve me," I reply in my toughest tone. I liked him better when he didn't speak.

Noah smiles awkwardly, obviously embarrassed. Good. I turn back to the wall and bounce my ball against it. It's only a millisecond before the car revs off down the road.

Sloopy

The boys laugh all the way to Maccas. They go on about Sadie, astonished that she would turn us down given that she 'isn't exactly popular.' I take deep breaths and concentrate on the road ahead. The skin on my face feels like it's burning. She looks really pretty today. I've never seen that much of her skin before. I've only ever seen her in the school or P.E. uniform. The team attire shows her body shape. Her arms are slender and I spied a white bra strap peeking out. I roll my window down to get some air.

Josh turns the radio over to Triple J. "I think you need to find someone else to fancy. I don't see Sadie giving it up for you anytime soon."

She is wearing her Road Runner scrunchie today; it's dark blue with mini-Road Runners scattered around it.

It matches the team colours and I wonder if that's why she chose it. She doesn't fold her socks down; she rolls them like a sausage. I literally hold up a ruler to make sure my socks are the same height from the heel up.

Adam and Josh talk but I can only hear her voice: *I fail to see how that needs to involve me.* Imagine being so certain of yourself, so confident, so brazen to voice your thoughts without fear of consequence or fall-out.

"It's weird, I mean, considering who her friends are and everything. Me and that Mya girl went at it in the holidays. And word is that Callie will fair dinkum hook up with anyone these days now that she's lost some weight."

I turn the radio up and try to estimate the distance between me and the semi-trailer up ahead. Sadie's white bra strap flashes through my mind again. I wonder if her whole bra is white or if maybe it has little pink flowers or patterns on the cups.

"Can you guys roll your windows down?" I ask, flustered. "Is it hot in here or is it just me?"

I pull up on a side street, behind McDonalds. Josh and I swap seats before he drives us into the car park.

"You're going to have to get over your fear of car parks one day."

I think about all the parked cars and how easy it would be for me to drive too closely to one of them. What if I scratched one? Dad would never forgive me. I would bring him so much shame.

Josh parks and I can't get out of the car fast enough. I order hot cakes, hash browns and a Coke slushie. I pay for Josh and Adam's order and inhale my breakfast in three seconds flat. I hope I remembered to put the radio on for Mum before I left. I can't drive in car parks and Sadie's white bra strap keeps flashing through my mind.

I wish I had put on more deodorant today.

Sadie

I get to school half an hour earlier than I need to. I'm disappointed to see I'm not the first one; the opposition are already here, doing drills. They're probably the best school we play against. Their team is confident. Together.

I drop my bag by the bench and head over to the drinks table off to the side of the court. I'm surprised to see Mrs Carrington standing there. She never comes to basketball. She pours green cordial from a large glass cannister into a row of white plastic cups.

"Morning, Sadie! Want to slice the oranges for me? I got roped into volunteering today, none of the parents were free to set up the half-time station."

Everything about her is annoyingly perky as usual, especially her voice. She talks like a Disney princess. I smile from the side of my mouth and commence cutting the oranges into quarters, placing them on the floral serving tray waiting to be filled. It feels weird to see Mrs Carrington outside of school hours, dressed in what I guess are her normal clothes. I have the same Just Jeans t-shirt but in red. Hers is white. I didn't pick her for the jeans sort, especially not fitted ones. Her legs are narrow and her waist is tiny. She looks prettier than she does in school; younger and more relaxed. She is wearing pearl drop ear rings. I don't think I've ever noticed her wear ear rings to school.

She talks non-stop about the movie she saw last night with her husband. I slice the oranges with more force than is probably required as I listen, uninterested.

"It was so emotional for me, I guess because I loved the book so much. Seeing it up on the big screen gave me goose bumps. Have you read How to Make an American Quilt, Sadie? It's not on the curriculum but I wish it was. Do you read much?"

Great. Her conversation is trying to become two-sided. "No, I haven't read it. Yes, I read a lot."

Far out, she asks so many questions. I look to the bench by the water taps, where I sit at recess and lunch with Mya and Callie. I don't know why. I guess it's just nice to see it, just to know it's there. It calms me a bit and helps me tolerate this verbal exchange I hate so much.

Mrs Carrington gasps and her theatrics make me tense my whole body. She might be the most annoying person on the planet.

"I'll bring you in my copy on Monday! You will love it!"

I smile with my lips pressed firmly together. I'm not sure you could even call it a smile. "Thanks. Oranges are done."

I aggressively slide the serving platter in her direction, drop the knife on the table and make a move for my inevitable spot on the bench.

Sloopy

We park outside the school and I exit the passenger side cradling my stomach.

"I shouldn't have eaten so much. I might seriously throw up."

Adam sniggers and Josh belches; loud and prolonged. I feel slightly queasy at the sound, more so at the smell that wafts over to me.

I walk two steps behind Josh and Adam. I'm nervous.

Adam hangs back and loosely drapes his arm across my shoulders. "Come on, you'll be fine. You won't even get much court time. Probably none."

I know. That's why I'm nervous.

Sadie

I'm never selected to play in the starting line up, so I'm not disappointed when Coach picks the same five players he usually does. Josh and Adam are on fire today. I think they're showing off for their friend, Noah. He must feel a bit self-conscious being the new guy on the team.

He's sitting next to me on the bench. He sits behind me in homeroom but now he's right next to me. He keeps rubbing his hands up and down his thighs and gee it's irritating. Even more so because he does it once and then it's like you can hear his brain ticking over and he quickly does it four more times.

Naylene scores the first goal of the game and I leap up to cheer for her. Some jerk on the other team pretends to flick his hair off his shoulders in an immature attempt to mock her. I add him to the list of people I hate.

When I sit back down, Noah wipes his hands along his shorts again, an action predictably repeated four more times.

I take a deep breath and watch on.

Sloopy

If I rest my hand in the space between us, I could literally touch the material of her shorts: that's how close our bodies are. She follows the ball so intently, her gaze never faulters. She looks more relaxed than she does in school. She is looking straight ahead at the game, not straight down into her lap.

"Could you move over?"

I panic and slide slightly to the right. She looks down at the widened space, raises her eyebrows and goes back to watching the game. I sense she may have wanted me to move over more.

It is already pretty warm. She brings her hand up to the side of her face, shielding her eyes from the blazing sun. I hope. It kind of feels like she did it to hide herself from my sight.

The other team scores. Sadie says "bummer" under her breath. I like her voice. She speaks her words adamantly, with conviction and void of possible regret. She speaks her words with full intention of backing them up.

The ball travels down to our team's end and Sadie turns her head to follow. The sun has dipped behind a cloud and I am desperate to absorb every detail of her face before she hides it again. Her side profile is dominated by her full cheeks; they almost swallow her narrow, deep blue eyes. Her thin lips part ever so slightly as she watches on. She has a few freckles scattered on her nose. Sitting this close now, I can see her better than I have ever been able to and God she's so pretty. Her hair is the colour of the sun right before it kisses the sky goodnight. Some strands aren't quite long enough to tie into her ponytail and hang around her face wildly. I get a glimpse of her white bra strap again. I wonder how many different bras she has. My cheeks suddenly get hot and I feel my breathing hasten.

Sadie

Adam's shot misses. Bummer. The other team grab the ball and take it back down to their end. We've got five spares today; me, nervous-wreck Noah, Craig, Lachy and Sam. Sam is shouting out things like *get it back, guys!* and *excellent!* He is sitting on the bench just like me and he is still part of the team. Just like me. He cheers and supports the team because he still belongs, even just by sitting here. He doesn't get the glory of playing but he feels the win or loss of the game just the same. It's amazing to me. He's on the list of people I like, for now anyway. It's a bit shorter than my other list.

Basketball is a team of people sharing the same passion to win. Everyone works towards the same goal, together. Like a family.

I swallow my thoughts and cheer as Josh slams the ball through the hoop. Not for himself, but for his team.

I swear Noah has moved closer to me again.

Sloopy

"Nice hey! That's two for us now, right?"

Sadie turns her head far too slowly to face me. My voice or face or both have annoyed her, I can tell. I wish I could pretend I didn't say anything at all but my words are out there now and I can't get them back. I contemplate sliding back over.

She smiles a pretty unfriendly smile and merely nods in response, giving me a look as if to install fear in me; warning me not to speak to her again.

"It'd be pretty cool if we won, hey?" I don't know why but I can't stop talking now that I've started even though I know that I need to. "It's my first game, so it'd be awesome if we win. I mean of course it would be awesome regardless of whether or not this is my first game, but the fact that it is my first game would just make a win even more awesome than it would ordinarily be." I despise myself. Sadie frowns and for some reason I just keep on talking. "My friends told me I wouldn't get much court time today, probably none, but that's okay because it's my first game, I don't know if I told you that, but yeah, it's my first game so I'm not expecting to get up and play but it's pretty awesome to watch anyway. And like I said, it would be even more awesome if we win."

I'm really panicking now. It's so hot and Sadie is still frowning at me.

Sadie

"I don't get much court time either." I consciously try to sound confident yet a little blasé. "I'm usually just a reserve."

Noah's face is frozen in a stupid-looking grin. He's weird.

I clap vigorously as Naylene scores for the third time. Noah claps a second after me, almost as if he is copying me. He's so damn smart in class, all the teachers love him. Yet he can't even decide when to clap on his own. I wonder if he's capable of making any sort of decision without checking what everyone else decides first.

Adam scores next and Noah cheers right on cue: directly after I do. He looks at me out of the corner of his eye and for some strange reason, it feels right to smile back. I guess I feel like I should, since he's trying to get into the game and all. He smiles right back, like in relief, and he suddenly resembles someone much sure of himself, like this layer of nerves has just been stripped away.

Sloopy

Right now, this could very well be the most perfect moment in my entire seventeen years on Earth. The sun's rays catch the side of her face and give her an almost luminescent glow. She is smiling, and she is smiling at me. I feel like no one else has ever seen her like this: happy. Maybe I'm the only person she's ever looked at this way before.

She sort of does a little laugh to herself and goes back to watching the game. I stare at her for a second longer, then return to the game too, only for fear of her biting my head off if I keep watching her instead.

Sadie

"You're up, Sadie and Will!" Coach shouts.

I want to squeal but I just walk up to Coach like it's no big deal. Our first game of the year and he is letting me play. I'm dreaming. I must be.

"Bec! Josh!" he bellows across the court. "Take five!"

Will and I run out onto the court as Bec and Josh come off. I take over defending the dude who made it onto my hate list only a few minutes ago. He passes to his friend but I get a finger on it and it veers off course. It bounces once before Naylene swoops in and scores. I jump into the air with as much elation and excitement as I would if I had shot the damn goal myself.

Noah is cheering louder than usual and it feels bizarre and too egotistical to think that maybe it might be directed at me.

Sloopy

I drum on Josh's shoulder. "Did you see Sadie's awesome defence? "

Sadie got some court time and she helped us score. She must be so ecstatic.

Josh just chuckles. "Keep it in your pants, Sloopy."

I look around anxiously, making sure no one heard his comment.

Sadie gets the ball three more times while she is on the court, but she never takes a shot. I'm surprised when Coach calls her name what must be less than five minutes later and swaps her again with Bec. Sadie was playing really well and Naylene has been on nearly the whole game. Why take Sadie off over her?

Mrs Carrington approaches Coach by the side line and hands him a clipboard. He signs something on it and then she leaves. I didn't know teachers came to basketball.

Sadie sits on the other end of the bench now, because stupid Josh took her spot next to me. Five minutes ago, I could touch the material of her shorts if I tried. Now there are two human beings between us.

I watch the last ten minutes of the game with little interest and only clap when I notice she does. We win by three points.

"We won!" Sadie says to me as she picks up her bag to leave after the game. "Just like you wanted. Being your first game and all."

Her voice is playful and it stumps me. I can't get any words out to offer a witty response. I cringe when I hear myself merely reply, "thanks." Her eyebrows tense in the middle and she turns to walk away. She swings her back-pack over her shoulder and doesn't look back at me. My awkward and nonsensical "thanks" lingers in the air and I agonise over what on earth she would think I was thanking her for.

I roll my eyes in abhor of myself.

Sadie

The house is deadly quiet. I knew it would be. He is never here on Saturdays. He gets up after I've gone to basket-ball and works most of the day doing courier deliveries, then heads straight to the pub. I don't see him at all. It's almost as if he doesn't physically exist, but still there is always an underlying presence, like a dark cloud that constantly hangs over this shitty house. I can never feel truly free because I know he is eventually coming home.

It's just after midday. I open up the curtains in every room and leave the back door open to let the breeze flow through. The house smells musty. I wash his dishes from last night and spray Windex around the place, hope-lessly trying to make everything at least *smell* clean. I make myself two vegemite sandwiches and sit on the floor in front of the telly in the lounge.

I was nine years old the first time I watched this television, sitting in probably the exact same spot I sit now. A lady in a dark grey three-piece suit brought me here. He sat on the couch next to her, signing paperwork. She told me to *watch some shows* while they sorted out *grown-up stuff*. He asked her when he would get his first parenting payment while I watched Double Dare, daydreaming that Eden Gaha could come adopt me instead. I couldn't bring myself to watch Looney Tunes yet. I stayed off that channel altogether.

I was hoping the lady would come back to visit but she left me there that day and never came back once, not even to check if I had settled in, or if I was okay. Or if he was okay.

Because he wasn't. He had no business in looking after a child and clearly didn't want me around. He would go straight to the pub after work, leaving me on my own every night at just 9 years old. I learned pretty quick how to get myself a vegemite sandwich for dinner.

My legal guardian was merely just on paper. There was no one to look after me.

I was scared of him when he did happen to come home; of his temper, his erratic moods, his hostility. He couldn't stand the sight of me so mainly lived behind the closed door of his bedroom. I figured I must be the most irritating person on the planet.

Every now and again on a Sunday evening, he would sit on the couch while I curled up on the floor watching The Comedy Company. I did my best impersonation of Con the Fruiterer in the hopes that I would hear him laugh behind me. But whenever I turned around, he would be staring into space, sleeping or looking at his knees. I wished I could run away and go live with Kylie Mole.

During those first few years, I knew he didn't like me but I had this pathetic desire to make us a real proper family. The more I felt he wanted me to go away, the more I tried to get him to like having me around. I cleaned up after him, made sure I didn't ask for anything and tried to learn his ways so that I could do little things to make him happy, like leave the backdoor unlocked. But rejection set in eventually and I completely gave up on the concept of family. I continued to clean up after him and warned him when he was running low on beer but beyond those obligatory efforts, I blocked him out. I had tried to mean something to him, to be a part of his life. But I'm what made him hate his life.

He did have fleeting moments of happiness, usually when he got the royalties owed for sharing his house with me. The cheques made me happy too: it meant he stayed at the pub for longer, drinking them away.

Rage is playing heaps good songs today. I want to get up and dance but I'm scared that he might come home, even though he has never come home before 11pm on a Saturday. But that's the thing when you are scared of someone. You can never fully relax. Even when they're not here.

Sloopy

The guys wanted me to go to Sheree's party tonight but Dad didn't approve. No surprises there. Mum made tacos for lunch and now I'm cooped up in my room writing about Earth's supposed first known human beings.

My desk is bare bar a pad of paper and my pen. I put a Nirvana sticker on it once. Dad ripped it off because he said their music was trash and would only distract me from who I am supposed to be. The brown laminate came off with the sticker. Dad said when I see that spot, it should remind me of who I really am, not who I am tempted to be.

I'm onto my second page now. I just want to get it done so I can go for a walk to take the DVDs back, and maybe get another new release for tonight since I can't go to the party. Then I remember that Dad put me in charge of Sunday school tomorrow. I sigh at Jesus, pinned to the cross on the wall above my bed, drop my pen and rest my head on my infamously perfect handwriting.

Sadie

Mya tears open her packet of barbecue chips and offers me the packet. I half-smile and shake my head.

"You should have come on Saturday night, Sadie. It went off! The whole year was there! Sheree throws the best parties. I made out a bit with that guy in your basket-ball team."

My smile fades. "What guy?"

"Can't remember his name now!"

"Slut!" Callie teases and they both giggle obnoxiously as if she said something that was actually funny.

Well, it wouldn't have been Noah. I know that.

"That guy!" Mya points excitedly across the court.

I'm surprised and confused to feel relieved that she is pointing at Sam. He is walking across the court towards the library and nods his chin up in recognition of Mya's point.

"Looking good, Mya."

Mya smiles and moves her tongue to the side of her cheek. I hate sitting with her.

"Lucy's having a party this weekend, come with us!" Callie asks excitedly.

I bite hard into my apple, deliberately trying to be unpleasant. "That's a no, in case you can't tell."

Callie and Mya chuckle at my expense.

"Oh Sadie, we do so love you!"

I nearly choke on my apple. You do not, I want to scream. You tolerate me because you know I've got nowhere else to sit.

"Uh-huh," I mumble.

At the end of the day, I wait around in the classroom for my tutoring session with Mrs Carrington. We spend nearly an hour doing my maths homework together. She sits at the desk next to mine and leans her whole body in towards me. She smells really pretty, like she takes the time to put on perfume when she gets dressed in the morning. I wonder if she buys it herself, or if maybe her husband buys it for her.

As promised, she proudly loans me her book, How to Make an American Quilt. It doesn't look like the kind of book I usually like but it's a nice gesture and I don't want to offend her. Being responsible for someone else's property makes me anxious but Mrs Carrington tells me, 'I know you'll take good care of it.' She reckons I'll really like it. Just like she always does when she's excited, she daintily claps her hands together, then giggles that we've got our own little book club going on.

In spite of myself, I smile.

Sloopy

"Can I please push open the window, sir?" I ask Cameron from the third row in the bus. "It's scorching hot in here!"

"The latch is broken," he firmly states, looking straight ahead.

I roll my eyes and then quickly smooth over the creases in my shorts five times for fear that he may have noticed my attitude. The bus continues to wait at the stop. It's just about full, but it's like Cameron is waiting for someone in particular.

And then she steps on.

I see her before she sees me, but I always do.

Sadie

"Thanks for waiting. Sorry, I'm a little late."

"You know I'll always wait for you, Sadie."

Cameron only ever wears a white short-sleeved business shirt. He never turns from the wheel so I can't see if it has a logo on it but I assume it's his uniform. His hair is receding and he keeps it trimmed super short. It occurs to me that I've never seen him standing up before. How bizarre that someone can exist solely in the capacity that we see them. To me he just exists from the waist up, sitting behind a wheel.

I look down the aisle; the bus is chockers. There are only ever a few seats taken on Fridays; usually just an elderly lady coming back from the shops and a few office workers on their way home from work. Public transport is evidently more in-demand on Tuesdays. There are even a couple of people from school but I take it they didn't have tutoring with their homeroom teacher. I'm not sure what other after-school elective there is on Tuesdays. Maybe debate?

Noah slides across to the window seat and puts his bag at his feet. I sigh and begrudgingly sit down next to him. I hug my backpack on my lap and look straight ahead. There must be something else after school on Tuesdays then, not debate. There's no way Noah would do debating.

"H-hey. D-did you have a good day?" he kind of stutters.

I don't answer. The bus pulls away from the curb and I stare at the back of some bald guy's head in front of me. For the entire ride, Noah constantly fiddles with the hem of his shorts and it bugs me so much I can barely stand it.

Sloopy

"I'm going to assume that you all finished Of Mice and Men last night as per my very reasonable expectations?"

It's been above 35 degrees all week. Thursday, last lesson of the day. I don't mind English. I just can't concentrate. There are two ceiling fans in the classroom and they've been pushed to their limits this week. One of them wobbles as it goes around and I look at it periodically expecting it to come flying off.

"The essay questions will be distributed Monday," Mrs Carrington continues. "Today we're going to hold an open discussion. I want to hear your thoughts. I want to know how George and Lennie's relationship made you feel. So, first off, let's partner up with the person in front and discuss how you interpreted George's final decision. Did he do the right thing by Lennie or do you think his actions were driven by a more self-serving need? What is an alternate ending that you would have perhaps preferred to read? Or were you happy with the way it ended?

Pick a representative to present your key points to the class. You've got fifteen minutes to discuss. Off you go, partner up!"

A ruckus forms while half the classroom drags their chairs to the desk in front of them. I pull my chair up next to Sadie and she moves hers over to the right, I don't know whether to make room for me or to be further away from me. I scratch my ear lobe five times and envy the ease of conversation echoing around me.

"So, what do you think? Do you think George did the right thing by Lennie?" I almost whisper.

Sadie circles the tip of her pen in a dent on the top of the desk. "I think he did the right thing by himself. And that doesn't necessarily make it wrong."

"Seriously?" I'm surprised to hear myself respond. "You think murder is okay? George was the only family Lennie knew. He was all he had."

"Lennie made his life hard," she replies, a bit too stoically.

"George was meant to protect him and keep him safe. He failed Lennie. And then he damned himself."

I seem to have piqued her interest and she looks at me for the first time since this conversation started. Her eyes burn into me. She wants to argue.

"Damned himself? If you want to go down that road, Lennie is the one who damned himself. There was no redemption for him after what he did. George was worth saving, Lennie wasn't."

"Everyone is worth saving. George was his whole world; his family. He was meant to protect Lennie. He is a murderer."

Sadie's eyes narrow. "Some people deserve to die."

"I don't think it's ever okay to kill someone."

She glares at me; poised for a fight. "You think it's better to just let someone keep hurting you until they finally kill *you*? Because that's what would have happened. Lennie would have eventually got George killed."

I dig my thumb into my palm five times and look down at the desk. Sadie's hand rests on the surface, fist clenched. She has four tiny bruises just above her elbow. It looks like she's put make-up on her arm but it's so hot today and the make-up has smudged against the sleeve of her school dress.

"I guess I just can't think it's ever okay to kill someone. My dad's kind of like, well, he's a priest, I don't know if you know. So, I sort of can't...I don't know, I can't- "

"Think for yourself and form your own opinion?"

It's not a great feeling when you realise that the first and only girl you've ever liked doesn't actually like you. At all.

I study her hands, too nervous to look her in the eyes. They will just be giving me their usual daggers, anyway. "I was just going to say, I don't know how George could be okay with killing the person whom he mattered the most in the world to."

Sadie's stern expression relaxes and she suddenly resembles the girl I've only ever seen a glimpse of at basketball. "That's why he did it. It was inevitable. It was more dignified for Lennie this way." Our eyes meet and I feel the tension in the air ease. "And just because your dad's a priest, doesn't mean you have to be one, too."

Sadie

He wraps his fingers around my arms and squeezes until the pressure feels like it will crush my bones. He clenches his teeth together, smirking as I wince at the sensation. I'm pushed back against the fridge. His breath heats my forehead.

"Go live with your ma, she's lonely down there and I'm sick of the sight of you."

He relieves his hold. I'm desperate to lift my arms to get the blood flowing again but I'm frozen in fear so leave them dangling by my sides.

He slams the back door on his way out. Off to the pub, no doubt. Thursday night, probably five-dollar schnitzel and pint night. Or maybe they do a parmigiana special. I wonder if he has friends that he meets there. I wonder if he has ever told them about me. Or does he act as if I simply don't exist, because he hopes that one day I won't.

Good on you, George.

You did the right thing.

Sloopy

"Friday today, baby," Mum reassures me as I drag my feet to the front door.

Mum is touching up her make-up at the hallway mirror. She doesn't need it; she is pretty without it and I tell her all the time. But I know she doesn't feel that way around Dad.

He likes it when I make an effort.

Your father likes me to look presentable.

He has to maintain a certain image.

I'm part of his image, too. We all are. As long as everything looks good on the surface, he's happy. Doesn't matter whether we actually are or not. Happy, I mean.

"Yep, finally!" I call back as I head out the door.

I start the short walk to the bus stop. It's been a long week and I'm not in the mood for the world. I turn the corner to see the bus pulling away from the curb.

"No!" I shout, running faster than my feet are prepared to move. "Wait! Please!"

Cameron sticks his arm out the window and waves in the air, honking with smugness. I really do hate that guy.

I get to school late again but the office lady tells me she won't record it. That's about the only good thing that has happened all week.

I wave to Sadie at lunch time. She is sitting with Mya and Callie under the veranda by the court, as always. She sees me but looks away.

The end of the day can't come quick enough.

"Alright, class," Mrs Carrington announces, "pack up time! I get two days of peace from y'all now. Start tidying up."

There's a mad flurry as everyone starts shoving books into their bags and desk. I scrunch up some scribbled-on pages of scrap paper and walk to the front of the classroom to put them in the bin. Sadie has her head bowed and doesn't look up as I pass her desk. I don't even get daggers.

I said a prayer for her last night. I prayed that whatever it is that makes her so sad or angry will go away one day. And that whatever it is that makes her happy, will become a more prominent presence in her life.

Sadie

"Well, it must be Friday, since you have detention."

Mrs Carrington sits down next to me. She folds her arms and puts her feet up on the next desk over, like some sort of rebel student. I'm amused but I don't let her see that.

"I was wondering to myself earlier, when Mr Harris told me that you'd need to stay back twenty minutes because you were late for his class, why you seem so determined to get a twenty-minute detention every Friday. But then it occurred to me, I know Mya and Callie aren't the sporting sort, so who would you wait with before basketball practice? If the rest of the team are hanging out on the court, who would you wait with? Anyway, so I was thinking, why don't you just stop getting these detentions, that stay on your permanent record I might add, and just hang out here for twenty minutes on a Friday?"

My mouth drops open and I look to her with sheer gratitude oozing from my every pore. "Really?"

"Really. I've got marking to do anyway. You're not in the way."

Her words pain my heart. I'm not in the way. But I'm always in the way.

I make an effort to sound sincerely grateful. "Thank you, Mrs Carrington."

"My pleasure, Sadie. Use the time to read my book."

Sloopy

My second basketball practice today and the weather is on my side. Coach said he'd have the school board breathing down his neck if he made us run laps like last week because of the heat. So, lucky for me, we're just doing chest passes.

Sadie is partnered with Naylene and seems to be in a brighter mood. She attempts a smile every now and again when Naylene says something, obviously trying to ease the awkwardness. Basketball really does bring out the friendlier side of her.

We spend the entire session practising our ball skills. It bores me really but it's worth it to be around her.

And to see her happy.

Sadie

I take the single seat directly behind Cameron. He hasn't rubbed the sun cream into his arms properly and for some reason I find it endearing. I imagine his wife scolding him this morning when he tried to leave without it so he begrudgingly smothered it on. Or maybe he forgot altogether and just now remembered, hastily rubbing some on so he can tell his wife tonight that he did.

"How was basketball?"

A rush of warmth washes over me. How special it is to have someone ask about your day.

"It was slow, because of the heat. We just worked on our ball skills mostly."

I wedge my bag between my feet. There are only four other passengers today. No one from my school. An older lady with some shopping bags, a man in a business suit and a mum with her toddler. My kind of bus. I didn't like it on Tuesday. The bus was way too full. I felt self-conscious. I just wanted to close my eyes and disappear.

"I wanted to ask how your tutoring went on Tuesday," Cameron says, not turning from the wheel, "but the bus was pretty full. Did you get much out of it?"

"Yeah, my homeroom teacher is very sweet. She annoys me a bit, like she's always in such a good mood. But she's nice enough, I guess."

Cameron looks at me in the long vertical mirror and chuckles to himself. He strikes me as someone who wasn't exactly the teacher's pet back in his day. He cocks his head to the side, directing my eyes to the black backpack resting by his feet. He scoots it back towards me.

"The Mrs made me a big bowl of pasta for lunch but I wasn't hungry. It's just plain tomato. Sprinkle some cheese on it and pop it in the microwave for a couple of minutes."

I take out the Tupperware container and push the bag back to his feet. "Looks so yummy, I'd even eat it cold."

We pull up at a red light and I look out the window, down to the car in the lane next to us. I recognise that hoon mobile anywhere. Josh is driving and Adam is up front. Noah is sitting in the back seat, with his head resting against the window. He has a nice face. He always looks like he's trying to figure something out. I stare at him and smile without realising.

The light changes to green.

Sloopy

I manage nine push-ups before my arms collapse from under me. I've always known I was lanky, but the basketball uniform really highlights how scrawny I am. My appearance has never really bothered me before. Well, I didn't even think about it so it's not that it didn't bother me, it just wasn't even an issue. But I think about Sadie a lot. And thinking about her makes me think about what I look like. And I don't really get why.

I force one more push-up, knowing that I stopped at an odd number. I add another five to compensate for my big pause between nine and ten but it's not enough. My head feels manic because I initially stopped before completing a group of five. I struggle through the torture of five more push-ups to make my brain calm down.

Josh and Adam are rolling up their sleeping bags.

"What exactly are you hoping is going to happen be-tween you and Sadie?" Adam pries.

"You know your dad won't let anything happen anyway," Josh says before I can answer.

Adam stuffs the rest of his belongings into his overnight bag. "And I hear she's a bit messed up, man." He hesi-tates. "Like, mentally."

I summon the last of my energy, get up from the floor and flop onto my bed. "She's just shy."

"I heard from Eva, who has Maths 2 with Callie, that she's got like anger management issues or something. Like, she's on a proper mental health plan and every-thing. That's why Coach doesn't leave her on the court too long. She punched some guy during a game once and literally broke his nose! Right before Josh and I signed up."

I hastily sit up, absorbing this information. "Are you being serious?"

"Yeah, she punched him right in the face."

"What did he do to her?" I ask.

"Dude, who cares! She punched him in the face!"

Josh waves his hands about excitedly. "Yeah, and apparently, she kneed a *teacher* in the balls! A teacher, man! The girl's a psycho! She's got like this history of getting into fights and stuff. Notice how all the teachers tiptoe around her, like they're scared to call her out on her bullshit? No one else would get away with her attitude."

"When did you find all this out? You guys never mentioned any of it before."

"We asked around a bit at Sheree's party last weekend," Josh shrugs. "Just looking out for you."

I stare into my lap and shake my head. "They must be getting her mixed up with someone else."

Adam and Josh exchange glances.

"Alright, man," Adam says quietly, "your call."

An uncomfortable silence fills my room.

Sadie

We're in an awesome position; six points in front nearing the end of the first half. Noah is sitting next to me again. He's quiet today. He hasn't tried to talk to me even once. Guess I scared him off.

Adam scores for the third time.

"Your friend's playing real good today."

Noah looks at me cautiously. "Are you-," he stutters, "are you speaking to me?"

I look right at him and his eyes seem to twitch. "Yeah."

"Adam? Yeah, he's doing alright hey?"

His face looks panicked. I'm nervous around *everyone* and he's nervous around *me*. I like that.

"He has his moments," I reply nonchalantly.

"I hope you get to play again today. You were awesome last week. Remember, back when I mentioned just once that it was my first game."

He nervously fiddles with his ear and I can tell he's anxious about how his attempt at self-mocking will be received.

"Was it your first game last week? You should have said something."

He smiles and I can't help but smile back.

"Do you catch the bus home every Tuesday now?" he asks eagerly.

"Yeah, Mrs Carrington is doing a bit of extra tutoring with me. You do too?"

"I get the bus every day, unless Josh has his mum's car. But I have debate on Tuesdays, so I get the later bus. Unfortunately. That driver hates me. I get stuck with him on the morning route, too."

He gets to see Cameron every morning. I'm not sure why he'd whinge about that.

"I can't really picture you on a debate team." I look away shyly when I notice him looking at my lips.

"Why's that?" he presses, his voice laden with uncertainty.

"You're too nervous," I reply firmly.

He smooths his hands over his knees multiple times. "That's mainly just around you."

Sloopy

Sadie looks down into her lap and feels her hair to ensure she has some strands framing her face. I think I said the wrong thing. She was happy a second ago and now I've blown it. I have no idea how to talk to girls, particularly ones as pretty as her. All I can think about is kissing those same lips that just told me I am too nervous. I've never kissed a girl before, never even wanted to. But looking at her now, it's all I can think about.

"Sorry, I didn't mean that to sound mean. I'm not all that great at talking to girls."

Sadie watches the game without focus. "Do I make you nervous? I don't mean to. I know everyone thinks I'm a bitch."

"I don't," I quickly reply, "I think maybe you're just a little bit lost, like we all are in our own way. Like I am."

Sadie smiles, not turning away from the game. "So, we're lost together," she says in that certain voice of hers.

Sadie

"You're nothing but a little leech!" he spits. "You'd be out on the streets if it weren't for me. You'd owe me a god damn fortune by now."

I stand stiffly in the backyard, hands clinging together in front of my waist. The washing basket is half full with wet clothes. I was hanging them on the line before he got up.

"I could be married by now if I didn't get stuck with you. I could have had a life, a decent one. Instead, I've got a lazy, pathetic leech taking up all my time and money!" He sways from side to side, wanting me to engage. Wanting me to fight. He bends his knees so his face is level with my bowed head. "I know you think you're better than me, filthy little bitch. Just like she did. You think you're going places just because you go to school? You're going nowhere, girlie. You'll be a dole bludger, that's all you'll be." His breath makes me feel nauseous. The stench of stale alcohol clings to his clothes.

He takes a step back and I bend down to pick up my nightie from the washing basket. This angers him and he lunges forward, grabbing my arms tightly.

"You really think you're better than me, don't you, ya fucking upstart!"

He digs his fingers into my arm and I hate myself for crying out at the instant pain. He shoves me backwards and storms back into the house, slamming the back door behind him.

I pick up my nightie from where it fell on the grass and hang it on the line.

I hate Sundays.

Sloopy

She is already sitting at her desk when I get to the class-room. I see her before she sees me, but I always do. I stop next to her, fuelled with self-confidence after what felt like flirtation at the game on Saturday.

I can't even hide how excited I am to see her. "How was your weekend?"

Sadie folds her arms across her chest and keeps staring at her desk. She shrugs her shoulders. I'm desperate to keep talking to her. I thought about her all weekend.

"I think we get our essay questions today," I ramble on.

Sadie finally looks at me. She narrows her eyes and tenses her lips. She wants me to go away.

I nod to myself, embarrassed that I thought she was starting to like me. I sit down at my desk and look over to Adam, two rows over. He scrunches up his face as if to say *what's her problem?* She is wearing a Tweety Bird scrunchie today, her hair loosely tied into a low ponytail like always.

"Alright, kids!" Mrs Carrington claps. "The weekend's over, now the real party begins! I have four different essay questions to randomly distribute. I can tell you're all so excited to see which one you'll get."

Sadie

The bus is packed again on Tuesday. I'd start walking home instead but then I'd be getting home about the same time as him, and I need to be in my room by then.

Noah moves over to the window seat and wedges his bag at his feet. He looks straight ahead and tilts his head towards the empty spot next to him. I look to a woman in a Hijab down the back. I walk past Noah's seat and take the only other vacant spot next to her.

Sloopy

"Eat your tea, darling, it's getting cold."

Mum pushes my plate closer to me then heads to the sink to wash her own dishes. Tuna mornay. Mum makes the best mornay.

I close my maths book and put my plate on top of it. I dig in.

"It's delicious, Mum! Like always."

Dad enters the kitchen and I instinctively sit up straight. He takes his usual seat at the head of the table; his throne from which to rule us, and waits to be served. "How was everyone's day?"

"Fine. Even better now with Mum's famous mornay."

Mum puts a plate in front of him and he starts eating without thanking her. He has one mouthful then traces his fork over the top.

"It's a bit dry. Well, my day was busy, busy, busy!" Neither Mum or I asked, but Dad's conversations only ever include himself anyway. "I visited the new day-care centre. Lovely staff, beautiful kids. We start our new Sunday session for the under eights this week, too. Noah, I expect your help in setting up. It doesn't look good if we're not all involved."

"I was going to come straight home after the morning service to work on my English essay."

Dad stops eating and stares at me intensely. I tug my middle finger five times under the table.

"Well, that's very disappointing, son. If you didn't take up that silly basketball, you would have enough time for your school work and still be able to help out on Sunday. How can I expect anyone else to volunteer if my own son doesn't even get involved?"

I know where he is heading with this. "Actually, I'm probably pretty close to finishing it up. I'd love to help out on Sunday."

Dad nods in approval, whilst simultaneously studying my face with a look of disappointment. "Do you shave yet? I know Adam started shaving last year, his dad told me after the service last week. No doubt Josh does too."

I smooth my hand over my chin, with a look reminiscent of his own disappointment. "I don't think I need to yet."

One more thing I can hate myself for. Thanks, Dad.

Sadie

Mrs Carrington sweeps around the bottom of the desks and I thank her for letting me hang out in the classroom before practice. "I guess it's nice not having to come up with new ways to get a detention every Friday."

"You're funny when you want to be."

She is wearing a blush-pink blouse with a long pearl necklace and a black pencil skirt with tan stockings: not a single crease on anything. She looks like she's been ironed.

"Do you want me to do that?" I ask, thinking that she looks far too pretty to be sweeping up after a bunch of teenage brats.

Mrs Carrington rests the broom against my table. "That would be lovely, thanks dear." I grab the broom just as she lets go of it. "What happened here?" she gasps, running her finger tips over the small bruises on my arm.

I recoil my arm quickly and take the broom to the other side of the classroom. Adam's desk is filthy underneath it. I start sweeping up the hefty collection of crumbs under his desk and try to start up a conversation to distract Mrs Carrington from thinking what she might be thinking.

"Did you read Of Mice and Men back when you were at school?"

Mrs Carrington sits herself down at my desk, looking pained. "No, we did The Great Gatsby and all of Shakespeare's works. What happened to your arm, Sadie?"

I drop the broom and hastily grab my bag. "I get eczema. Thanks for letting me wait here."

I rush out the door.

Sloopy

Coach tells us to partner up and I instinctively make a beeline for Sadie but Sam grabs her attention before I can. My whole-body slumps in disappointment. Naylene smiles and waves her hand at me so I partner up with her.

Coach blows his whistle. He seems to like doing that.

"Stretches, first up! Sit facing your partner, feet to feet. Then holding hands, stretch back and forth, slowly. Make sure you feel the pull in your back, arms and leg muscles. Hold the stretch for at least fifteen seconds. And go."

The asphalt is hot against the back of my legs. I rest my sneaker soles against Naylene's and we hold hands. Her feet are smaller than mine. I wonder if Sadie's are. She gently pulls my arms and my torso follows, leaning in towards her. I hold the stretch for fifteen seconds like Coach instructed, pleased to be counting to five three times in my head, and then pull back, bringing Naylene with me.

I look over to Sadie; she has her back to me and is stretched forwards over Sam's lap. He catches me looking at her and smirks. He pushes his tongue against the inside of his cheek and looks down to Sadie's head as it bows over his lap. The way he looks at her stirs a reaction in me that I have never experienced before: rage. Without hesitation, I leap up and lunge at him, shoving his shoulder hard. He tips backwards onto the asphalt.

Sam jumps up, anger smothering his face. "What the hell is your problem?"

I shove him again with all my might and he shoves me right back. Coach jumps between us and forcefully grabs holds of me.

"Enough!" he bellows. "Noah, front office, NOW!"

Sadie

After practice, I wait outside the front office. I'm anxious about the bus. I lean against the red bricks and kick the loose pebbles by my feet.

Noah roughly pushes the office door open and storms past me.

"Noah!" I call after him.

He turns back and is visibly surprised to see me waiting for him. "What are you doing here? You'll miss your bus."

"Probably. Just wanted to make sure you're okay. Not like you to pick a fight." I apprehensively hold his eye contact. "So, are you? Okay?"

He is out of breath. "I am now that you're here."

Sloopy

Josh and Adam are waiting in the carpark. I approach them with Sadie lingering behind me.

"All good, Rocky?" Josh teases.

"All good, you guys can go on without me. I'm going to walk Sadie home because she's probably missed the bus."

"We can drop her home?" Adam suggests.

"Nah, we're gonna walk. I'll catch up with you guys tomorrow, yeah?"

Josh smirks at Adam before getting in the car. I'm already not looking forward to the next conversation I'll have with them.

Sadie leads us around the corner, presumably in the direction of her house. She doesn't say anything and I suspect she doesn't want me to either so I don't. We walk in silence, but it's not awkward. When we turn onto the street of the bus stop, the bus is there. I look to her in surprise and she smiles knowingly, as if she was expecting it to be.

The doors of the bus open and the driver's whole face lights up when he sees Sadie. I follow her down the aisle.

"I know, Cameron," she says casually, heading for a seat down the back, "you'll always wait for me."

I've never seen that guy smile before but he looks mighty happy to see Sadie. I climb into the seat next to her and notice him watching in the vertical rear-view mirror, as if he is checking that she is sitting down before he pulls away from the curb. Sadie doesn't try to start up a conversation on the drive, so I don't either. She gazes out the window and I look straight ahead at the back of the seat in front of us. My stop is first. I stand from the seat and nod goodbye but she keeps looking out the window and gives no indication that she even realises I am leaving.

I'm running late come Monday morning because I cut myself trying to shave my perfectly smooth face. Every time I took the toilet paper off my chin, it started to bleed all over again. Then I forgot the cheese sticks. I run all the way to the bus stop. Cameron doesn't deliberately speed away when he sees me frantically running up the street, like he usually does.

He waits for me.

Sadie

"God's sake, stop talking already!" I grumble at the radio, innocently sitting atop my chest of drawers.

I anxiously rest my fingers on the play and record buttons, mentally willing Ugly Phil to shut up. They're playing the proper long version and I want to get the orchestral intro on tape, too but he won't stop talking! Axl is going to start singing any second! This is the fifth night in a row that I have been trying to get it. I jig my feet on the spot and impatiently apply a tiny bit more pressure to the buttons, ready to push down hard any second now.

"So here it is, kids," Ugly Phil bellows across my bedroom, "Guns n Roses with their new masterpiece, November Rain. Nine minutes of sheer genius. Your kids will look this one up one day. Signing off on this Wednesday's edition of the Hot 30, over to you Axl!"

I quickly push my fingers down, locking in the play and record buttons. I miss Axl's first word because of Ugly

Phil's intro. I'm annoyed but still, I've finally got it! I silently squeal and lower myself to the carpet in extreme slow motion, so as not to add any background noise to the recording. Finally! I've got it! I jolt my head back in relief and satisfaction, just as the play and record buttons pop free and the tape starts rewinding.

"What?" I panic, leaping up. "No!"

I press stop and eject the tape. The ribbon is all the way at the end. Night five has been yet another failure. I rest my head in front of the radio and want to cry.

My tummy does a little flip as Axl's vocals wrap themselves around my despair, creating an inexplicable sense of comfort and hope. Hope for everything. Not just that I'll manage to record the song one day: hope that I will actually have a *one day*. Every single musical note makes me ache for a life I wonder if I will ever have the chance to know again.

I listen to the majority of the song, chin resting on my folded arms, mere centimetres in front of my ghetto blaster: the only kind of front row tickets I'll ever likely experience. The guitar solo heightens my disappointment that the tape didn't work. I wish I could listen to it whenever I want.

His truck pulls into the driveway and I have no choice but to return to this life. He's home. I flick the radio and bedside lamp off and retreat under the covers, and keep listening to November Rain in my head.

Sloopy

Adam flicks an ant off his knee. "Look I'm just saying be careful, man. My parents gave me the biggest lecture ever after your dad's epic sermon on Sunday. They think you're heading off the rails and I should watch my step around you."

We sit cross-legged on the oval in a triangle, feeling the spray of the sprinkler when the warm breeze sends it our way.

Josh unwraps his sandwich and tucks in. "See me over here in my happy little life, just eating my fritz and sauce sandwich without having to worry about all that religious crap?"

I roll my eyes, recalling the pre-sermon rehearsal that Dad had subjected Mum and I to before its seemingly infamous Sunday premiere. "At least you only had to watch the premiere, Adam. He practiced on Mum and I the day before. I had front row tickets to my own hate show two days in a row."

Josh is visibly annoyed. "It was literally the first fight you've ever gotten into and you didn't even deck him,

107

you just shoved him a couple of times. I hardly think that means you're going off the rails. And what a dick to bring it up in front of the whole church, just to make himself seem like your goddamn saviour. It's called parenting. I don't care if he's a priest or not, it was a dick move!"

I rub my apple on the thigh of my school shorts five times and take a bite. "Yeah, it sucked."

"You know what I did on Sunday?" Josh gloats. "I stayed in bed and watched Video Hits. You know what my parents did? Gardening. You know what we didn't do? Go to church and judge everyone else to make ourselves feel good."

"We never said we aren't jealous," Adam laughs. "But nah, mate, it's not that bad. Mind you, my old man isn't the priest."

Mum told me that Dad's old church lost most of its constituents a few years back in some kind of protest, which is why he had to be relocated to the new one. Dad's self-esteem took a blow and he has been obsessed with rebuilding his reputation ever since. He cares more about what strangers think of him than what his own family do. Mum and I are never good enough for him, never up to scratch. Everything that goes wrong for him is because of us. Everything is our fault. It's his life, not ours. We just stuff it up.

Dad knew word would get out that his son got into a fight at school. So, he got in first. It's like when you have a massive pimple on your face: you announce it, just because you know that everyone is going to notice so you'd rather just say it first. 'Look at my huge pimple' is easier on your ego than someone else saying, 'Gross, is that a pimple or a boob on your face?' I realise this analogy likens me to a pimple. Or a boob.

Father Blean played it well, determined that his congregation wouldn't find out that we are not a perfect family. He rehearsed his sermon in the lounge. Mum and I sat on the couch, hands on our knees, listening to him preach about how hard life is for him, but how he perseveres because of the love of God in his heart. *My son may fight with his friends, but he does not fight with his faith. He will repent his sins and I will not give up on him. I will do everything I can to raise him to be a man of God and a lover and a friend to his fellow man, not their adversary. I accept the challenges thou hath given me and I aim to be worthy of the faith He has in me. I try, Lord, I try. Thank you for entrusting me with the arduous task of bringing my family back to the path of the Lord.*

His official performance was well-received by the congregation. Dad lapped up the attention.

Oh, Father Blean, you do such a good job with that boy of yours.

Oh, Father Blean, you are an amazing role model.

Oh, Father Blean, what would your family do without you?

Oh, Father Blean, we are so lucky to have you.

Oh. Father. Blean.

They actually swarmed on him like he was some kind of celebrity. Mum and I stood waiting by the car, watching him mingle with his private fan club. We were his props, used to make himself look like a hero. I was the bad guy, led away from the path of destruction by my righteous father.

I used to go to the local Catholic primary school but when we moved churches, we moved everything. Home, school, church. Friends. Dad put me in public school because he wasn't sure his new church would cover the school fees like before. Mum tells me I'll understand when I'm older: life hasn't worked out the way he planned for us and he is working hard to ensure it does now.

After the service on Sunday, Mum gave Dad a shoulder massage as he sat at the kitchen table. She praised him for all the work he is doing in getting the new programs up and running. She *thanked* him for being such a wonderful husband, father and leader. It made me sick to my stomach. He'd just spent the last hour telling the whole church how hard his life is because of us. He tears her down and she puts him on a pedestal. Does he even notice what that is doing to her? Does he even notice how sad she is? I had to get out of there before I gave him my own sermon so I grabbed the New Releases and took my time walking to Video Ezy to return them.

"Have you ever been to church, like even once?" I ask Josh, genuinely interested.

"Nope, not even once. Would *you* have been even once, if you weren't forced to go?"

His question throws me. I stretch out my legs on the grass, taking quick notice that the tops of my socks aren't parallel. I push down my right sock slightly.

"I've never really thought about it, I guess."

Josh inhales another mouthful of his fritz and sauce sandwich. "Maybe you should. I wouldn't automatically believe in something just because I was told to. Think for yourself, man."

I look across the oval, out to the street. On the other side of the road, a lady with a pram strolls by the wire mesh fence. The primary school kids play on the monkey bars and I think back to when I first came to this school, wondering if I would ever fit in with the other kids. Fast forward to my last year of high school and I am still wondering the same thing.

Adam catches me pensively staring across the oval and seems intent on getting the focus off of me. "Oh yeah, hey Josh, I heard Mya was talking about you."

Sadie

The whole class line up in pairs outside Room 12, waiting for Miss Logan. I can't believe Typing isn't an elective. I don't have a computer at home so I'm never going to be able to get up to twenty words per minute like we're supposed to. I linger at the back of the line while everyone mucks around with their friends. I pathetically start wishing that Mya and Callie were in my homeroom so that I wouldn't feel so alone and awkward.

Noah moves from his spot in the middle of the line and comes to stand right next to me.

"Nearly Friday!"

I take a step to the side and press my shoulder into the exterior brick wall, willing myself to get sucked into it. Lucy is flirting with Daniel up ahead and Sarah and Bec are giggling behind them. The whole class is happy, like that's just their natural disposition.

"Have you had a good week so far?" he persists.

I stare ahead and shrug my shoulders. I don't know what else he wants me to say. I am very aware of how mean I must come across to him but I don't know how to stop it. I want to be friendlier, like at basketball but there are so many people around me now and I want the ground to open up and swallow me whole. I need someone now, and it can't be him. It's bad enough that I had a fleeting moment of needing Mya and Callie. I don't belong here; I don't fit in and I never will. No one likes me, everyone wishes I wasn't around. Or that I never existed in the first place.

I bring myself to look at him and narrow my eyes. I want him to talk to me, to stay with me, and I hate myself for that. No one is meant to notice me. I need to be invisible. I need to be quiet. I need to disappear.

Bec laughs loudly and stumbles backwards, pushing into me. I instinctively shove her back and she calls me a bitch.

Miss Logan rushes past us to the head of the line. "This is hardly what I would call waiting quietly!" She fiddles with her keys and unlocks the classroom.

Noah is still standing next to me.

He didn't leave.

I make a conscious effort to be invisible every single day. He notices me when I'm scared to be seen. And when he sees me, when he sees who I am, it doesn't scare him off.

Sloopy

Coach pats me on the back, hard and nearly knocks me to the ground. I need to bulk up. "You're up, Noah. Stick with your opponent and do a quick scan before you pass."

I follow Josh and Adam out onto the court and take my position. I press my thumbs into my palms five times, mentally psyching myself up. Although it's too late now: the ball is heading right for me. Shit.

I instinctively grab it and dribble down to our end. I pass to Naylene and she takes a shot but misses. Josh grabs the rebound and scores. Everyone cheers but I can only hear Sadie.

I get my hands on the ball a few more times before the whistle blows for half-time. I grab one of the orange slices on the table and a green cordial and sit with the team while Coach picks the players for second half. I'm left sitting on the bench to catch my breath, next to Sadie.

I try to shallow my breathing so it's not glaringly obvious how exhausted I am. I count to five between each breath.

I haven't spoken to her today and this week has been dead average, so I'm not really fishing for yet another rejection. I'm just going to sit here, time out my breathing and support the team.

My promise to myself is almost instantly broken.

"You played heaps good," she says, looking straight ahead at the game.

An excessively stupid grin takes over my face. It is such an alien feeling when she speaks to me. I don't know what it is, what to call it. I'm told by my friends that it's a crush and maybe they're right. But it feels like something far more visceral than that. A crush seems so simple, so easily defined. I don't understand the way she makes me feel. I understand what a crush is. I don't understand this.

I concentrate on sounding nonchalant. "Thanks." I want to keep talking but I leave it at that.

I'm so grateful when she keeps the conversation going.

"My week was pretty average, actually. You asked the other day."

She pulls her ponytail over her shoulder and aimlessly twirls the ends of her hair. She is wearing her Foghorn Leghorn scrunchie.

"I've been trying to tape a song all week but every time, something goes wrong. Like I so nearly got it the other night, then the tape ran out. Last night was the worst; I pressed play on its own. The record button didn't stick down. So, I still haven't got it yet."

Her words drift from her lips to my ears with a defiant yet graceful melody, and I want to bask in their coveted magic. They were gifted to me and the offering feels so rare that I almost start to panic.

Her cheeks flush the colour of the dahlias in Mum's flower bed. I know she is getting annoyed because I haven't replied yet. I'm still lapping up her words. The sound of her voice has drugged me. She turns her gaze from the game and looks at me with a frown starting to form. I need to reply.

"What song are you trying to get?"

"November Rain."

"I've got their album. You want to borrow it?"

"Nah it's okay, thanks. I'll get it. It's like a personal vendetta now."

I love her voice. She smiles, as if she likes the way I am looking at her.

"Have you heard of The Cranberries?" I ask. "I just got their CD and all their stuff is pretty good. I could lend it to you if you want?"

"Sure, then I'll let you know whether or not you've got good taste in music. They've got that Zombie song out yeah?"

"Yeah, that's the one. Their other stuff is heaps good, too."

The game ends and it's a win for us. Sadie claps excitedly and giggles when I attempt to pull-off a manly wolf-whistle.

The boys rush up to the bench and Adam aggressively rubs the top of my head. "You did awesome!"

Coach gathers us all together in a huddle and we chant our team's name. *Warr-i-ors. Warr-i-ors. Warr-i-ors.* Sadie joins in and I'm mesmerised by her smile as she looks from player to player, subtly adoring everyone around her.

Most kids in school would describe Sadie as withdrawn, unsociable, maybe even depressed.

Angry.

Scary.

If only they could see her right now.

Being part of the team really does do something for her.

Sadie

The urge to wee wakes me up at 6am. I was hoping I would have the chance to clean the toilet before I needed to use it but I'm so busting. I heard him throwing up in the middle of the night, right after he stumbled through the back door and made a heavy-footed dash to the bathroom.

Chunks of regurgitated food fill the bowl. I quickly flush and squat my legs, hovering above the seat. I hold my breathe against the repulsive stench of vomit and try to expedite the speed of my wee.

After my shower, I get dressed in loose-fitting linen pants and a white t-shirt. The water bill came on Friday so I strip my bed, wash my sheets and hang them out on the line. I wash them once per water bill.

Today is the day I'm finally going to get November Rain. I've plugged in the extension cord so I could move the radio onto the end of my bed. I've checked a million times that the tape is on the right spot. Plus, they're doing a competition to win a double pass to see How to Make an American Quilt. I don't want to see it, but it might be nice to give the tickets to Mrs Carrington so she can see it again, considering how much she said she loved it. You have to be the first caller when they play the designated song every hour. I'm on the listen out for Peter Andre's Gimme a Little Sign. I sit cross-legged on my bed, coiling the telephone cord around my index finger, excitedly waiting.

The dude on the radio is talking, and I just know it's going to be the song straight after. I key in the phone number, bar the last digit. I hover my finger over the 9 and impatiently wait for him to stop speaking.

Accidentally Kelly Street starts playing. I relax my tensed shoulders and put the receiver back down.

It's 12.30pm and I'm hungry. I open my door just enough to peak out. No sign of him. I can't see a light underneath his door so he's still asleep. I tiptoe the few steps across the hallway into the kitchen, make myself two vegemite sandwiches and quickly retreat back to my room.

Bugger. Gimme a Little Sign is half-way through.

Sloopy

I wrap my arms around Mum's shoulders, cuddling into her as she sits at the table sorting out her new batch of Avon orders.

"I wish the shops were open on Sundays. We need to get your dress for the party! Maybe we can go to Arndale after the game next Saturday?"

Dad enters the kitchen, carrying the Sunday Mail. He sits down opposite Mum at the table. "I already bought your mother a dress."

"Yes, it's lovely, dear, thank you."

Mum pats my arm and I'm annoyed that he doesn't detect the disappointment in her voice.

He opens up the paper and starts reading. "It wasn't cheap either, so make sure you don't cram it in the wardrobe. You'll get it all creased and ruin it."

"Yes, dear. Would you like a cup of tea?"

"That would hit the spot. I received some lovely feedback forms from this morning's service so I'll be in the office filing them before the bible reading seminar at four. Noah, I'd appreciate you keeping the noise down so I can concentrate."

"I'm heading down to the court soon. I'm meeting Adam there to get some practice." I feel good knowing that he won't be able to blame me for not getting enough peace.

"Good, and your mother will need help with the washing later. She put too much powder in the machine last time and everything needs to be rewashed. Not sure what she expects people to think if we all walk around with clumps of washing powder stuck to our clothes."

Mum dutifully places his cup of tea in front of him.

Dad is a devoted, attentive and loving family man.

Just ask everyone at church.

If only his actual family thought the same.

"I'll take you driving again after dinner," he says into the newspaper. "You need to learn to watch your speed. The road isn't your personal race track."

I did drive us home after church. 40 all the way. But he still thinks I go too fast. He put down 10 minutes in my log book. He wouldn't even exaggerate the time by 5 minutes. If I ever get my Ps, it'll be a miracle.

Sadie

School is dragging and my attention is waning. The heat of the afternoon has drained my energy. I wish I could have a shower tonight to wash away the remnants of the day but there won't be enough time before he gets home. I could skip tutoring with Mrs Carrington; just tell her I have something else on today. But she gives up her time for me and I guess it would be kind of rude.

I look to the clock; only another couple of minutes before the bell goes. I run my hand over the back of my neck, wiping away the sweat.

Sloopy

She is wearing my favourite scrunchie today: Bugs Bunny himself. Her skin glows from the humidity of the afternoon and it's mesmerising. Every tiny droplet hypnotises me and seduces my thoughts away from the classroom.

Her ponytail sticks to her neck and she gracefully smooths it away, stirring something inside me. I'm kicked out of my own body. I feel my blood pulse through my veins, sending my organs into overdrive. Her hand pushes the back of her collar down, trying to get some air on her neck.

My shorts suddenly feel too tight against my legs, compelling me to look down. This can't be happening. Not now. Not here. Sadie rubs her neck again. The pressure builds against my zipper. More and more intense. I tent my geography book across my lap and frantically try to regain control of my thoughts which are currently plotting against me; intent on inducing irrevocable public humiliation.

Think.

White collar.

Turn the radio on for Mum.

It's not going away!

Whitecollarwhitecollarwhitecollar. *Get used to it, Noah; you'll have to wear one too soon.*

Turn the radio on for Mum. She is sad without it. If I forget, she will be sad because of me.

White collar. Radio. White collar. Radio.

Oh god.

Why won't it go away?

Sadie

The bell goes and everyone makes a mad dash for the door. Excited to go home: what a strange concept.

I lift open my desk and take out my maths text book, noticing that Sloopy hasn't left yet. Mrs Carrington is finishing up something at the head of the classroom. I wait patiently for her, growing more and more irritable that Sloopy hasn't left yet. He has debate. This is my time with Mrs Carrington. He is always one of the first to leave. What is he doing?

Sloopy

White collar.

Radio.

I am sweating profusely, and not because it's 39 degrees.

I count to five between each breath, pinching and releasing the skin between my thumb and index finger in time with the breaths.

White collar.

Radio.

"Everything okay, Noah?" Mrs Carrington enquires, ready to start her time with Sadie. I am messing up their thing.

My eyes snitch on me and my voice is laced with anxiety. "Yes."

Mrs Carrington subtly notices my geography book pitched across my lap. "I forgot you were late for geography this morning! That's so unlike you, Noah. I was surprised when Mr Roberts told me you'd need to make up some time after school. Go when you are ready; I know you won't go before you've paid back the time that you owe."

Sadie gives me daggers as Mrs Carrington pulls a chair up next to her. This is her time and I am ruining it. I am ruining something important to her.

That thought alone is more powerful than any white collar, and my body finally agrees. Rampant relief energises me. I hastily pack up my things and rush to the door.

"Thanks," I utter as I rush past Mrs Carrington.

Sadie

"Noah wasn't late for geography. You should have picked a class that we don't have together."

Mrs Carrington smirks. "No fooling you."

"So, what was that about? Why didn't he go when the bell went?"

"Maybe we should have a little talk, Sadie. Woman to woman."

You're not my mother, I want to scream at her. But I don't. There's so much I don't understand about life. There's so much no one ever got to tell me.

"Okay, I'm listening."

Sloopy

My hormones have made me late for debate, but Mr Gates doesn't notice.

"I've made up some cards, each with a random topic; controversial, of course. Once you get your card, choose if you're for or against and you'll have two minutes to convince us."

I slip into the back of the room, sitting low in my chair, wishing myself invisible. It doesn't work.

"Noah, you're up first today. Come grab a card."

Sadie

Mrs Carrington daintily claps her hands, just like she does. "I'm so proud of you, Sadie. You are really starting to get a handle on this."

I close my maths book and smooth my hand over the cover. "Thanks." I mean it. This must be how everyone in class feels when their parents say they're proud of them.

Mrs Carrington stands from the desk next to me and straightens out her navy pencil skirt. I enjoy these Tuesday tutoring sessions a little too much. It's quiet. Everyone else has gone home. I don't feel self-conscious or paranoid that everyone around me wishes I wasn't here.

"Do you feel like you're grasping everything a bit more now?" she asks in that perfectly pitched voice of hers.

"Yeah, thanks."

Mrs Carrington leans over onto my desk and I arch back in my chair to compensate for her close proximity.

"Sadie, can I make an observation?"

"O-kay?"

"If you concentrate more on the work, and shut out all that noise going through your head, you will find it much easier to find your way."

I tense my face and fold my arms across my chest. "I do concentrate."

"I know, I see that you try, but you lose your way. What do you think about? Like, here in class. Are you thinking about maths, or are you just worried about what everyone else is thinking of you?"

I want this conversation to be over. I shift uncomfortably in my seat. I would walk out but she has been so nice to me and she is the last person I want to fight with.

"I think I'm just a nervous person," I shrug.

"What are you nervous of?"

"People. I don't know, I'm better at being on my own. I guess I'm not good at being around people."

"I speak to the guidance counsellor sometimes, because I care about you, Sadie. I know you've been in a lot of fights over the last couple of years. You broke someone's nose in a basketball game. You castrated your geography teacher."

I suppress a chuckle and Mrs Carrington does the same.

"Well Mr Roberts is a blithering idiot anyway."

Mrs Carrington presses her lips together. "Yes, he is, but that doesn't mean it's okay to knee him in the balls."

My eyes widen in shock at words like that coming out of the mouth of such a lady. She smiles knowingly and it relaxes me.

"I haven't got into any fights for like a year now. Coach has hardly put me on court since that day anyway. I was only on for like ten minutes last game."

"Do you wish you could play a bit more?"

"I guess."

"The wheels are in motion. There are progress reports and things like that in place. Coach just needs to see that you can cope and control your anger. We're trying to protect you, Sadie. I know it probably doesn't feel that way. Can I ask, why did you punch that boy in the face last year? In the middle of the game?"

I roll my eyes and exhale loudly, trying to sound a bit tough. But I feel embarrassed, realising I probably just look like an immature brat to her. I'm annoyed to realise that Mrs Carrington didn't come to basketball because they were short on parent volunteers. She was obviously just being a spy for the guidance counsellor.

"I didn't like what he said to me." Mrs Carrington encourages me with her eyes. "He said that my parents would have been eaten by worms by now."

Mrs Carrington nods and gently puts her hand on top of mine as it sits atop my desk. I recoil instinctively, flicking her arm back. I feel bad. I can tell I've hurt her feelings.

"I know that you lost your Mum and Dad, Sadie. I understand why you would be so protective of them."

I abruptly jump to my feet and Mrs Carrington sits back in alarm.

"Stop interfering in my life," I firmly tell her. "I'm not your responsibility."

She looks gutted. Because of me. I hate that.

"Look, it's fine." I try so hard to sound softer. "It was ages ago. I'm going to miss my bus. I need to go now. Bye."

I run toward the door and faintly hear her whisper, "you won't miss the bus, Sadie."

Sloopy

I check my watch. 4.30pm. The bus should have left ten minutes ago. I rest my head against the window and pull out my new MAD magazine.

A man in a grey suit sitting three rows ahead of me complains loud enough for Cameron to hear. "Any chance we can leave some time today?"

Cameron turns back and shoots him an authoritative glance then looks at me and nods in strange recognition.

Sadie steps onto the bus. Cameron reaches back and gently grabs a hold of her hand. "You okay?" he asks.

"Stupid teacher wanted to have a counselling session."

Cameron chuckles as Sadie makes her way down the aisle. An elderly woman sits close to the front and a loved-up couple sit at the back. The bus is practically empty and I can't hide my shock when she sits down next to me. She slips her backpack off her shoulder and wedges it between her feet.

"Doesn't mean I feel like talking," she says, looking straight ahead.

The bus pulls away into the street and I bite the inside of my cheeks five times to stop myself from grinning like an idiot. Her thigh is pressed against mine. Her plaid school dress rests above her knees. I run my eyes along her legs, imagining what her skin feels like. My head starts to spin. I abruptly drag my stare to the bald guy's head sitting in front of me.

"I saw that," she announces confidently.

Sadie

I've had almost every class with Noah since the bus ride home on Tuesday. I've caught him looking at me a few times, but he hasn't tried to talk to me. Not even once. I guess I appreciate that. He gives me space. But still seems to look for me.

On Thursday, I watch him a bit at lunch as I sit with Mya and Callie. He is on the court in front of us, shooting hoops with Josh and Adam.

"This is our last year in this shit hole, Sadie," Mya chats, seeming not to care about the visible half-chewed up sandwich in her mouth. "I'm not leaving this school without getting you to at least one party."

"Pass," I reply without emotion, watching Noah try too hard to look cool. He scores and instantly looks over to me. I quickly turn my gaze to the water taps. I smile, almost unbeknownst to myself. His grey shorts and white short sleeved shirt emphasise his lanky arms and legs. He reminds me of a spider. "Looks like you're stuck here forever in that case."

"Trust me, this one is going to be epic," Callie insists.

Josh runs past us and runs his whole head under the water taps. He guzzles from the spout like a lost hiker who just stumbled upon a lake in the dessert.

Mya follows him with her eyes and adjusts the hem of her dress, hiking it up a little. "Yeah, that Charlie guy's organised it. You know, the hot dude with the little sister in year eight. He's got his grandma's property up in Crafers for the weekend. I met up with Nick at Time Zone on the weekend and he told me all about it. She's having a hernia taken out or something so Charlie's house sitting. It's going to be wicked. Come with us, please! I've got my brother's car. I can pick you up Saturday at five."

"I'm busy, my loss."

Josh leaps in front of us and shakes his head like a wet dog, spraying water onto us. Mya and Callie squeal and shield their faces with their hands. I stare at him, unimpressed.

"You're stupid if you don't come," he gloats, turning back to the court. "Sloopy will be there."

Sloopy

"It's been very hard for me to repair the damage you caused, Noah," Dad reminds me as I pile into the back of Josh's mum's car.

Josh puts the keys in the ignition, failing to hide his impatience, or intolerance. Adam clicks his seat belt in and they both sit waiting, obediently. Dad shuts the back door with both hands and motions for me to roll the window down.

He sticks his head through and rests his arms on the open window.

"My life is so demanding; my community expects a lot from me. I need you to be upstanding, to set an example. I want to be proud of you. Can you imagine how humiliating this whole episode has been for me? No more fights. This has to be a one-off."

"Yes, Dad."

"Your mother tells me you're staying over at Josh's house this evening. I expect you home by ten on Sunday. We leave at half past for the eleven o'clock service."

"Yes, Dad."

"And I need you to run the kids club at three this week. You need the practice. Seminary school will be looking for things like that. Which reminds me, I need to contact them again about the application."

"Yes, Dad."

"And if people are drinking tonight, and you give in to peer pressure, I *will* find out about it and there *will* be consequences, understand?"

"I understand, Dad. I don't drink."

"Just like you don't get into fights. Remember whose family you belong to." He leans back from the window and taps the roof of the car. "That goes for you too, Josh. Just because you're eighteen doesn't mean you can drink and drive. A full license comes with even more responsibility. Speed kills. Okay, off you go then."

Josh drives off and waits until we are half-way up the road before mocking him. "Yes, Dad. Fuck off, Dad."

I panic and look back out the window. I can't even see our house now but I'm still freaking out that Dad will hear him. I tug at the collar of my basketball top five times, suddenly too tight against my chest.

"Maccas?" Adam asks.

"Maccas!" Josh rejoices.

Up ahead, Sadie bounces her ball back and forth against the new housing estate wall.

"Don't stop," I instruct Josh. "Keep driving, she doesn't like being bothered."

Sadie

He always smells like McDonald's on game day. I'm sure this bench is getting shorter; he seems to sit closer to me every single Saturday. Our thighs are basically right next to each other. It annoys me. I wouldn't let anyone else get away with that.

Noah doesn't pester me, so I'll let his lack of knowledge about personal space slide. He doesn't talk to me unless I talk to him first. He lets it be on my terms.

We're playing really well today but the other team is better. We never beat them. It's a home game but they are dominating us on our own court.

"Your friend Josh said you're going to that house party up in Crafers tonight."

Noah's face lights up like one of those kids in the John Martins Christmas ads. I can't get used to how excited he gets when I talk to him. I suppress my smile though: I could never let him get a hint of how much I like it.

"Yeah, I thought I might go. Are you going?" he replies too eagerly.

"No. I mean, Mya and Callie are. They want to pick me up on the way but it's not really my scene."

"What is your scene?" he presses, and he's so damn interested it puts me off talking to him.

"I don't know," I shrug.

Noah nods to himself and looks down into his lap. He fiddles with the stitching on his pocket and starts to pick at a scab on his wrist.

Great, I feel bad.

"I like being in my room, listening to music. I like going through my CDs. I like reading. I really love basketball. I don't know, I'm not much fun, I guess. I don't really go out or anything like that." I hate talking about myself. The flow of blood in my veins accelerates to a frantic gush. *I go to school and then hide in my room because my uncle is a drunk and I'm scared he will really hurt me one day. That's my scene.* "Well, what about you? What do you like?"

He resumes fiddling with the hem of his shorts and looks up at the game. "You. I like you."

Part of me wants to punch him in the shoulder, warn him to never speak to me again. Another part of me, the most dominant part, is desperate for him to keep talking to me. "Why? I'm rude to you. I'm rude to everyone. No one likes me."

He looks around nervously. "I like you. I like you and I like music I'm not supposed to. They kind of go hand-in-hand."

I press my lips together and hate myself for liking his answer so much. He opens his mouth to speak, pausing in hesitation.

"When we're in homeroom, I look at your scrunchie when I find myself feeling a bit out of it. Like sometimes I just don't have the mental energy, you know, to get through the day, doing everything I'm expected to do. *Being* exactly who I'm expected to be. I don't know if anyone else feels it, but it's all a bit exhausting to me, particularly because I don't really know yet who I even want to be. I focus on your scrunchie, bizarre as that may sound and just wonder who the girl that wears them really is. Your scrunchies slow my brain down a bit."

My brows tense and my lips move to speak but I don't know how I'm meant to put the necessary words together to form an appropriate reply. It's a big thing to let someone see that you're actually a mess. I don't know if it's my turn to speak and I'm relieved when he continues.

"You have five different Looney Tunes scrunchies. I've tried to work out if you wear a particular one on a particular day but it seems pretty random. Anyway, guess what I'm trying to say is, I notice you. I know you don't really want anyone to notice you, but I do. Noticing you is what stops me from wanting to disappear. Noticing you makes me want to figure out who I am. So, you asked what I like, I like you. You are the only thing in my life that I have chosen to like for myself." He glides his finger back and forth vigorously over his wrist. "Well, you and Nirvana. I don't know if that makes sense."

I study his face for a hint of what he expects me to say in return but all I can read is a rampant fear of exposure. "My, ah, my Mum and I used to watch Bugs Bunny together," I almost whisper. "Every day at four. She loved Foghorn and Miss Prissy. I loved Yosemite Sam. She bought me the scrunchie collection on my eighth birthday. It was a set, there was one for every day of the week but I lost the Sylvester one at swimming carnival one year."

"So, you obviously still love the show then? You still watch it together?"

"My Mum died." The words float out of my mouth and I swallow hard, wishing that would retrieve them.

"I didn't know that. I'm heaps sorry." He cautiously reaches his hand onto my lap and strokes the back of my hand. I flinch and he recoils. "So, is it just like, you and your dad, then?"

"No, he died with her. They were killed by a drunk driver. We were on our way home from a Christmas service my

Mum dragged us to. I just had a concussion but, yeah, they um, kind of died at the scene. I live with my uncle, Mum's brother. I was told that he was the closest living relative but I'd never actually met him when I came to live with him. I think he was estranged or something like that. Mum never really mentioned him."

The whistle blows and we've lost the game. I feel like I missed most of it and I'm annoyed at Noah. He made me talk about myself for nothing. We can't even finish the conversation. Josh pulls Noah up by his guernsey and drags him over to the line-up, ready to high-five the opposition.

"Can you come to that party tonight, please? Please come," he gushes. "I'll look for you."

Sadie

"Hey, cool house," Callie lies as she nosily looks around the hallway entrance. "It's, um, retro!"

"Your uncle not home?" Mya pries, stepping into the lounge room.

The floorboards creak under the carpet and it's a sound that I normally don't even notice when he isn't home, but everything about them being here is irritating me.

"Not usually. I'll just go grab my stuff."

Mya and Callie seem compelled to touch everything and I regret calling Mya after basketball asking her to pick me up. She literally squealed into the phone and it felt kind of nice at the time but now I just wish I'd never called her.

I hastily head to my room to get my bag, contemplating whether I should invite them to come, too. I like my room and it might counteract the shame of the rest of the house. It's my home, really. The walls are painted faded pastel purple, from long before I lived here; as if it knew I would come one day and need a pretty place to call my own. I plaster my favourite singers all around and a large cream rug with faded flowers stretches across the whole floor. I want them to see my room because it's the only space I am proud of in this house, but it is *mine*. It is my safe place. Maybe it's just best to leave them fossicking in the lounge.

I shove my lip gloss and Impulse in my bag and stand at my dressing table, giving my hair a quick brush before dumping my brush in too. I don't wear my hair down very often and I feel different looking at my reflection now.

The kiddie counsellor they made me see after the accident once told me that I look 'softer' with my hair down. The insinuation that I traditionally looked harsh in comparison was not lost on me, even back then. Did she expect a nine-year-old to walk around smiling when she'd just lost her entire world?

I saw her once a week for three months. Some woman I'd never even met before picked me up every Saturday morning and drove me to the appointments and then 'home' again afterwards. She told me that everyone from Mum's church had collected money to pay for trauma counselling for me. I don't think it helped but I did eventually join the basketball team, like she had suggested I do.

Mum used to love going to church. She took me a couple of times but I don't really remember it. I just recall not really being into it, but that didn't bother Mum. She always said people should believe whatever feels right for them, so Dad and I stayed home reading Choose Your Own Adventure books. He would tease her when she got back, saying things like, 'are you allowed to be a Christian if you're this sexy?' When they kissed, which was often, I'd tell them that they were gross. Dad would bowl me over and tickle me and Mum would try to 'rescue' me. All of that is still with me: the memories, the *feeling*. Family is not a tangible object so you can never technically lose it.

Mum and Dad loved their life and they loved their family. A drunk took it all away and then I was handed over to another one.

I step into my black, chunky Doc Martens. They're old now. The yellow stitching has faded but I need to make them last a little while longer until my traditional birthday money comes. I push my striped short-sleeved skivvy into the waist of my jeans. I had it out but I like my white belt, so I decide to go with it tucked in. I look myself up and down in the mirror and practice my smile. It's prettier with a closed mouth, I decide. I hear Mya continuing to rummage in the lounge so I put my arms through the straps of my backpack and rush out.

I want them both out of this house.

Sloopy

Josh's bedroom is tiny. There's just enough room for his single bed and mirrored wardrobe. His walls are covered with TV Hits posters: Alyssa Milano, Tiffani Amber Thiessen and the odd Wesley Snipes visible. His TV rests atop a short cupboard next to a faded black bean bag laden with white cat hair; it's simultaneously the ugliest and most comfortable thing ever. I sit watching Josh squeeze a pimple on his forehead and try to hide my disgust when he starts making embellished side effect noises.

He wipes off the remnants of his squeeze on the mirror. I dry heave into my chest, hurling my whole torso forwards, and both he and Adam roar with laugher.

"Pretty sure you should have been born a girl, Sloopy."

Josh has the smallest bedroom and the smallest house out of the three of us. He lives in a two-bedroom semi-detached dwelling a couple of streets down from the train station. My bedroom is probably bigger than his whole lounge room and Adam's parents take him on an overseas holiday every year, yet Josh is probably the happiest out of all of us.

Josh's dad enjoys spending time with his wife and son. He actually opens his arms for an embrace when he comes home, like the TV dads do. I can't recall the last time Dad hugged Mum. Or me.

Josh isn't a nuisance to his dad. Everything his parents do for him is done with joy and pride, not resentment. The mere sight of me is an instant downer for my dad. Last week I asked him to take the lid off the vegemite jar because it felt like it was superglued on. He sighed and dropped his shoulders, as if mentally wishing I would just go away and leave him alone. He unscrewed it with relative ease, and then just left it on the counter and walked away without a word. I ruined his whole day. Just like I ruin his whole life.

I was ten the first time Josh invited me round. I was still new to the school. I knew Adam from church so it was nice to already have one friend here. Josh was Adam's best mate and he first greeted me like I was already his best friend, too. He was a year older than us, I soon found out. The teachers held him back in year 2 because they said he was too small to move up a grade. I wonder how being judged solely on your height can impact a kid's self-esteem. Josh caught up but I think there's a part of him that constantly feels like he has to prove that he's got enough testosterone.

I didn't think anything in particular of his house back in those days, it was just a house like any other as far as I was aware. All I remember thinking is how awesome it was that we got to play Super Mario Brothers in the lounge room and that his mum made popcorn for us.

I wish I was still like that kid, still blissfully unaware. I wish I still viewed the world like a ten-year-old. Just seven years later and I can't help but wonder if he feels embarrassed by his house when Adam and I come over. I notice things now that I never used to, like the size of Josh's bedroom, what his parents do for a living, and I hate myself for it. I can feel myself becoming someone I don't want to be, someone I don't like. But I guess that's just what growing up is.

Josh's dad works at the Holden factory and his mum at the local fish and chips. They work hard yet I know they struggle a lot. My dad looks down on them, pities them even: materialistically poor and all that. Lower socio-economic status. Don't go to church. Certainly not a family of merit or class, like ours. We tick all the boxes; he makes sure of that. Such a loving dad in public. Straight A son. Dutiful wife. Two storey home with modern appliances. Tick. Tick. Tick. Perfect.

"What do you guys think?" Adam ponders, making room for himself in front of the mirror next to Josh. "Gel, or leave it scruffy?" He runs his fingers through his curls and checks out his profile from all angles.

"Scruffy," Josh and I reply in unison.

Adam pushes his glasses back up by the bridge and flops backwards onto Josh's bed. "I reckon most of the year eleven and twelves will be there tonight! It's gonna be huge!"

Josh agrees. "I'll be pissed off if I don't get some action, considering I'm the one who'll have to drive your drunk arses home."

"I can't drink, just let me drive," I remind him.

Josh grabs his white Levi's t-shirt from the chest of drawers and pulls it on over his head. "Nah mate, no way. The cops will be out in force tonight. Even if you drive home, I still can't drink. Hurry up and get your Ps then we'll be sweet. You'll be the designated driver every weekend."

I run my hands over my bent knees and pinch my jeans in between my fingers. Josh says it's time to go so I quickly pinch the material four more times and Adam calls out shot gun.

Sadie

Mya parks her brother's metallic brown Torana next to an old picket fence, which I suspect was white many moons ago but which now bares the marks of years' worth of sun damage and neglect. Everything out here feels old and somehow forgotten. You would have to actually drive down to your neighbour's house or else take a ten-minute walk just to say hello to them. Which strikes me as ironic: out here, I imagine people actually want to say hello to their neighbours.

Callie slides the passenger seat forward so I can climb out from the back.

"Make sure you lock it!" Mya panics. "My brother will kill me if anything happens to this car. It's his baby. I had to give him two weeks' allowance just to borrow it."

It's crazy that we're less than an hour out of the city. There are crop paddocks all around us and the roads stopped being proper roads twenty minutes ago; everything is just dirt out here. There must be more sheep than people.

We walk in the direction of the music; The Prodigy's Voodoo People blares across the paddocks and I feel like we're in a real live horror movie. If it weren't for the thirty odd cars branded with P plates lined up along the fence, I'd be worried that we had been lured out here to the middle of nowhere by some suspicious old man with murderous intentions. I regret this. I don't belong here. I hate that I'm reliant on Mya for a ride home. I'm stuck out in the sticks until she decides she's done enough tarting around for the night.

"Get a load of all the cars!" she squeals. "Dibs on the year twelve guys! And you know I mean all of them! I wonder if Josh will be here?"

Mya's black boots stretch all the way up to her thighs, only leaving a small gap of leg before the hem of her A-line red chequered mini skirt. Her black, long sleeved ribbed crop top emphasises her toned abdomen. I feel frumpy walking behind her.

Callie is dressed more like me; baggy jeans and a pink skivvy tucked in under a thick black studded belt. I love her chunky-soled Sketchers and I'd probably tell her if it didn't feel so unnatural to start a conversation like that.

The three of us walk towards the house, down a long loose-gravel driveway. Mya kicks her feet as she dances a few steps ahead of us. You can nearly see her bum cheeks every time she waves her arms above her head. I stare at the back of her and feel perverted checking her out. She has the most perfect body and she knows it. Puberty was kind to her. I wonder what it feels like to be so perfect. She could easily be on the cover of Dolly.

Callie giggles, no doubt at my obvious stupor, and loops her arm through mine. I wince but she doesn't seem to notice.

"Come on," she nudges into my side, "party time!"

The music bounces off the trees and booms across the paddocks around us. I'm surprised the sheep aren't running away in fright. I shudder to think how loud it's going to be inside the house.

"You ready girls?" Mya prances back to us. "Best night ever because our third amigo is finally out with us! Only took her five years!"

I wish she wouldn't bother to pretend that she likes me. I know she doesn't. Nobody does, I'm just in the way. My bottom lip attempts a smile, but it must look sarcastic: Mya seems disappointed that I don't reciprocate her banter. I don't see the point in pretending that we're actually good friends.

The front door is held open by a six pack of beer. I instantly feel tense, realising that people are going to be drinking. We walk in single file, squeezing our way through what feels like the entire student body. Callie stretches her arm behind her, probably not expecting me to grab it. But I do. I hold onto it. I hold onto her.

Mya oozes out a *hey, you* as we pass Josh but he just nods and walks straight past us without stopping to chat. Judging by the look on her face which almost resembles hurt, Mya isn't used to rejection. And rejection from Josh specifically, really seems to bother her.

We stumble on a vacant brown leather couch at the back of the adjoining sunroom. It's too comfortable and I sink into its embrace between Mya and Callie. I feel myself relax; being able to watch the party around me feels more natural than trying to be a part of it.

Leigh from our year sits himself down on the arm of the couch and starts chatting up Mya. She crosses her legs and curls her fingers along the top of her thigh high boots. She's so aware of herself, so confident in her own body. But she keeps looking around the room instead of at the boy who is chatting her up. I get the feeling she is just flirting with Leigh in the hopes that it will get someone else's attention. Maybe someone who just snubbed her. I don't know why she is so determined to get Josh to notice her.

I unconsciously loop my arm through Callie's, because apparently that's what we do now. I'm disappointed in myself for thinking how comforting it feels.

Sloopy

I see her before she sees me, but I always do.

She's got her hair down, pushed back behind her. She seems to suddenly feel exposed and self-consciously drapes it forwards over both shoulders. Leigh is trying to score with Mya. I heard he and Cane were both going to try to.

I thought she'd wear jeans and I feel good that I got it right. Makes me feel like I'm getting to know her, even though I'm aware of how very little I actually do.

The boys and I are chatting to Sam and his group of friends in the kitchen. I can see Sadie through the large archway which opens into the lounge and through to a little sunroom up the back. It looks and sounds like the whole senior school is here but I found her. I move my head around to keep her in my line of sight.

The music clicks over to Nirvana's About a Girl, blocking out everyone around me. Dad hates this band. I love them. But in secret. He scolded me once before for liking them. In my head I can still hear the sticker being ripped off my desk; the remaining hole in the laminate surface forever representing Dad's disapproval of me.

I watch Sadie from across the room, with the band I'm not allowed to like egging me on. I wonder if it's a sign from God.

Church always bored me. When I was younger, like around 9, I used to hide my Choose Your Own Adventure book in the bulletin, secretly reading it instead. Even back then, I was hiding who I wanted to be. Maybe it's time to start making some of my own choices. *Keep pretending that you fit in with your friends while they talk about sex...Fill out the seminary school application...Stare at Sadie's scrunchies all year and do nothing like the wimp that you are...Fuck it, live your life and get the girl.* Nirvana wants me to go and talk to the girl I want.

"I'll catch up with you guys," I shout over the music.

Adam and Josh look puzzled. I feel their eyes on my back as I make my way through the crowd to Sadie, with what now feels like our song fuelling me with confidence.

Nirvana and Sadie have a lot in common: I *choose* them both for myself.

Sadie

His tongue must be tickling the back of her throat. They barely even spent ten minutes together before Leigh latched on to Mya's face. That can't feel nice, surely. How does she even breathe like that? I try not to look at them and make a conscious effort to keep my eyes on the party. I look straight ahead: straight ahead at Noah, walking through the crowd, heading right towards me.

He looks more grown-up than he does in school. The uniform hangs off him; his jeans and red marbled Stussy t-shirt look like they're actually his size. His hair is a bit shaggy, not brushed back like in school. He's not fidgeting. He looks calm.

"Don't worry about me," Callie whispers in my ear, "I'm going to go catch up with Bec and Susie." She nudges my side. "Go say hi."

I stand robotically at her command, waiting for him to reach me. I feel like an idiot and want to sit down again. But before I know it, he's holding my hand, leading me out the back door.

Sloopy

The whole field sways against the warm evening breeze. The blades of dry grass flatten and rise in unison. Mother Nature is our own personal optical illusion.

We sit in silence, balancing atop the rustic split-rail fence. The distant sound of the party creeps across the field and I'm sure we are a million miles away from it, and everyone. But I always feel like that when I'm next to her.

The cow in front of us lets an absurdly large bowel motion drop to the ground and I dry-heave, unintentionally making Sadie laugh.

"Feel the romance," she says in that defiant voice of hers. "I take it you're not going to try to kiss me, what with the cow dung and you trying not to vomit and all."

I raise my eyebrows, planning to look as classic as River Phoenix. Sadie just giggles at me and another heifer relieves herself of what must surely be an entire week's worth of food in our near vicinity. We rest our feet on the lower beam of the fence and Sadie grips the top of the wood.

The trio of cows moo at the sunset and the smell of manure dominates the air. And amazingly, everything seems completely perfect. Even with my odd dry-heave.

Sadie

"I finally got November Rain last night, well, most of it. They played the long version so the tape ran out."

"Yeah, they really didn't want that song to end hey?"

The sound of the crickets is peaceful and that's exactly what I feel like right now, sitting next to this boy on an old fence, out in the middle of nowhere: peaceful.

"I can't tell you how glad I am that you came tonight," he rushes.

He sounds a bit pathetic, desperate, but it doesn't irritate me like it normally would.

"It makes me uncomfortable that you seem to like me. It feels more natural when people don't."

He lowers his head and laughs a little into his chest. "That's pretty messed up, you know."

I roll my eyes and laugh a little at myself, too. "Whatever, you're pretty messed up, too you know. Future priest and all that. I'm not sure you even believe in all that stuff."

"What makes you think that?"

"I mean I guess I don't really know you that well, but it doesn't seem like it's your kind of thing. I mean it's fine if it is, but would it be if it didn't have to be?"

Noah shifts on the fence and presses his lips together five times. "I told my dad once that I didn't believe in God. I don't know why. I don't even know if I do or not but I wanted him to think that I didn't."

"How did that make you feel?"

"Pretty amazing actually. Like I stood up for myself for the first time ever. It was right when he wouldn't sign the permission slip to let me join the basketball team this year. It was the only way I could think of to get to spend time with you, just to be around you even. It's all I wanted. When he refused, I told him I didn't believe in God. It scared him. I took away his power. He signed it the next day."

"You joined the team because of me?"

"Yep. Obviously. Only because of you. It's the first time in my life that I've done something because I wanted to, not because I was told to. I hate arguing, yet I have to do debate because Dad says I need to be able to listen to other sides. I don't even know if I believe in God yet I have to go to church every week. I don't know who I am because I've always been told who I have to be. I don't know what to think because I've always been told what to think. I don't even know what I like doing because I've always been told what I should like. Joining the team, chasing after you, that's me. For the first time, it's just me."

"Why does everyone call you Sloopy?"

"Because it's the one thing my dad never calls me. It started when I was about ten, I reckon. Mum and I were dancing in the kitchen to that 60s song, you know, Hang On, Sloopy?"

I nod and encourage him with my eyes to keep going. I'm not used to enjoying an actual conversation so much. Or someone's company.

"Mum and I were having the time of our life, being silly, dancing around the kitchen. Just existing in the moment. Dad had started getting irritable the last few months at home. Mum and I seemed to have become his least favourite people. But she danced around that kitchen with so much joy and spirit. She was happy, free. Like, with her own personality, not just presenting herself like she'd started doing. We busted out of the box that he kept trying to squeeze us into. So then in comes Dad and tells Mum that she hasn't finished the dishes yet. *What would someone think if they came over and saw our house was a disgrace.* Mum dutifully turned off the radio and told me to go get ready for bed while she tidied up. I knew she felt sad but she still smiled and acted as if she was the happiest woman alive, because that's what kids need to see from their mums, right? After that day, she started to call me Sloopy when Dad wasn't around, and it felt like it was this secret code, her way of telling me that everything will be okay. That *she* was okay. It was my superhero name. The boys heard her one day and it just kind of stuck."

"Do you want me to call you Noah or Sloopy?"

"What do you think suits me more?"

"Whatever feels more like you. Do you want to dance around the kitchen or do you want to follow in your dad's footsteps?"

"Sloopy it is then."

Sloopy

I motion at the marks on her arm. "What did you do here?"

Her skin is so soft and pale, like it never sees the sun. I imagine she would bruise pretty easily.

Sadie nods at the healing scabs on my wrist. "I suspect nothing as interesting as what you did here."

"Yeah, it's a bad habit, that's all. I don't even realise I'm doing it most of the time. I just look down every now and again and I've picked at myself so much, I'm bleeding."

She cups her hands over the marks on her arms and the evening breeze pushes the loose strands of hair off her face. I hesitate before placing my palm over the back of her hand. I feel her hand turn over in my own and suddenly, amazingly, we are holding hands, fingers entwined.

Sadie

I jump down onto the dry grass below us.

"I should probably head back to Mya and Callie. I think there's like etiquette rules or something about ditching your friends at a party."

Sloopy hops off the fence after me, disheartened. But he reaches for my hand again anyway. I panic and instinctively swat him away. I want so desperately to be like everyone else. I don't want to freak out every time someone tries to get close to me. Especially him.

Without hesitation, I rush my body against his; swiftly before I have a chance to think too much and inevitably talk myself out of it. I lean into his chest and his arms instantly wrap around me, completely engulfing me in his embrace. My cheek rests against his; I almost have to stand on my tip toes to reach him. I am taken aback by the instant warmth of his skin. We stand perfectly still, cheek to cheek. My breath is loud and panicked; his is soft and calm.

The physical sensation of being held by him evokes an ache in my heart. I swear the universe lifts my feet off the ground. I am floating and I allow myself to be completely dependent on another person. If he lets me go, I will surely fall.

I breathe in his scent and it compels me to close my eyes as if to better absorb it. His cheek presses deeper against mine and for just a second, I wonder if maybe he isn't trying to find my lips. The touch of a fellow human being feels ironically alien, as if I am really from another species. I never knew how much I craved the sensation of an embrace until this very moment. To be held by someone. To be so meaningful to another person that they may never want to let you go.

But then he did. And just like that, the first hug I have had in nearly eight years is over.

Sloopy

I didn't want to be the one to let go. But I knew I had to be. Holding her in my arms had blocked out everything; the noise in my head, the constant rush of nerves, the panic that makes me frantic every day of my life. She was in my arms and I exhaled. Calm. She was my peace.

But then the calm became something else. I felt desperate. I wanted to kiss her. And keep kissing her. I wanted to kiss her until we fell to the ground, madly exploring under each other's clothes. She felt so small; my arms wrapped all the way around her. For the first time, maybe in my entire life, I felt like I was doing something right. Like I could protect her. Keep her safe from whatever makes her so sad. It felt like I could love her and it absolutely terrified me to think that perhaps I already did. Is that what this is?

"S-sorry," I fumble. "Sorry."

I tug at my index finger five times. She is going to storm off. I've ruined it. I lift my eyes, expecting them to find hers in an enraged state. She frowns and I wait for her to tell me to piss off and to never speak to her again.

"Me too. You can hug me again one day, like if you want, I mean."

She looks at the ground. I've hurt her feelings and I hate myself for it. I don't know what's happening to me. All I can think about is whether or not she's wearing that bra with the white straps.

I take her hand again but I don't know what I can say. I think about my dad and his white collar. I think about Mum pretending not to be sad for me because her husband's an arsehole and she doesn't want me to realise that my father is one, too. But I do realise it, Mum and I try to make up for it for you. I think about the girl holding my hand right now who shuts everyone out but lets me in.

Her midnight eyes study my face. "I'm not mad at you."

"I'm sorry. I'm always disappointing someone." Just like how I'm disappointing her right now.

She pulls my arm to follow her and starts walking through the field back to the house. "That's enough talking now, Sloopy."

Sadie

Mya is nowhere to be found when we get back to the party. Callie tells me that she left half an hour ago with Leigh. She cosies up to my side, back sitting on what has evidently become *our* couch.

"We'll go look for her if she's not back by eleven. You're so nice to cuddle and I think I'm a little bit drunk and I need to tell you that Mya and I really do love you."

I tense my eyebrows and try to inch myself away from her. Sloopy has re-joined his friends in the kitchen. He constantly looks through the crowd over to me. I wish I could hear what he is saying. I miss the sound of his voice. I would give anything to be listening to it now over Callie's bullshit ramblings.

"I'm so glad you finally came out with us," Callie whispers right in my ear.

Her drunken breath is warm and I'm angry at her. She was my comfort tonight and now she's drunk. She fiddles with my hair and giggles. "I think this might be my most favourite-ist night ever."

"You don't need to pretend that you like me," I find my-self saying. It's not like she'll remember this anyway.

She is drunk, and I hate drunks.

She pats my tummy as if swooning over a pregnant woman's belly. "You're so pretty, Sadie. You're so much prettier than me. Everyone is so much prettier than me. I wish you wouldn't joke around like that, saying we don't really like you. I think about you all the time, hoping you are okay, hoping you know that I'm here if you ever need a friend. Cos that's what we are, you know. We're just the friends that you need. We just let you be. I think I'm gonna throw up."

I had started to tune her out but her last words make me leap to my feet. "Quick, let's get you some fresh air."

I pull her up from under her arms and she flops her head onto my shoulder.

"I love you, Sadie," she slurs.

I smile at her words. They don't irritate me. I lead her to the back door, holding onto her and telling her that everything will be okay and that she will be able to vomit outside in just a minute.

Sloopy

Cane fills his plastic cup from the keg before joining Adam, Josh and I by the sink. The benchtops are dark green and the kitchen tiles have pictures of squirrels on them.

"I can't believe she went straight for Leigh! I didn't even get a 'hi' in before he got his tongue in."

I look around anxiously, expecting to see Dad rushing towards us to tell Cane off. The squirrels judge me, reminding me that we are in a grandparent's home.

Josh nudges him, beer splashing from his own cup. "What about Callie? She's probably hot for it now that she's lost some weight."

"Now there's a thought," Cane ponders.

I'm disgusted by this conversation but confused too because I'm not actually sure I even get what they are talking about. The sleeves of Cane's Bon Jovi t-shirt end right on his bi-ceps. He actually has genuine muscles. He's not the sort of person I need to be confronting about morals.

I self-consciously tug down the sleeves of my own t-shirt, hopelessly attempting to cover up my measly arms.

Adam chugs the rest of his beer. "Nikki is looking good tonight."

Cane slurps from his beer and the sound repulses me. "Don't hesitate. I took a breath and lost to Leigh. I heard Mya's really hot for it, too. Could have been a good night!"

I am incredibly uncomfortable and shift awkwardly on the spot.

"Her friend Callie's a bit of a babe," Josh persists, seeming to not like the focus on Mya. "She went through an ugly duckling phase last year, but she's coming good now. I reckon she could do with a confidence boost. We should see which one of us can make Callie get all hot and bothered. The four of us plus we'll get Sam and the carry-over champion, Leigh, in on it, too."

I can't hide my shock at what I'm hearing. "Come on, Josh, time to take off soon, yeah? You're driving remember. Country roads are harder at night."

Adam catches my eye and I know he wants to abort this conversation just as much as I do. "Yeah, mate, I'm about ready to go, too."

Sadie

We reach the grass just in time. Callie heaves her whole body forward a millisecond before I intuitively sweep the hair back off her face into a high ponytail. Green vomit erupts from her mouth and I try not to scream when a chunk lands on my shoe.

"Thatta girl, get it all up. You'll feel so much better soon."

Another explosion pours onto the ground, with more force than its predecessor.

"Oh man, I am never drinking Midori again!" Callie sighs, but then I'm relieved to hear her laugh.

I find myself laughing along with her, but more so at the absurdity of not even caring that I have vomit on my Doc Martins because I'm actually being someone's friend right now.

She drapes her arm across the back of my shoulders. "Let's get me a glass of water to gargle and go find Mya."

We only take a few steps back towards the house before I stop and motion Callie to do the same. "Did you hear that? I swear that was Mya."

"I didn't hear anything," Callie whispers back. "What?"

"I thought I heard Mya's voice. She said stop." We stand perfectly still in the dim radius of the porch light. "I'm sure I heard her."

I mentally will the music of the party to hush so I can hear better. I feel a rage burning inside me and I'm ready to kill.

Cut it out, Leigh! Please! Come on, I said stop! I don't feel well!

Mya! I'm coming. I drop out from under Callie's arm and frantically run towards the sound of Mya's voice, resonating across the crop field. Callie chases after me but she struggles to match my pace.

I don't want to, I've had too much to drink, please stop!

My legs move faster than even I can keep up. I run into a row of mini trees held up by sticks and listen intently. The full moon tries to illuminate the field for me but darkness prevails. I put my trust in Mya's voice.

Leigh, please. I want to stop. Please.

You can't say no now, it's too late.

Get away from her, you bastard! I'm coming, Mya!

I run into the next row, confronted by the stomach-turning sight of Mya pinned down on the ground, squirming underneath Leigh as he roughly runs his hands all over her body; under her top and up her skirt. I edge closer towards them, now able to make out her flushed cheeks, stained with mascara. She makes eye contact with me as I rush up alongside them with a small branch gripped in my hand. I can't read her expression; scared, humiliated...grateful? I reach their bodies with the branch poised high and whack Leigh across the head in a frenzy.

"She said NO!"

Leigh cradles his forehead and stands to face me. "The fuck is your problem? Get your own slut, lesbo!"

My anger is palpable and I lunge at him with the branch again. He ducks and I miss. His laughter makes me livid.

"You're so pathetic. Run along, little miss psycho Sadie. This isn't your business."

I jerk my knee forward and relish the sheer satisfaction of it colliding with his groin. He moans and drops to the ground, curling his whole body into a ball.

"Only her friends can call her a slut. If you ever touch her again, I'll kill you, got it? And if you tell anyone that you scored with her tonight, I'll make damn sure that your mother, sister, aunty and every single woman in your life finds out what you tried to do."

Leigh rocks his whole body back and forth and I devour the sight of him in pain. I reach my hand down to Mya and she grabs it like it's a lifeline. I pull her up and she cries in my arms. Callie wraps her arms around us both. I don't know why but I start crying, too.

"Alright, come on," I finally say, "which one of you are going to teach me how to drive us all home?"

Sloopy

"It does look really nice, Mum. Do *you* like it though? The party's not until next Saturday, we could go late night shopping on Thursday and get you something more *you*?"

The day after I sat on a fence with the girl who I'm pretty sure I'm falling in love with, I now sit on my parents' bed, supporting Mum as she fights with the lady in the mirror. She's tried on the dress that Dad bought for her to wear to Adam's mum's birthday. It's a nice dress...for someone else. It looks beautiful on her simply because everything does, but it's not *her*. It's not her style and she doesn't look comfortable in it. It's black. Mum never wears black. Fitted. Mum likes loose clothes. It's just not her at all.

Mum rummages through a drawer in her tallboy and pulls out a few coloured belts. She straps the pink one around her tiny waist and sways her hips, trying to convince herself that the belt makes a difference.

"This could work?" she says to herself.

I sit up and tell Mum that she always looks beautiful, because she does. It kills me that the person who should be telling her that every day, never does. And seems to want her to feel the exact opposite.

Sadie

The first note of Nirvana's About a Girl plays and I quickly take my finger off the 9. It rings! Holy shit, it's actually ringing! I twirl the cord of the phone around my fingers and jiggle my feet excitedly.

"You're our first caller! Congratulations, tell us your name!"

"Oh my god! Oh my god! Sadie! I'm Sadie! Oh my god, have I won?"

The radio announcer laughs. "Hey love your enthusiasm, Sadie! You've just picked up an in-season double pass to go see How to Make an American Quilt!"

I bounce up and down on my bed. "Thank you so much! Oh my god! I can't believe I actually got through!"

"Hey, no worries! Stay on the line, Sadie. We'll grab your details in just a sec."

"I can't believe I actually won, oh my god. Thank you so much, just thank you so much," I blubber into the phone.

The announcer puts me on hold and I listen to the rest of the song. It's become my favourite now. I wonder if Sloopy likes it, too.

"Hey I'm back, Sadie. Thanks for holding there. I'm throwing in a couple of snack bar vouchers so you can get some goodies for the movie. Let's get your address so we can get these sent out to you."

Sloopy

I see her before she sees me, but I always do.

I've been anxious about this morning. I don't know if she's going to recoil after we got so close at the party. I beam with childish anticipation as I head to my desk but I prepare myself for the daggers that she traditionally gifts me.

And.

She.

Smiles.

Right.

Back.

At.

Me!

I take my seat, feeling on top of the world. She is wearing her Tweety Bird scrunchie today and it reminds me how she said she lost the Sylvester one. I rip a piece of paper out of my exercise book, write Sylvester on it and put it in the front pocket of my school bag.

Sadie

"I think Tuesdays are becoming my favourite day, Sadie," Mrs Carrington coos during our tutoring session. "I like hanging out together."

I soak up her words as I finish the last question. *She likes hanging out together. She likes me being around.* "I get 97. Is that right?"

Mrs Carrington studies the calculation on my page. "That's right, Sadie. I'm incredibly proud of you."

She's proud of me.

"I guess I um, I don't know. I never really cared about getting it right before. I didn't even try."

"I'm not following, dear."

I stare at the complex fraction so perfectly worked out on the page before me. "I just didn't think it mattered. Like," I shake my head as if deciding not to carry on, "nah I don't know, forget it."

Mrs Carrington sits at the desk to my right, side-ways on the chair to face me. She reaches across and rests her hand on my lap. "Please go on, Sadie. Tell me what you mean. You can't say anything wrong to me."

I cross my arms to stop myself from hitting her hand away. I hugged Sloopy. I can handle her hand on me.

"I mean, like, if I did get it all right, what would be the point? When you don't have anyone to be proud of you. When you've got nowhere to go at the end of it all. Like uni or Tafe or something. Like what's the point? When you're proud of me, it makes me want to try. So, yeah, that's all I wanted to say." I clear my throat and mentally talk myself out of leaping up and running out the room. "I guess I just wanted you to know that I appreciate you giving up some of your time for me. And it's, well, it's kind of made a big difference."

I can't bring myself to look at her but I think I hear her swallow.

"It's my absolute pleasure, Sadie."

Sloopy

Sadie sits next to me on the bus ride home and it feels like I've just won the lottery. There are a dozen other empty seats.

I notice that she didn't swipe a ticket and it occurs to me now that she never actually does. Cameron looks in the rear-view mirror and waits for her to push her bag under the seat in front. He gives her a second to settle comfortably and then drives. I am desperate to talk to her but want to let her speak first, and only if she wants to.

"Did you have debate?"

Her voice makes me squeal excitedly on the inside. "Yeah, hated it. I always hate it."

It's just impossible to suppress my smile: she is sitting next to me; she is talking to me. It spreads even wider when she smiles back.

"Then don't go. Tell your dad that it's not you."

I don't really know how to reply. I don't know if debate is or isn't me because I don't know who I am. All I know is that I need to get more time with her because she makes me feel like I can figure it out.

"Um, h-hey, I was wondering if maybe you want to get off at my stop today and come over for a bit? I've got heaps of CDs we can go through. Mum will drive you home."

I spill all the words out as one and I've probably scared her off again. I pinch at the skin on my wrist. Sadie flings her arm across me, landing her hand on my knee. She motions with her fingers for me to put my hand in hers, which of course I do, too eagerly. I forget how many times I have pulled my skin. I contemplate starting the count over again but I hold on to her instead.

"Figured I'd have to be the one to make the first move again," she says ever so adamantly. Just like Sadie. "Thanks though, but I can't. He gets home around six most weeknights and I like to be in my room by then."

"Your uncle?"

She nods.

"So, you just stay in your room all night?"

Her fingers close tighter on my hand. "Mostly. I try to co-ordinate my movements with the sound of his door closing. If I hear him go into his room, I can quickly sneak to the toilet, or grab something if I need to. I normally walk home but I don't like getting home too close to him, so I get the bus on Tuesdays and Fridays, when I've got something on after school."

"That's a lot. Like, that's a stressful way to live."

"Yeah. Just the way it is I guess."

"Is your uncle not nice?"

She glides her fingers across the skin I was pulling at only seconds before and tilts her head so it rests on my shoulder. I skip a breath. I look straight ahead, frozen: scared to make even the slightest twitch for fear of making her think she needs to move.

Her hair drapes down onto my arm. The soft tickling sensation makes my breath shallow. I have never really comforted a person before and I am very aware that Sadie has never sought it from anyone, likely ever. And it's my shoulder that she chose. She must miss her parents so much.

I stare at the back of the seat in front of me to help me focus on keeping my body perfectly still. I say it in my mind alone, wondering if I will ever be able to say it out loud: I'm so in love with you, Sadie.

"If you still want me to, I could come over after the game on Saturday?"

She doesn't sound like herself; she is nervous. She sounds like me.

I deliberately pause, consciously wanting to feel this moment for as long as I can.

"I definitely still want you to."

Sadie

I wipe my apple on my school dress and take a bite. Callie opens her brown paper lunch bag and pulls out a cheese sandwich. Mya crunches on her barbecue chips. I catch myself appreciating the moment; weirdly content.

None of us have mentioned anything about last Saturday night. It's Friday, so if something was going to be said, you'd think it would have been said by now.

Leigh and Cane walk past us and Mya looks down at her knees. I glare at Leigh and he quickens his pace. They are heading for the boys' toilet block.

"Did you guys watch Heartbreak High last night?" Callie asks as she bites into her sandwich.

"I gotta pee." I chuck the rest of my apple in the bin and head towards the boys' toilet block.

Sloopy

"Come on," Josh whinges, "don't be such girls!" He rips the end of the sausage roll packet between his teeth and spits the plastic onto the grass. "It's just for a bit of fun and it's pointless unless we all do it."

We sit out on the football oval behind the goal posts in lunch break, chasing a sparce spot of shade. Josh has been going on about "getting" Callie all week and I can barely stand it. I'm not sure if he has always been this obnoxious and I just didn't see it or if he is just destined to become a total sleazebag.

"Callie could do with it anyway!" he sniggers.

Adam tries to sound casual. "Nah, it's a bit lame betting on girls like that. Callie's cool."

Josh looks across the oval, uncharacteristically pensive, and bites into his sausage roll. I hope it's too hot and burns his mouth.

"Whatever," he scoffs, "you guys are getting boring. What's eating you this week, Sloopy? Never seen you so quiet."

"Nothing."

"You got a problem with me or something?"

"What? No? Well, yeah, no, I'm just preoccupied with the Kids Club preparations. I don't have a problem with anything."

Josh scrunches up his face and rolls his eyes. "Whatever, Father Blean."

Sadie

The boys' toilet block reeks of urine. I sneak in and wait outside the urinals, where Cane and Leigh went. Their voices echo off the concrete walls.

"I thought for sure you were going at it!" Cane laughs. "Good on you for being honest though, mate."

"Yeah, nah nothing happened. I was drunk as and she just sat with me while I puked."

I close my eyes and exhale with relief. I was ready to beat the shit out of him if it worked out that I needed to.

Sloopy

We change into our P.E. gear after school in the locker room, ahead of basketball practice. Sam is going on about the new girl in year eleven, Ally.

"She let me rub my bits against hers, but she wouldn't let me in."

I lose track of my thought process and untie my shoelace so I can start to tie it up from the beginning again.

"You won't get any further than that with a year eleven," Josh sniggers.

Sam chucks the basketball at him. "Yeah, I realise that now!"

Josh catches his throw and cradles the ball on his hip. "We'll see you slow pokes out there."

I'm relieved to watch him follow Sam out.

Adam sits with his legs either side of the bench, pulling his P.E. top over his head. "You okay, mate?"

I stretch my legs out to make sure my socks are even. "Yeah, all good. Just getting a bit sick of that kind of talk, I guess. Seems to be getting worse."

"Josh is going through a bit of a phase, that's all. He's been hanging out with Cane and that on the weekends. It'll pass. Hey, you still got your eyes set on Sadie?"

"Yeah, we're sort of friends. It's nice."

He rolls his basketball back and forth between his legs. "Friends. Nice. Anything you want to ask me?"

I laugh awkwardly and shake my head. "No."

"You sure? Josh is gone. I won't say anything. Promise."

My socks are even but I pull them both up and start to ruffle them down again. "Geez, Adam. I don't know. No."

"Have you kissed her yet?"

"No. But I think I could have. I think she wanted me to. At the party. But I just couldn't get the timing right in my head."

"Don't think too much about it. If it feels right, just do it."

"Yeah, I guess. I don't even know how to do it properly."

"It will come naturally. In the right moment, you'll just know what to do."

"Nothing ever comes naturally to me," I admit self-consciously.

"She likes you. It will happen. Just try not to plan every-thing."

"Yeah. Okay."

Adam picks up the ball and tosses it back and forth from hand to hand. "Anything else?"

I've been friends with Adam my whole life. We were the bratty four-year-old kids play-fighting in the aisle before the church service began. We were the cranky seven-year-olds dragged out of bed by our mums to attend midnight mass. And he was my only friend when I had to change schools. We grew up together. Only, I fell behind. Because my dad determines how much I am allowed to grow up, and who I have to grow up to be.

I wipe my hand across my forehead and shake my head in annoyance with myself. "I don't know. I'm starting to think there's a whole bunch of stuff that I just don't understand."

"Like what Sam said?"

I roll my eyes. "Whatever. It's nothing."

Adam stuffs his school uniform into his bag. "You don't just go up and down," he says nonchalantly and without looking at me, no doubt for my benefit. "You go in and out. Get it?"

My hands are sweaty and I wipe them on my P.E. top five times, then five times again.

"Like, in and out, of her, you mean?"

Adam zips up his bag. "Yep. That's what happens. Get it now?"

I nod, even though he isn't looking at me.

Out on the courts, the prettiest girl I have ever seen sits waiting on the bench, feet either side of her basketball, toes pointing inwards. The fact that she is waiting for me makes everything Adam just told me seem even more terrifying than it already is.

Sadie

The house is in darkness when I get home. Three rays of sun shine through the holes in the lounge room curtains, stretching all the way across the room like spotlights. Light shining through something it's not meant to shine through feels inherently inspiring.

Practice was amazing today. Coach said he'd spoken to my school counsellor and they both agreed that I'm ready to get more game time. I see Ms Becker every Monday in last period, which means I miss Italian. The school made me start seeing her after I punched that dick that had a go at me about my parents. He deserved it and I don't regret it. In fact, I only wish that I had punched him harder, and twice. But I don't tell Ms Becker that.

They said I have 'anger management issues'. It always seems incredible to me that standing up for yourself can be construed that way. I remember once when Ms Becker was doing her usual 'trying to understand me' act, she said something like, 'there are some things in life that we can't control, so we go about controlling the things we can control the wrong way.' I guess she meant well, but really, what a crock of shit.

I make myself a couple of vegemite sandwiches and eat sitting cross-legged on the floor in front of the telly. I watch The Simpsons, then Neighbours and Home and Away, and wash his dishes from last night plus my own knife and plate. The wind picks up outside and rattles the back door. It scares me but I need to leave it unlocked for him, so I retreat to my room to feel safe.

In my room, I take the luxury of turning up my radio loud. It's nearly 8pm but because it's Friday I've got a couple of hours of guaranteed freedom. I listen to the Top 40 countdown and go through my wardrobe, anxiously trying to find the best outfit to change into tomorrow at Sloopy's house. I decide on a white short sleeved t-shirt with my pink floral, spaghetti-strap dress. I grab my sandals and put the whole outfit into my backpack, placing it right next to my bedroom door so I don't forget it in the morning. I lay out my basketball uniform and put my favourite bra on top.

Sloopy

It's almost half-time and Sadie has been on the court the whole game so far.

Her bra strap is different today. It has a pink tinge and I swear I saw a little tiny bow peep out when she put her arms up. I grip the edge of the bench and squeeze it five times, harder than usual.

Sadie

Josh scores and I'm so happy to still be on the court I could literally scream. We're playing against an Eastern suburbs school, the one we thrashed last year in the final. They still seem bitter about it. I guess kids with corporate lawyer mums and general surgeon dads aren't used to not getting everything they want.

It was our week to play away but their court was being re-surfaced, so we're playing at home. I would have needed to catch two buses to get there and it wouldn't have been Cameron's route so I'm not sure how I would have snuck by the driver without a ticket. Mum would tell me that someone was looking out for me, but it's just luck that it worked out this way.

They get the ball down their end but I steal it back from a girl with an undercut. I pass to Naylene and she takes it all the way to the basket for a lay-up.

"I didn't know they taught basketball in orphanages!" the girl with the undercut sniggers to another girl on her team.

I turn back to face them, a bit flabbergasted by their desire to be mean for no reason. Snobby little rich kids who have everything and yet still choose to be bitches to someone who has nothing. I bet they go home to play Uno with their sisters and have sleepovers with their friends. I bet their mums kiss them goodnight. I bet their dads bring home chocolate on Friday nights. I try so damn hard to just breathe like Ms Becker tells me to do. I even try to pinch my skin five times like Sloopy. But then the girl with the undercut sings a line of It's a Hard Knock Life and before I have the time to coax myself out of it, I'm on top of her and we're rolling around on the court trying to smack each other in the face.

Sloopy

The referee's voice is assertive but lost in the ruckus. "Foul!"

I leap up from the bench and lunge towards Sadie. Some girl with a really bad haircut is on top of her, yanking on Sadie's ponytail. Sadie roars with rage and pushes her to the side, shifting both of their bodies so they lay facing each other; arms and legs flailing everywhere. Both teams have formed a circle around them, egging the fight on.

I reach the crowd just as Coach breaks through and pulls Sadie up from the ground by her guernsey and holds her back. The other team's coach grabs the girl with the undercut.

I'm only an arm's length away from Sadie when Coach takes hold of her hand and leads her over to the bench.

Sadie

Coach buries his head into his chest, shaking it slowly. "Dammit, Sadie."

I want to run away but my ankle hurts.

He sighs heavily. "I shouldn't have left you on for so long. I'm sorry."

His unexpected apology confuses me. I thought he was mad at me.

"Sadie, you can't let people know that they can get to you like this." His tone is gentle and his whole manner feels peculiar, like, parental. It's so damn nice. "Don't give anyone that kind of power over you."

I roll my eyes but I want to fall into his chest and cry. My ankle really hurts and I miss my mum and dad. I shift all of my weight onto the other foot.

"You've hurt your foot. Go home and rest, Sadie. Do you want some money for a cab?"

Sloopy

"I'll help her get home, Coach!"

I already have her backpack on my shoulder.

Coach glares at me. I've never seen him like this before. I wouldn't say he's angry, but he's worked up. Almost like he's disappointed or something. But it's not directed at Sadie, it's directed at himself. He nods once in my direction and then turns back to the court.

The game has resumed and the girl with the undercut girl is standing on the foul line for two free shots. I put my hand on Sadie's back, quickly guiding her away so she doesn't notice.

Sadie limps to the school gate and I trot along slowly beside her. I catch myself unintentionally limping in sympathy and I panic that she might think I am making fun of her. I pick at the baggy bit of skin between my thumb and index finger. Sadie whimpers, seeming to put too much weight down on her sore ankle and suddenly I don't feel the need to pick at myself anymore.

I pass her bag to her. "Here, put this on your back."

She looks pissed off with my lack of chivalry but obliges anyway. I step in front of her and squat down.

"Hop on."

I've startled her. "What? Get out of here, no way!"

"Come on!" I laugh. "There's no way you'll be able to hop all the way to my house."

"I'll crush you!" she chuckles. I'm disheartened to realise that she obviously thinks I'm scrawny. "And I mean that, like, as in, I'm probably heavy, not that you're not strong or anything."

She felt bad. She cares about hurting my feelings. My smile must be visible from the moon.

"You're tiny, Sadie. Come on, hop on! My knees are getting sore down here!"

If rolling your eyes made a noise, I would have heard it from Sadie. I turn my head back to face her and she is pressing her lips together like she is actually nervous.

I try my hardest to look irresistible. "Come on, it'll be fun!"

Sadie resigns and puts her legs on either side of me. "Oh my god, I can't believe I'm actually doing this."

She wraps her arms around my neck and I hop up the same time as she hooks her legs onto my waist. She squeals and then laughs as if laughing from a place deep inside her that didn't even exist until just now.

I walk all the way to my house with Sadie riding piggy-back. Her boobs push against my shoulder blades. I bite the inside of my cheeks five times and bask in the sound of her voice as it serenades so close to my ear.

"I think I'm getting a bit too used to you liking me so much," she says playfully. "It's rubbing off on me."

Sadie hardly stops talking, as if she is hearing her own voice for the first time. She talks about the nasty girl with the undercut. She talks about her parents, and Eden Gaha and Kylie Mole. She talks about Mrs Carrington and the way she reminds her of her mum. She says so much, barely stopping to let me get a word in. I mentally file it all, almost like I'm scared that she'll never talk to me like this again.

Sadie

I feel my bum slipping so I tighten my legs' hold around his waist and push myself up as he instinctively lifts with his hands under my thighs. I'm very aware that he is touching my skin, not my shorts but I don't panic. I giggle at the absurdity of it all. I'm riding piggy-back on Sloopy. I don't think I have ever had this much fun. I might be delirious, or maybe I have a concussion. But I'm falling for him. My ankle is throbbing but I have never felt happier.

"I hope the movie tickets come soon; I can't wait to give them to Mrs Carrington. Do you think she'll mind? Like, it won't weird her out or anything?"

"She will love it."

It feels weird to hear him speak without hesitation.

I squeeze my arms tighter around his neck and rest my cheek against his. His skin is warm and I hear his laboured breath but I'm selfish: I don't want this piggy-back to end.

"You and I should go to the movies one day, too," he suggests, but I'm not sure if it is a question.

I'm still trying to figure out how to respond when he scratches his forehead five times. I don't want to be another person in his life who compels him to pick at himself.

"We should." I make a real effort to sound excited.

Sloopy brings his hand up and wraps it onto my wrist, squeezing a bit too hard. I instinctively flinch and he self-consciously returns his hand behind my knee.

"Sorry, I wasn't pushing you away. My wrist is a bit sore."

"Did you fall on it?" he asks, obvious in his concern.

"I must have." Never in a million years did I ever think a boy would carry me home because I twisted my ankle. This moment is everything to me. When you're so used to being hurt, you can really sense when someone not only has no intention of hurting you, but will somehow protect you from anyone who does. I want to tell him that my wrist was already sore before the altercation, that it has been sore for days. Because the man I live with saves up all his hatred and anger and the probable disappointment with his own life, and then he explodes. "Or maybe the girl with the undercut fell on it."

He didn't hurt me in the beginning. Not physically. I loved him for the first couple of years, because I yearned for my family and he was the only one that I had. I was desperate for him to love me. He drank a lot and ignored me mostly, but sometimes he would shout at me. Sometimes he would cover his ears when I spoke. My voice annoyed him. Maybe it was just a reminder of how my very existence was ruining his life.

One night, he was doing the dishes and I came up behind him to say goodnight. I reckon I was about 11 or 12 then. It was the first time he hurt me. He slammed the bowl into the water, spun around with an intense rage already burning in his eyes, grabbed both of my arms and shoved me against the wall. He clenched his teeth and made a chilling grunting noise and squeezed his grip so tight...I wanted to cry out in pain. I managed to struggle free and ran straight to my room. He came in about ten minutes later and said he was sorry. He never came in my room again after that night and I started making sure that I was already in there by the time he got home.

I also started washing his dishes.

Sloopy cups both of my knees but he doesn't rub them five times like I expect him to. He just holds onto me. "I like you so much, Sadie."

I rest my chin on his shoulder, bringing us cheek to cheek.

I think about that night often. He said that he didn't realise it was me, as if he had merely just jumped in surprise, nothing more. No one else lived with us and he looked right into my eyes and squeezed harder and harder whilst he *held* my gaze. The moment of realising it was only me had passed yet he kept hurting me. He saw the fear in my eyes and it urged him to squeeze harder, not to let go. I had to pry my way out of his grip. None of it added up to him not realising it was me.

If I hadn't run away to my room, I'm not sure he would have stopped. That was the night that I realised: he could really hurt me one day. That was the night that he realised: he can.

I sometimes wonder what he was thinking about, standing at the sink, mindlessly scrubbing away at the remnants of cheese baked onto the rim of his bowl. Before I interrupted him. What was he thinking about to make him react with such disproportionate anger and hostility? Was he standing there wondering what his life would be like if he didn't get stuck with a child he never wanted, from a woman I sense he always hated? And then there I was, standing right behind him.

But now here I am. Literally being carried by a boy who should have given up on me the first time I gave him daggers and every time after that I scowled at him or shot down his attempt at conversation.

I tighten the grip of my legs and ruffle Sloopy's thick hair with my nose.

"I like you too, my Sloopy. Now giddy up!" I laugh with a click of my tongue.

Sloopy

"Alright, this is my house then."

I crouch down on the driveway, trying to offer Sadie a delicate dismount. She hops off and I straighten my knees to stand but I must have gotten used to the extra weight of another person. I overcompensate the strength required to stand up and tumble into Mum's flower bed. Sadie holds her sides and bends over, roaring with laughter.

I love that sound.

I pull a daffodil out from under me and hold it out for her.

I've never felt so damn smooth.

Sadie

Sloopy's house is a two-storey. I've never been inside a two-storey house before. It seems most of the houses around here are though. He lives just one suburb over from me but wow, what a difference a few streets can make.

His front door has a panel of stained-glass, with some sort of green vine entwined through red and pink flower buds. It feels reminiscent of an evil, cursed forest I read about in a book once.

"Mum!" Sloopy bellows as he lets us in. It's the first time I've ever heard him shout before. "I'm home!"

A lady in a capped sleeved, mustard polka dot dress comes rushing out of nowhere, as if she has been waiting all day for Sloopy to come home. She has thick black hair just like Sloopy's, cut in a shaggy bob. She is incredibly pretty; I find myself staring at her longer than is probably considered polite. Her eyelashes are impossible not to notice; prominent against her icy blue eyes. If someone drew a picture of her, they would have to colour her eyes blue and then use an eraser to fade the colour out. I wonder if the blue of her eyes would still look as pale if her features weren't so dark.

She rushes up to Sloopy, very obviously her most favourite person in the world, and pulls him in to her delicate frame for a hug rampant with motherly love and adoration.

"Hello, my boy! You're home earlier than I was expecting! Did you win? Is this Sadie?"

She lets go of Sloopy and wraps her arms around my shoulders. My arms tense at my sides.

"Are you Sadie? You must be, silly me! Let me look at you, my goodness, you are beautiful. Welcome to our home, darling."

Sloopy clears his throat and his mum laughs. She looks at me as if she is wanting to ask something, only she is not sure what she actually wants to ask.

"Well, I best not embarrass my boy by telling you how glad I am that you're here."

"We're gonna head upstairs, Mum. Have you got any frozen peas?"

Sloopy

Sadie holds onto the rail and hops up each step. I offered to carry her but she adamantly told me *no way!* and I was kind of relieved. As much as I want to hold her again.

I open my bedroom door and Sadie limps straight over to my bed.

"I'm going to change my clothes," she informs me, unzipping her backpack. I smile at the fact that she is kicking me out of my own room.

That's so Sadie.

Sadie

His room has no personality at all. It's like it's made up for an open house inspection. No posters on the walls, nothing left lying around. Mere furniture; a bed, a wardrobe, bedside table and a desk. He does have a telly though but that's hardly enough evidence that a teenage boy is growing up inside these four walls.

I limp over to his desk and open the top drawer. There is a pad of paper, a pencil, a box of Band-Aids and a Bible. The Bible is stunning; black cover with orange, embossed lettering. It must surely be a family heirloom. My mum had a Bible. I never knew what happened to her things. I wonder what they did with her clothes. Mum loved clothes. She had so many books, too. She used to read to me every night. Mum was a big fan of the classics but I always got my way and we read The Twits and Skeleton in the Dunny almost every night. She read them to me as if it was the first time: full of expression and wonder, even though I'm sure it was mundane for her. I did cave in one day and let her start Alice in Wonderland. We were half-way through it when I lost her and now, I will never be able to bring myself to finish the story without her.

I hope Alice found her way home.

I didn't.

I never got to go home after the accident. They kept me in hospital for a couple of days to monitor my concussion and then I was taken straight to his house. I wish I had some of Mum's things. Anything of hers, actually. Someone had delivered most of my possessions to his house before I even got there. They were kind enough to throw a few photos in a shoe box but I didn't get to see any of my mother's things ever again.

I hover my hand delicately over the Bible and try to remember what her own looked like. She kept it next to her bed, permanently resting on the base of a table lamp. I never saw her read it and I asked her once why she bothered to keep it out on display if she didn't even read it. It seemed odd that she kept it out like some sort of ornament just to collect dust when she put all her other books on the bookshelf in the lounge. 'Some things you just want to keep with you,' she'd told me. 'Some things bring you comfort just by being nearby. It's the same with people.'

Anyway. I close the drawer gently and notice remnants of a sticker or something like that on the corner of the desk. There is a patch where the laminate has actually been ripped away and it looks like Sloopy used a ruler or scissors to try to scratch the rest of something off. I smooth my hand over the remaining white flecks. It doesn't match the rest of his perfectly presented room. It's almost rebellious and I'm fuelled with intrigue. I wonder what was so awful that he had to rip it off, even if it meant ruining the desk; ruining such a perfect room. It kind of feels like the only piece of him in his own space. His own little mark, evidence that *Sloopy was here*.

"Knock, knock!" Mrs Blean opens the door just enough to peep her head in. "Is it okay if I come in, Sadie?"

"Um, I think Sloopy went to another room to get changed," I awkwardly utter.

"Oh, I know, I just came to visit you!"

"Oh, um, yeah." I don't understand why she still hasn't come in and then I realise that she's actually just that nice and will wait until I say it is okay. "Yeah, of course, come in."

I lean with my back against Sloopy's desk and his Mum almost skips towards me with a bag of frozen peas.

"I heard you need a nurse!" she gleefully explains.

I hold my hands low on my tummy and feel my insides get tighter and tighter the closer she moves towards me.

"Nah, I'm all good. I just twisted my ankle a bit, it'll come good."

Mrs Blean sits herself down cross-legged on the floor right in front of me and pats the side of her knee. "Here, come on, give me your ankle."

"I'm fine, really," I shake my head.

She pats her knee again and winks at me. I roll my eyes and put my foot on her knee. The cool relief of the frozen peas feels incredible against the pain in my ankle.

She looks up at me. "It might seem simple, but I find that simple solutions are usually the best ones."

Her eyes really are breathtaking and I'm certain that she's the prettiest human being I have ever seen in my life. I bet Sloopy's dad treats her like a Queen.

Sloopy

After my tenth push-up, I don't get up. I lay face-down on the upstairs bathroom floor, catching my breath, and jiggle my arms by my sides to get the feeling back in them. I rest on the cool tiles and count to five, five times.

I change into my jeans and plain black tee and ruffle up my hair in the mirror. I guess I look okay.

The door opens without a knock and Dad glares at me, with that usual look of dislike on his face.

"What are you doing in here, writing a song? Come on, some of us need to use the toilet."

"Just on my way out. We won basketball today."

Dad lifts the toilet seat. "Out you go now."

I don't know if we won basketball or not because Sadie and I left early. I just wanted to see whether or not he even cared.

"Tell your mother that I won't be home for dinner tonight. I have to rush straight off to the office and I won't be home until late."

Sadie

Sloopy's mum's name is Loretta, she informs me when I keep calling her Mrs Blean. How pretty is that? Loretta. I love finding out people's actual names, I mean, as opposed to their title or whatever they are to us. My mum's name was Vivian. Dad called her Vivvy. His name was

Andy. Mum and Dad. Vivian and Andy. I wonder what Mrs Carrington's name is.

I sit on the edge of Sloopy's bed. Loretta is on the floor with my foot resting on her knee. She really seems to enjoy playing nurse and says I need to keep my leg elevated as much as I can for the next few days. She holds the bag of peas on my ankle and softly strokes my skin with her thumb. Her touch doesn't make me panic. I haven't been around a mother since I lost my own. There's an inherent feeling of safety that she creates, maybe simply because she's a mother, I don't know. She's good at it though, being a mum, I mean. Her spirit seems to shine brighter when someone needs her.

I insist that she closes her eyes whilst I change and she tells me all about her plans for tonight as I do. She hired True Lies. She's excited because Sloopy's dad never got around to seeing it when it first came out, even though he apparently really wanted to. She is surprising him with a night in together.

Loretta says she doesn't fancy the look of the movie herself and she is amazed about how keen her husband is to watch it.

"I think maybe he just wants to try something different. He's been in a bit of a rut for a while now. It's already a weekly. They don't keep them as new releases for long now."

She's cooking a lamb roast for him. She's a vegetarian. It's their wedding anniversary, she tells me.

When I'm dressed, I tell her that she can open her eyes. I scrunch my face and shoulders self-consciously, kind of secretly hoping that she'll reassure me that I look okay.

"What a pretty dress, Sadie. You look beautiful. And happy."

I want to tell her that my mum literally always wore dresses. I never saw her wear anything else, like jeans or tracksuit pants. Except when she read to me in bed at night. She always wore a nightie and her dressing gown then. But there is a knock on the door before I can.

"Everyone decent in there?"

Loretta looks to me for approval before answering, "come on in, darling."

Sloopy

Mum kisses my cheek on her way out. "I adore her."

"Oh, Dad said he won't be home tonight."

"Ah, all good, I'd planned to catch up on some reading anyway."

Mum closes the door behind her, leaving me and Sadie alone. In my room. I can't believe how cute she looks in her normal clothes. I can't believe she is actually in my room. I wish I had some posters on my walls to make it look cooler in here. They're all hidden though in a secret spot.

The quiet is deafening. I stand in front of the door completely dumbfounded. I have no idea what to do.

Sadie clears her throat and stands from the bed. Her arms are folded, her usual stance. Always wanting to create a barrier between herself and the world. She hesitates and then lets her arms fall freely to her sides.

Sadie

He looks just as uncertain as I feel. I clear my throat for the second time in ten seconds. I don't know why. "I like your top."

Sloopy looks down at his utterly plain black tee, no doubt thinking that I'm an idiot. He clears his throat, too. "Your dress is really pretty."

Another random throat clear, this time from me.

This is just all together completely awkward.

Painful.

My tummy is fluttering and I feel light-headed.

Why is he still standing at the door? It's his room. Just relax already.

Sloopy

My feet are heavy and feel like they're glued to the carpet.

This is ridiculous. Sadie is here to spend time with me and I'm wasting it. I don't want to be like him. I know that's where I'm heading. Sadie is my chance to change direction.

"Wanna see my CDs?" I don't even sound nervous.

Sadie nods.

I sit on the floor and Sadie copies. How absurd that she is following my lead and not the other way around. I pull out a plastic tub from under the bed.

"I keep my CDs under the bed, too!" she says excitedly. "But in a suitcase."

"Really? Weird, hey? Everyone else keeps theirs on display, like in a CD tower or something. It feels too exposing to me, like leaving your diary open for everyone to read."

I like the way Sadie is looking at me. I think she likes what I said.

Sadie

"No way!" I squeal. "You like Baby Animals? They're like my favourite!"

Sloopy's collection is so cool. He has way more CDs than me. Heaps of Nirvana.

He picks out a single and puts it in his player. "This one's the best."

Baby Animal's One Word kicks off. Sloopy drops his head low and starts banging it like some sort of rock groupie. I watch him move around the room that suddenly does feel like it is his after all. He is lost in the music. Found in the music. No one can see him except me, and that seems to give him the power to be himself.

I ogle his CD collection while he leaps about his room for the entire song. It's pretty amazing to know that someone can be totally themselves around you; I imagine Sloopy dancing like this only when he is completely on his own. Door closed. Hiding. Suppressing who he really is and who he really wants to be. And yet he is this person now, in front of me.

He's right, too; as I rummage through all his CDs, I really do feel like I'm reading his diary.

I hold out Silverchair's, Frogstomp.

"Can you put on Tomorrow next?"

Sloopy

It's nearly 4pm. I notice Sadie glancing at the clock every few minutes. I guess she wants to be in her own room now.

I walk down to my parent's room, planning to tell Mum that Sadie is ready for her ride home. Mum sits on the side of her bed, with her back to the slightly-ajar door. The clothes basket is next to her, as if she was about to start folding the washing. Her elbows rest on her knees, her hands cup her face. She is crying. Quietly. Privately. Secretively. She even has the curtains closed, as if she suddenly felt overcome with sadness and needed to hide from the world. I should have put the kitchen radio on when I got home.

I head down the stairs, calling out to Mum as I do.

"Hey, Mum! Are you downstairs? Sadie's ready to go now."

Sadie

Mrs Carrington's laugh is the polar opposite of my Mum's laugh. It's polite and ladylike, just like she is. My mum's laugh was loud, uncensored and completely unapologetic. I was always taken aback by how such a bold laugh could come from such a tiny body. It was always without hesitation and never toned down; if Mum wanted to laugh, she did so as joyfully as she wanted. But as different as they are, I sure do like the sound of Mrs Carrington's.

"This must make me the worst teacher in the world, but I bet it felt so good to knock that smirk right off her face!"

Our Tuesday tutoring sessions are my favourite part of the week. I may even look forward to them more than basketball. Maybe. Just maybe.

Mrs Carrington leans on my desk, sharing my space and I don't feel the urge to move backwards to compensate.

"I think Coach was really angry with me though. I don't like my chances of playing much for the rest of the season. But it was worth it. I can't pretend I'm sorry. She was such a bitch."

Mrs Carrington pats my knee and leaves her hand resting there. I form a fist and hope that she doesn't notice.

"Just make sure you tell the school counsellor that you tried to control your anger, okay? Make sure you tell her what she wants to hear."

Her encouragement throws me off guard, given that it goes against everything that a teacher is supposed to tell you. She senses my surprise.

"People change as you get older. In high school everyone is trying to figure out who they are and they think everyone is out to get them, when in reality, we're all here for each other. That's the way it should be. That's what life is. The girl with the undercut will wake up one day and she'll be forty years old with a home loan, kids running amuck, bills piling up, a job that sucks all her energy. She'll go to work and seek reassurance from her colleagues because she knows that they understand how hard it is to juggle everything. The older people get, the more they support each other. Right now, everyone is just caught up with being the prettiest and the most popular. One day they'll get it. We're all here to support each other."

Mrs Carrington really is just an angel on Earth. She always believes in the good in everyone. I want her to know how much I respect her.

"I don't think I'm a naturally smart person. Like, this maths stuff just goes completely over my head. I can handle English but anything to do with numbers, forget it. But I want to try. I want to try because you believe in me. And when I knocked that girl to the ground on the weekend, I wanted to tell you about it. Like, how I would have wanted to come home and tell my mum." I roll my eyes and shift uncomfortably in my seat. "Just wanted you to know that, that's all."

The length of silence that follows extends beyond my level of comfort.

"You have to know how proud I am of you, Sadie. I pray you know that."

Her gold wedding band has three rubies in a line and I forget myself for a second and run my finger over the tiny jewels.

"One for each of my angels," she whispers.

I frown uncertainly.

"My husband and I couldn't have children. It wasn't meant to be. My first two, I was blessed to carry for a few months before my body failed them. I gave birth to my last baby, but she was a sleeping angel and never woke up. It was brutal. It absolutely destroyed me. I couldn't put myself through it again. My husband had the stones set into my wedding band so that I would always have my angels with me. He is a good man. He gave up his dream of being a father for me. I live with that every day."

"I didn't know any of that. I'm heaps sorry." And I mean it.

"We, ah, we fostered children for a little while through the church. But eventually they chose to terminate their contract with the agency. I guess life just had other plans for us. We have a quiet life, just the two of us. We like to watch movies."

I don't know if it's the right time to give her the tickets I won. She is talking about major pain. Grown-up trauma. And here I am thinking I have some movie tickets and that will solve everything. But they are literally all I have to give and I want to give them to her.

I pull the envelope out of my bag and pass it to her.

She runs her fingers under her eyes, wiping her tears. "What's this?"

"I won a double movie pass on the radio, like, I mean for you. I spent all day trying to get through. And yeah, I won, so they're yours."

Mrs Carrington laughs and cries simultaneously. It's the first time I've seen the two emotions fused together like that. And then she hugs me. She keeps her bottom on the chair and leans her whole torso into me, wrapping her arms around my neck. I put my arm around her petite waist and I actually hug her right back.

Sloopy

"Come on, Noah! Make me agree with you! Make me see it from your point of view!" Mr Gates stands in front of me and grabs the podium with both hands, shaking it. "This is debate! Debate, not *let me read from this essay I wrote about the side I just happened to be assigned*. Make us feel it!"

I turn the page over and recommence reading, this time trying to look up more. "The second reason why we are in favour of voluntary euthanasia is-"

"Blah blah BLAH!" Mr Gates mocks me. I press my lips together and try not to blink as quickly as I feel compelled to. "Voluntary euthanasia is *essential*; it is *paramount* to society moving forward...doesn't that sound more convincing? You don't even sound like *you* believe in what you're saying, Noah so how do you expect anyone else to believe it?"

I pick at the corner of the page and twist it between my fingertips, counting five twirls. "I don't believe it, though. I can't believe in euthanasia."

"But this is debate!" he roars and I feel myself jump. "That's the whole point of this. To argue! To take a side even if you don't agree with it and *sell* it! I need to see passion, Noah. Conviction. Believe in what you are saying."

I drag myself to the bus after debate and take the only spare seat in the middle. I just want to sit here and forget about the world that I will never be able to fit into. I hate arguing. I hate talking in front of people. I hate pretending to believe in something I don't just to win a debate. Pretend, that's all I ever do. I pretend to be someone I'm not. From the moment I wake up to the moment I go to bed, I'm not me. I pretend. Unless I'm with her.

I want to be in my room jumping around to music I'm not supposed to listen to, with the girl who makes me feel brave and free to do so.

Sadie walks past the window and steps into the bus. I see her before she sees me, but I always do. I breathe out almost in relief when she sits down next to me. I can stop pretending now.

Sadie

I sense his sadness straight away. Cameron pulls away into the street as I hold Sloopy's hand and put my head on his shoulder. The scab on his wrist has completely fallen away and the skin underneath is healing. Without the patches of scab, the scar looks longer than I noticed before: it stretches across his whole wrist.

I don't speak on the ride home because I know what's it like to not want to talk. We all want to disappear sometimes. The irony is, he noticed me when all I wanted was to be invisible. He saw me when I was scared to be seen.

He found me.

But he needs to find himself, too.

Sloopy

Mum scoops the tuna mornay into my bowl and kisses me on the head.

"Thanks, Mum. It smells delicious."

She puts the casserole dish back in the oven and sits down to eat her own tea, adjacent to me at the table but the sound of the front door opening makes her drop her fork and leap to her feet. She rushes to the oven to pull out the dish again, scooping the rest into the largest bowl we own. Dad sits himself down at the head of the table.

"What's for dinner? I'm starving."

Mum serves Dad his meal and goes to kiss him on the forehead but he moves his head to the side as if purposefully trying to reject her affection.

"Mornay," he sighs. "Again?"

He picks up his fork and starts eating regardless. *Yeah, you seem really disappointed that we've got mornay again.* Mum smiles brightly for my benefit and sits down to eat her own tea.

"You didn't pass the pepper," Dad complains.

Mum obediently stands and grabs it from the cupboard.

"Sorry, darling," she says sweetly, handing him the pepper grinder.

I'm relieved that she sits down again and doesn't grind the bloody pepper for him. I don't have enough skin to pinch to get through that.

I hate that she apologised. I put another forkful in my mouth and swallow my growing hatred for him.

"What did you get up to today, Mum?" I ask, realising that her actual husband hasn't asked about her day yet.

The sound of Dad's voice immediately answers me.

"I did the communion round at the hospital and met with the new financial advisor to organise some extra funding for the chair-yoga I want to get up and running for the oldies."

Mum turns her fork over in her bowl, moving the mornay back and forth.

I want to annoy him. "We were talking about euthanasia in debate today."

Dad opens the paper and starts to read it next to his dinner.

Mum looks up at him somewhat cautiously. "Were you for or against, Sloopy?"

I look directly at Dad. "For. I have to agree with euthanasia."

"I'll speak to the school about that," Dad sternly pledges, not taking his eyes off the paper. "What a terrible look for us, condoning euthanasia. Do they know whose son you are? What do they want people to think about our family?" He looks straight at Mum. "And don't call him that. His name is Noah."

Sadie

Mya extends her arm across me, accepting Callie's offering of her sandwich. "Are you sure you don't want it?"

"Yeah, I'm really trying to give up meat. Mum gave me chicken and mayo."

Mya bites into Callie's sandwich. "It's good!" She never waits until she finishes chewing before she speaks. "I'd offer you mine but it's fritz and sauce."

I don't want to but I pass half my vegemite sandwich to Callie. I strangely find myself caring that she doesn't really have any lunch now. She takes it and nudges her shoulder against mine. I chuckle and I have no idea why. Mya nudges my other shoulder and for some reason we all laugh together, affectionately.

"Yeah, alright," I say as I collect myself.

Sloopy is shooting goals out on the court in front of us. He seems happier today and I can't help but wonder if he feels the Friday effect, too: basketball day. It would obviously mean something different to him, but maybe it is starting to mean *something*.

He takes a shot and then lifts the hem of his shirt to wipe the sweat off his face. I don't think he likes the feeling of being sweaty. His torso is so lean but it suits him and I swear his abs are starting to look more defined.

The faint lines on the sides of his stomach hint at the fact that he has been working out.

He catches me looking at him and amorously raises his eyebrows; almost as if he knew I was already looking at him. Like he always sees me first. I'm in my final year of high school and I finally understand how good it feels to have a boy flirt with you. Sloopy seems just a tad cocky; not nervous or wary of me anymore. I'm trying to figure out if that's a good thing or a bad thing.

"He's getting a bit buff!" Mya notices. "Plus, he's obviously got it bad for you."

Sloopy jumps to catch Adam's throw and trips over his own feet. We all laugh at him and I realise how much I am really enjoying my friends' company. I'm never the one to initiate a conversation, or get particularly involved in one, but for the first time ever, I crave to be that person. I want to talk about the boy I like with my friends.

"I don't know what to do about him," I kind of stutter. "Does he just want to be friends or like, go out or something? I've never made out with anyone before, I don't even know what I'm meant to do. I'm not like you two."

"Um, hello, what the hell is that supposed to mean?" Mya bites back.

I didn't mean to offend her. "No, I just mean like with boys and stuff. You've got heaps of experience and I have no idea what I'm doing."

"Heaps of experience?" Mya is suddenly worked up. "Are you calling me a slut? Is that what you think of me?"

"I think she just meant that she's never had a boyfriend before so she is nervous. Right, Sadie?" Callie encourages me with her eyes and I feel myself panicking.

"In comparison to me, right?" Mya narrows her eyes at us.

"Well, yeah?" I hesitate. "You've been with lots of guys. You brag about it all the time. You hook up with someone new whenever you want. I'm not saying that's a bad thing."

"I've made out with some guys, sure, but I've gone all the way literally like one time, with Josh in the Christmas holidays and he has barely said one word to me since so, yeah, no, actually I haven't *been with* lots of guys. Thanks a lot for thinking that about me. I've slept with one guy, one time and he snubbed me straight after."

I don't know anything, about anyone apparently.

Mya folds her arms high on her chest and stares across the court. She is angry but I don't feel scared of her.

We sit in silence until the bell goes a few minutes later. Mya and Callie walk off to their homeroom and I watch them leave, together. I can't identify what I am feeling. Guilt? I guess I'm pretty shit at all this. I've only just figured out that I have real friends, but now I realise that I'm a really bad one.

And it hurts more than I thought it would.

Sloopy

I can't take my eyes off her this afternoon. I feel feverish, like if I don't get close to her, I'll explode.

We stand opposite each other doing chest passes and I'm addicted to her coy smile. She fixates on the ball but looks up at me every few seconds. The instant her eyes lock with mine, I have to press my feet down five times to stop myself from rushing up and pushing my mouth onto hers. Not that I'm ever likely to figure out how to make that happen.

Her lips are so thin, like two parallel lines lightly etched onto her face with a sharp rose-coloured pencil. And they are. All. I. Can. Think. About.

She seems preoccupied and I'm anxious for practice to be over so I can ask if she is okay. I want to see her over the weekend. I'm desperate for her to come over again. I am my best self when I am around her. My self, period. And now that I've had a taste of who that is, I'm starving for more.

If I have any chance of figuring out who I am and who I want to be, it will be with her. It will be because of her.

Sadie

He is so hungry today; constantly looking at me, wanting more. I like it, but I don't know how to respond. I don't know how to flirt back. All I want to do is talk to my friends about boys and share vegemite sandwiches. My heart feels heavy and if I let myself, I could probably cry.

When I was in the eighth grade, I got my period for the first time. No one had ever told me about stuff like that. Mum hadn't quite got to it but I know she had been on the verge of filling me in.

I hid in the toilets all through second lesson, terrified. I thought I had somehow cut myself down there but the blood kept coming out, like actually out of me, and it was lumpy. I was petrified.

Mya came looking for me just before recess. We were meant to have Australian Studies together and I wasn't there. She knocked on the toilet door and asked if I was okay. I had been crying but I tried to sound fine. I was tough. Everyone knew that. Everyone was scared of me, even the two girls I sat with. That's the way I liked it. That's the way it needed to be.

"Yeah, piss off, I'm fine. I just didn't hear the bell," I mumbled through the toilet door.

"Do you need a pad? I've got one, or I've got some change for the machine if you want a tampon instead."

What on earth would I need a pad for? How is a notebook going to stop the blood coming out of me? "Nah, I'm okay, just piss off, alright?"

I'm not okay, Mya. I'm scared and I don't know what's happening to me. I scrunched up my face, trying to suck all my tears back in. I grabbed some more toilet paper and wiped, but there was even more clumpy blood, like more than before and my tummy was so tender. I put my hands over face and cried.

I wanted my mum.

There are some moments in life that you just know you will *remember*. Forever. Like twenty years later, you could be walking your dog, doing the dishes, falling asleep, and you just...*remember* that moment. I remember this moment.

Mya began to appear from underneath the toilet door. She squeezed her head, then her shoulders, arms and legs, underneath the gap. She slid herself on the dirty toilet floor and ended up sitting in front of me, resting her back against the cubicle door. She told me about periods. She told me what was happening to my body. And then she pulled out a packet from her pocket and unwrapped what I soon understood to be a pad, and lined it up in my underwear for me.

"You need to change it every few hours. Don't flush it, you've gotta wrap it up and put it in the bin. I've got a couple more in my bag and I'll bring you in a packet tomorrow. Then Mum can get you some every month."

I didn't say thank you. I didn't give her a hug or tell her what an amazing friend she is.

"Yeah, fine. I've got it. Can you just leave now?"

And Mya didn't get mad at me. She didn't accuse me of being ungrateful or call me a bitch, like she really had a right to.

She and Callie never did.

"I'll go put the other pads in your bag."

Then she carefully opened the cubicle door, checked that no one else was in the toilets and went back to class. I quickly turned the latch to *engaged* and got myself together.

Mya never mentioned that day again. I never got the impression that she told Callie either. And every month after, without fail, a packet of pads would mysteriously appear at the bottom of my school bag, with never a word said.

When Callie was drunk at that party, she told me that she and Mya were just the friends that I needed. They gave me space and let me be. It's only today when they thought that I was insulting them, or I guess that they thought I had no respect for them, that their seemingly infinite patience finally run out.

Because they care what I think about them. And for the first time ever, I realise that I care what they think about me, too.

I like my friends. So damn much. I didn't know that it was okay to like someone because how could they ever like me back? But they did anyway.

I throw the ball back to Sloopy.

"If Josh has his mum's car today, can I get a lift with you guys? I want to get home quicker to make a phone call."

Sloopy

Sadie buckles up next to me while Josh makes a crude remark about me finally getting a girl in the back seat. I panic and look to Sadie.

"Original." She is never phased.

Adam turns around to face us. "Wanna stop at Maccas on the way?"

Sadie softens her perpetual scowl and actually smiles at him. I can tell by his reaction that he realises how pretty she is.

"I just need to get home, thanks though, Adam."

Sadie is incredible and she should let the whole world see that, not just me. I know Adam wants to get to know her. I totally get why she pushes people away, at least I think I do. But when she lets you in, I can't imagine that there is anything else that feels so validating.

Sadie

Josh pulls up behind the bus and I quickly hop out. "I'll just be one second."

The doors open and I run up the steps to reach Cameron, sitting behind the wheel.

"I'm getting a ride home today, but I wanted you to know."

Cameron relaxes his grip on the wheel. "I appreciate you coming to tell me. You know I would have waited all night here for you." He bends forwards and takes a Tupperware container out of his bag. "Tuna mornay today."

Before I have a chance to think about what I'm doing, I lean in to hug him. I think I make him uncomfortable because he sort of does this little pat on my back and clears his throat.

"I love tuna mornay, thanks," I smile.

Back in the car, Josh cranks up the radio, all excited, when some song comes on that I've never heard before. I don't mind it; it's got a good beat.

"Who sings this one?" I ask.

Josh oozes cool as he drives one handed, drumming his free hand on the edge of the open window. "Reef!"

Aesthetically, he's pretty hot but he knows it and I find that a bit off-putting. Plus, my newly acquired knowledge that he hooked up with Mya in the Christmas holidays and then ignored her makes me naturally hate him.

"Place your Hands," he goes on. "You don't know it?"

"Never heard it. I like it though. I'm pretty sure they're Mya's favourite band."

Josh shoots me a look in the rear-view mirror and I'm smug with pride that I made him feel uncomfortable. Jerk.

Adam turns it up even more. I'm amazed the radio can even go any louder. Judging by the collective volume of their voices, the song has hit the boys' favourite part. I think the doors of the car are actually vibrating. I get the impression that Friday's drive home always looks and sounds like this. Sloopy is so young and happy and free, mucking around with his friends in Josh's mum's car as it goes way too fast over the train tracks. He stretches his hand across the middle seat to hold mine and it bestows me with a sense of comfort and protection and suddenly I feel like I can groove along, too. I wish I knew the words to scream along with them. For just a moment, I feel just as young and happy.

And free.

Sloopy

The car is brought to a sudden halt when Sadie points up ahead and announces that that's her house. I don't think any of us were expecting this to be her street. I thank God in my head when Josh censors himself and doesn't say anything.

Sadie had directed us up until this point but I don't think it clicked with me that she was navigating us through her own streets. It's a rough part of the neighbourhood; dole-bludger land as Dad would call it. The next street over was on the news last week; big drug bust that ended up in a hostage situation. I watched it on the couch with Mum, eating take-away and whinging that the air conditioner was taking too long to cool the house down.

I walk Sadie to her front door, stepping over the piles of rubbish decorating her front yard. An old fridge, broken bar stools, a vacuum cleaner and too many toasters and kettles to count litter the sides of the cracked cement driveway. It's a minefield of broken electrical appliances amongst dry blades of grass that tickle the backs of my knees.

The washed-out weatherboard house seems to sway as we walk up the two steps onto her porch. It feels like it could collapse any second. I only let myself believe this is her house when she actually opens the front door. I was hoping she was just dropping something off and then we could take her somewhere else. Anywhere but here.

She notices me looking around.

"Yeah, um, he doesn't like to throw anything away. He always reckons he's gonna fix them up one day. Anyway, this is me then." She seems embarrassed as she looks back from the ajar door. "So, see ya, I guess."

"Hey, I'm going to Adam's mum's 40th tomorrow night. It's at Sunnybrae, one of the big event rooms there. There'll be a band and everything. Do you maybe want to come, too?"

Sadie looks up from the shadow of the door and smiles to herself.

"I can't, I'm having friends over."

Sadie

It's only just before 5. I know I've got between 4 and 7 hours before he stumbles through the back door but when I've got something I want to do, I need to be able to do it without the slightest possibility that he will come home early. I want to call Mya and Callie and tell them that I'm sorry. I want to ask them to still be my friends even though I know I don't deserve it. I want to talk to them, knowing for certain that he won't come home. I want to invite them over.

I feel irritable and a bit frenzied. I want Sloopy to go away. I know what he thinks of me. I know what his friends think of me. I don't care. I don't care if he doesn't like me now that he has seen where I live.

He lingers by the front door and I frown impatiently. I know he is judging me and it's pissing me off.

He shuffles his feet. "Well, uh, I might walk down to the court on Sunday for a bit of extra practice. Do you want to meet me on the bench? Like around 4?"

He picks at the skin around his finger nails and I feel bad for being in such a bad mood. Sloopy thinks I'm feral and my friends think I'm a bitch. And what if *he* comes home early for once? I can't relax, ever. The fear lays dormant in the pit of my stomach all day and the second I am home, it rises up my throat and I hate everyone.

"I'll see you tomorrow at basketball anyway, yeah?" I kind of snap.

"Oh, yeah, for sure. Okay. Well, bye then."

I close the door quickly. I don't say goodbye. I just want him to go.

The front steps of the house creak, confirming that he is leaving. Soon yet another person I care about will be gone. Just five minutes ago I was riding in the back seat singing a new-found favourite song with three boys, happy and carefree and now I'm annoyed and angry. And scared. Again. Like always.

I want to be the person I was five minutes ago.

Sloopy

I'm not going to look back. She wants me to go. She doesn't want me here. I should have picked up on that earlier. I shouldn't have walked her to her door. I keep my eyes focused on Josh's mum's car. I pinch the vein on my wrist five times and just keep walking. Past the fifty toasters.

Adam sticks his head out the front passenger window. "Good to go?"

The engine revs. When it subsides, I make out Nirvana's About a Girl playing on the car stereo. Of all the songs in the world, this song comes on. Of course it does.

I hastily turn back to her house and run up the driveway. I have no idea what I intend to do, but I just know that I can't leave it this way.

I knock on the door and she opens it instantly, like she was waiting right behind it.

"I want to kiss you so much, but I don't know how," I blurt out.

Our eyes study each other. I rush my mouth towards hers but come to an abrupt halt close to her face. I've thought about it too much. I've gone against everything Adam said. I look at Sadie hopelessly, almost asking for help. I have no idea what I'm doing.

Sadie sighs impatiently and lightly touches her lips to mine. Her kiss barely connects so I press in further and she presses back. Neither one of us move: frozen together with tightly pursed lips, rampant with uncertainty. My mind is racing. I didn't check my breath first. I didn't moisten my lips. Maybe they are too dry.

Sadie pulls away slowly and studies her feet, trying to hide her smile it seems.

Our first kiss was pretty awkward. Hardly perfect. Just like us.

I wrap my arm around her waist, a physical gesture which symbolises my exact feeling at this moment: I never want to let her go. I am desperate to kiss her again, better this time. Properly. But I still can't get the timing right in my head. My fingers involuntarily press against her side five times and my eyes apologise for being such a gutless wonder. But she forgives me: her mouth finds mine for a second time, with a touch so sensual I am instantly addicted. Drugged. Our lips move together, naturally aware what to do all of a sudden, independently, without my planning.

Thank you, Nirvana.

Sadie

I pick up the receiver and dial Callie's number. The adrenaline running through my body is insane and I feel like I can do anything right now. I pace around my room waiting for Callie to answer. I jump. I skip. I have to hang up the phone after the third ring to scream. Holy shit, I can't believe I just kissed Sloopy!

I sit on the edge of my bed, phone on my lap. My heart is beating so fast and I can't calm down. If I was brave enough to make too much noise, I would scream.

I just kissed Sloopy and I want to tell my friends! I need my friends. We all swamped numbers in year eight but I told them to never call me and they never have.

I dial Callie's number again. *Answer the damn phone, I have so much to tell you!*

"Walsh residence," a voice I assume is her father's sounds from the other end.

"Oh, uh, hi, it's Sadie, from school. Just wondering if I could please talk to Callie?"

"Caaaaaaalllllliiiiieeee!"

"Callie here."

The sound of her voice is the most reassuring sound in the world sometimes.

"Hey," I whisper close into the receiver, my lips grazing the mouth piece.

"Are you okay?" she rushes. "Mum can come pick you up."

"I'm sorry."

"Oh." Callie's breath is heavy, as if she was expecting me to say something else. "It's okay. I know you are."

"I really am, Callie. I'm sorry. I didn't mean it the way it sounded. You and Mya are my best friends. I love you, both of you. I don't deserve you. I'm sorry. I'm trying and I'm getting a lot of stuff wrong, but I'm trying, just like you guys have always tried for me. Please don't hate me."

There is a pause and it kills me.

"I could never hate you, Sadie."

Tears start pouring out of my eyes. I'm embarrassed by myself. I quickly wipe them away before I can catch a glimpse of myself in the mirror. "I'm sorry, so sorry. I know I'm a terrible friend to you guys."

"Shut up," she laughs, "I know. Call Mya and tell her too."

"I will, right now. Can you guys, I mean, if you want to, do you want to maybe come over tomorrow afternoon and hang out for a bit? I've got basketball at 10 so maybe like 1? Just like to 5 or so? I don't know how to hang out really but I think I'd like it."

It makes no sense to think that I can hear her smiling. But I can hear her smiling.

"We'll be there."

"Cool. I just need to make sure you go by 7."

"It's cool, we get it. Go call Mya."

"Yep, I will. Oh, and Callie?"

"Yeah?"

"I kissed Sloopy!"

Sloopy

The ball rolls fast towards the baseline and every player gives chase; a mad flurry of panic encapsulating the court, as if something dire will happen should it go out of bounds. The benched players on our team all call out *go!* and g*rab it!* but all I hear is Sadie: *go, Sloopy!* An aggressive determination engulfs me and before I can count to five or calculate my chances, I swiftly scoop it up and shoot a three pointer. I don't even aim properly but by some miracle, the ball bounces once off the backboard and then drops straight in. I try to act cool, suppressing my urge to do a cartwheel right here and now. The team cheers. Sadie cheers.

We are playing against the same team as last time; the one with the mean girl that Sadie got into a fight with. We are on their turf: they have an indoor gymnasium with two basketball courts. Their school has vending machines and fruit trees. Dad would automatically assume it is a better school just because of the wealth behind it. He would assume the kids that go here are nicer people just because of the wealth behind them. So, I'm meant to assume the same.

Whoever wins today makes it through to the finals. I can't believe first term is nearly over.

Their coach calls a time-out. We rush to our sideline and everyone but me pays attention as our own coach goes on about set plays. I think. I scored my first goal ever, and Sadie saw it. She is wearing her Road Runner scrunchie today and she looks so pretty and I am the only person in the world who knows what her lips feel and taste like and the whistle just blew again and I have no idea what Coach told me to do.

I run back onto the court, following Josh.

"Noah!" Coach beckons. I turn around sharply. "I told you to take five! You're off, Will's on now!"

I don't even feel embarrassed. I've got Sadie's lips on my mind. Everything else seems so trivial. Ordinarily, I'd die internally if a teacher caught me out for not doing what I was told to do.

I merrily take the spot next to Sadie. It's not our bench and it feels different. It's painted red to match the school colours. It's not our bench, but at least we are on it together: sitting somewhere we don't really belong. There's familiarity in that.

Sadie folds her lips in together and sits on her hands. Her cheeks are rosy; I don't know whether because it's quite muggy in here or if because she feels the same rush when she looks at me as I do when I look at her.

Sadie

I hate this bench.

It's not ours.

I wish he had been the one who initiated our first kiss, not me. I'm always going to wonder now if he ever would have. Would I have ever been enough to help him let go? Or maybe he never really wanted it to happen in the first place. He did stop himself. I'm the one who went for it regardless.

He said 'hey' when he got here after me today, with the same enthusiasm as he would say it to Adam or Josh. I guess that says a lot. No one could ever really like me once they saw the real me.

Sloopy

Sadie presses her lips together again and it's like someone physically shoves me on the shoulder, egging me to get closer to her. I desperately want to kiss her but my head grows louder and I don't know if anyone will see and tell my dad. I don't know if anything has changed for her. It has changed for me. Was the kiss just a once-off or is it something we just do now? Everything feels wrong, especially this bench.

Sadie is looking at me, waiting. I just can't get the timing right in my head. I pinch at the loose bits of skin around my fingernails, trying really hard to make it hurt.

Sadie

Air Jordans seem to be the sneaker de jour for the other team. I got my shoes at the Harris Scarfe Boxing Day sales for six dollars. The girl with the undercut keeps staring at me. Her name's probably something like Charlotte or Yasmine but she's Undercut to me.

I bet even the walls of the gymnasium whisper to one another that I don't belong here.

I need to feel home.

"Sloopy?"

"Yeah?"

I brush my lips against his; softly and then with more force. He kisses me back, without pause or hesitation, like he'd just been waiting for me to make the move. He can't do anything without first knowing for certain that he's not going to get into trouble. He can't think for himself. He lives for the future; someone else's. I live in the moment; my own. The moment is all I have.

I like kissing him.

This bench doesn't seem so bad now.

Sloopy

I cup the back of her head and the noise in my head turns down as her mouth moves with mine. I bring my hand to the base of her neck, resting it there against her soft skin.

"Okay, I've made my point," she breathes. "That's what you should have done today when you said hello."

"Okay," I breathe back. Are we still at basketball? "Noted. I need to man up."

She smiles at my immaturity. I love making her smile.

"Sadie!" Coach bellows. "Swap with Bec."

Sadie

Bec runs off the court and takes my spot on the bench. I replace her, carrying Sloopy's kiss on my lips. Straight away, Naylene passes to me and I dribble it up the court and pass off to Sam.

Undercut is on my defence. Great. We lock eyes and I give her my toughest scowl. She matches it with her own.

Sam is directly under the ring; he can't get a clear shot. He tries but misses. I instinctively grab the rebound and wait for him to get into a better position before passing it back to him. He scores this time and ceremoniously taps me on the behind, unintentionally making me feel sick with fear.

"Can't even shoot the ball yourself," Undercut sniggers. "Pointless anyway since Mummy and Daddy aren't here to cheer for you."

I nearly lunge for her, but I don't. I focus on the ball, now heading back up the other end. I focus on what Mrs Carrington told me. I mentally filed away her advice as if it was given to me by my own mum.

The other team score almost straight away and I clap a couple of times for them, unwittingly giving Undercut more ammunition.

"You're clapping for the wrong team, retard."

My chest tightens but I don't even look at her. She will feel bad one day, Mrs Carrington is right. I follow the ball back to our end. Adam passes it to me and I frantically look around for a teammate but no one is open.

Undercut is wrong. I do have someone to be proud of me. I have Sloopy: the boy who is too scared to be himself around anyone but me. And Mrs Carrington with our special Tuesdays. And Coach with his enthusiastic whistle. And Mya and Callie who don't even mind that I'm the worst friend ever. And Cameron with his Tupperware dinners, Loretta with her frozen peas and Mya's mum who has never even met me before but secretly buys me pads every 28 days. I have so many people who care about me. I really do. And maybe that should make me care about myself.

There is only one person who doesn't want me to exist.

He is outnumbered.

I stretch my arms high in the air, releasing the ball from my grip. Swish! Straight in! I stare at the ring in a stupor. Am I dreaming? Sloopy's screams wrap around me and Coach blows that whistle that he loves so much over and over again, jumping up and down on the spot. I laugh to the heavens and I don't even flinch when my whole team rush up to hug me.

The opposition are confused.

"It's just one goal, loser!" Undercut bitches.

Yes, it is. It's one goal. And it was mine.

My family are proud of me.

Sloopy

I button up my powder blue long-sleeved shirt and check myself out in the mirror. My hair isn't sitting right. I brush it back and flop my head forwards five times to ruffle it up. Better. I tuck my shirt into the waist of my trousers and then untuck it. It looks better in. I tuck it back in and out again four more times and then leave it in.

My brain is manic and I can't slow it down. Rushing, I open the drawer to my desk. The sheer sight of the bible bestows me with an impending sense of hope. Everything will feel okay in a minute. I open up to Colossians 3:20 and take out the kitchen knife wedged against the spine. I hold the blade lightly against my wrist and slowly increase the pressure until it pierces my skin and I start to bleed. Everything slows down. The sense of relief is instant.

"Are you ready, baby?" Mum's voice sounds through my door.

"One sec, Ma."

I hastily shove the knife back in the bible and take a Band-Aid out. I put it over my new cut and push down hard, making the fresh wound hurt. I put another Band-Aid over the top to cover up the stain of blood seeping through.

I ensure everything is back in its place, adjusting the bible and the Band-Aids on top so that they sit at perfect right angles in the back corner of the drawer.

Adam's mum turning 40 seems to be the event of the year. Most of the church are going to be there. Adam tells me close to a hundred people all up. Dad has worked really hard to build up the congregation after the numbers dwindled a few years ago, back at his old church. Well, so Mum tells me anyway. We have to be our best tonight. We're on display.

Just outside my room, Mum shyly waits, visibly in need of a self-esteem boost. We're meeting Dad at the venue. He's been playing golf with important associates all day. It's up to me to make Mum feel beautiful.

"You look stunning, Mum. You could easily be Kevin Costner's date for the Oscars."

I offer her my arm like a gentleman and hum music reminiscent of Bach as we make our way down the stairs. Mum giggles. Success.

Independent of being my mum, she really is beautiful. I see the way other men look at her when we go to the shops. Women, too. Like they envy her.

She's obediently wearing the dress Dad bought for her to wear, even though she hates it. Even though she would never choose it for herself.

I get it, Mum.

If she had been allowed to shop for her own dress, I think she would have picked something bright. Mum loves pink. And florals. She loves long, flowy maxi dresses with bright flowers on them. She is always gardening. Always putting fresh flowers on the table. This is the only time I've ever seen her wear black. She hates fitted things.

She has tried to make the outfit more her with a patterned clutch and dangly ear rings that look like sunflowers. But even her shoes are forced; black strappy high heels. Mum likes flats.

I feel bad that Dad is just going to meet her there. He should be with her now, telling her how beautiful she looks, how beautiful she *is*. He should ask her to dance with him before they even leave the house and make her feel special and safe and adored before they go out into the world. Together.

At least, that's what I think a husband should do.

Instead, Mum is on a date with her son.

"You really do look amazing," I praise her.
Mum twirls around on the spot, then sighs at the high heels already making her feet ache. She picks up the keys from the entrance table.

"Grab your Ls, you're driving."

Sadie

I have done the best I can with the house. I've tidied up but he has so much stuff, like everywhere. It's just impossible to organise. Piles of records, old magazines, 'collectable' stubby holders, tin signs (like literally stolen road signs, go figure). In everyday life I'm sort of just immune to it, but knowing my friends are coming over to hang out, the evidence that I live with an alcoholic hoarder is depressingly obvious.

And yet there's no impending sense of embarrassment or shame like I predicted and guess there probably should be. I know for certain that Mya and Callie are not coming over to judge. They are coming over to spend time with me. The first time I let them see where I live, they looked around, sure, but the more I think about it, there was no bitchiness or snobbery behind it. They just wanted to check out my home, because whether I like it or not, it is a part of me.

I've got my favourite Smash Hits CD playing. I bought it last year when my traditional birthday card came in the mail, with vouchers for all my favourite shops. Last year, the card read, "Sweet 16, how blessed the world is to have you in it." As always, the card was merely signed with a love heart. I sort of just assume they are from Mum's old church friends. I even get them at Christmas. I keep the cards, every single one, with my CDs, in the suitcase under my bed. It's the same suitcase that someone packed all my things in and delivered them here when I was 9 years old.

It's sunny outside so I've opened all the windows. I really like the t-shirt dress I'm wearing; it's black with big bold sunflowers on it. Nice and flowy for a warm afternoon. I wish Sloopy could see me now. I feel happy and excited and I want him to see me in my nice dress. I wonder if he thinks about me as much as I think about him.

Sloopy

The estate's car park is packed. The lane between the rows of parked cars is too narrow for my nerves to handle. Mum gently directs me while I grip the wheel so tight my fingers start to ache. I repeatedly recite *brake is on the left* in my head. Sweat drips onto my eye lid but I don't blink. I have to focus; if I don't, my flight response will kick in and I'll jerk open the door and jump out of the moving car. I repeatedly press my tongue up against the roof of my mouth in groups of five.

"You're doing good, baby." Her voice is purposefully soft, calm. Gentle. I can only faintly hear her, really. "You won't hit anyone. Have confidence in yourself."

I let my mind drift to thoughts of Sadie. Again. Always.

I wonder what her afternoon has been like. I wonder if she really is going to have Mya and Callie over like she said. Part of me finds that really hard to believe. I wonder what clothes she changed into after basketball. I wonder, just wonder. I wonder about her all the time.

I check in the rear-view mirror to see if anyone is behind me before bringing the car to a slow halt. "I can't do it. Can you park?"

Mum doesn't say anything. She just gets out of the car and takes the driver's seat as I climb over to the passenger side.

"Here's one," she whispers, evidently still in keeping-things-calm mode. She parks and then documents the time in my log book. "Two hours, easy."

"Except it was a fifteen-minute drive."

Mum writes two hours down. "Same thing."

The invitation is for 5 o'clock onwards. *Come celebrate Holly's 40th birthday. An evening of music and dancing. 3-course meal served at 6pm.* It's just gone quarter past 5. The band is loud enough to hear from the landscaped gardens we walk through on our way to the function room. They are playing old rock n roll stuff; songs that always swoon over some girl named Carol or Donna. Mum excitedly announces that she loves the one on now. I don't recognise it but she tells me it's called Poetry in Motion.

We reach the grand entrance hall. A blackboard rests on an artist easel: Holly's 40th. Mum looks at me and tightens her grip on my arm.

"Do I look okay, really?"

It kills me that Mum feels the need to seek validation from me.

"You always look beautiful and the dress looks incredible on you."

She slides her hand over her hip. "Hope your father thinks so." She smiles. "I'll tell you a little secret: I hate it."

I smile right back. "I know, Mum. I totally get it."

Sadie

Callie holds the can of hairspray like a microphone, speaking the opening words of Brownstone's If You Love Me as it blasts from my stereo. Mya and I stand either side of her, performing for ourselves in front of my dressing table mirror. We provide the back-up vocals while Callie sorrowfully recites the verse, before the chorus kicks in and the three of us audition for the best bedroom girls group there ever was.

Callie has borrowed my white hat to complete her desired superstar look. It has a purple flower sticking out the side. Paired with her denim overalls and cropped, black skivvy, she looks just as pretty as Alison Brahe. Mya's white midriff top and wide-legged Tencel jeans show more of her tummy than I have ever seen before. Her chunky blonde bob is held back off her face with tiny pink and purple butterfly clips all in a row. Her belly button is pierced. I never knew that. I try not to stare at it but it's enticing. It feels ironic that something can be on display for everyone to see yet still retain this weird sense of intimate femininity. I wish I could get mine pierced.

Mya is naturally amazing, of course; oozing her body up and down like a pole dancer. Callie sings into the hairspray with so much power and passion you'd think she was the lead singer of 4 Non Blondes. Callie normally radiates an underlying shyness. She is self-conscious and unsure of herself. Or maybe she just seems that way in comparison to Mya whom is currently gyrating her pelvis on my hair brush. The three of us are completely at ease in each other's company. Free to shine. No judgement. Friendship is empowering.

We fall onto the floor, laughing at each other, laughing together. Callie snorts and we lose it even more.

Sloopy

Mum and I stand at the entrance to the function room, arm in arm, looking around at the fancy tables laden with champagne glasses and gold foil centre pieces. Every man here is wearing a suit. The women have all got their hair professionally done and no doubt feel like they should be on the red carpet in their $300 David Jones dresses. It's quite the affair. Adam's mum is evidently really excited about turning 40.

I spy Adam over by the band, talking to Nikki. Her name's really Nikita, like the ABBA song apparently, but we all call her Nikki. She's one of the prettiest girls at school. Or so Adam mentioned excitedly when he heard that she fancied him.

Adam waves me over. Mum scans her eyes across the room, somewhat nervously. No doubt looking for Dad. I spot him by the bar and point him out to her. She smiles, relieved it seems. The band start playing one of Mum's favourite songs; 20 Miles by Ray Brown. I know it well. She plays it on LP almost every Sunday when she's cleaning and somehow it feels like the universe is playing it just for her.

Mum kisses me on the cheek. "Have fun, baby."

She heads over to Dad, who is talking to a woman I recognise from church, but I wouldn't know her name. She comes to the service on her own, or sometimes with an elderly woman I just assume is her mother. She is curvy and judging by her current body language, she purposefully chose her shiny, slinky emerald green mini dress to fully accentuate her womanly frame.

Dad is hanging on her every word and it makes me feel sick as I watch him lap up her attention while his wife is walking straight towards them, looking absolutely sensational, desperate for him to give her the same attention, wearing a dress that she hates just to please him. And he doesn't even look at her. I think about how Mum must be feeling as she walks towards them, trying to look proud and excited to see him. Deep down, I bet she is pulling at her skin in lots of five, too.

Adam shakes my hand as I join him and Nikki. "Looking sharp, my man!"

"You don't scrub up too bad yourself. Nikki, looking lovely," I nod.

Nikki starts rambling on about her upcoming gymnastics showcase and I feign an interest whilst looking directly over at Dad. Mum greets him warmly but he just keeps talking to that other woman. He doesn't put his arm around Mum or make her feel welcome. He has totally ignored her. No, *'wow, honey, you look incredible!' 'Mystery woman, you know my beautiful wife, Loretta.' 'Lovely talking to you, but my stunning wife is here now and I'd love to get her on the dance floor.' 'Darling, come join us, you look amazing, I'm so glad you're here now.'* Instead, Mum just stands there, awkwardly, like she's the third wheel in her own marriage.

She looks down at her shoes and then back up again, smiling politely and dutifully as always, as if the high heels that she hates gave her a hasty pep talk. Adam's mum catches her eye from the other end of the bar and Mum touches Dad on his arm to let him know that she is going over to say hello. I don't know why; it's not like he noticed she was even there anyway.

"Do you know what table you're sitting at?" Adam asks.

"No, but it better not be the same one as that woman in the green dress."

Sadie

"Oh my god," Mya wheezes, "this has been the best afternoon, can't believe it's nearly time to go."

Callie looks up at the Looney Tunes clock on my wall, a little conscientious. "We'll rack off soon so you can get settled in for the night."

I have never had a friend sleep over before. It occurs to me now that I never will be able to, and I realise how much I wish they could stay. I glare anxiously at the clock. I remind myself that he never comes home before 10pm at the earliest on a Saturday and it's only just gone 7.05pm, but I don't want to take my anxiety out on them. I know I will get more and more irritable as the time gets closer. I need them to go now.

Callie begins to tidy up. "Cane said he was going to call me tonight. I'm hoping he'll ask me out. Cane and Callie sounds good, yeah?"

"He's friends with that dick, Leigh," Mya reminds her. "Just be careful. I don't trust him or his friends. They're all sleazebags."

Callie scoops up my scattered CDs and starts putting them back in my suitcase. "Speaking of his friends, you know what's weird as? Sam was behind me in the tuck-shop line the other day and started chatting to me. He's never spoken to me before. He asked me if Cane or Josh had spoken to me recently."

Alarm bells sound in my head and from the look on Mya's face, in hers too.

"Josh is a jerk, Callie. I thought he was interested in me too, but it was just to get what he wanted. He's getting in with the wrong crowd. Be careful, hey? I mean it's about time the boys noticed how hot you are, but just be careful."

I feel like I'm meant to say something supportive and empowering too but I don't know how. But as usual, my friends don't seem to mind.

I walk them to the door and they both hug me at the same time. I tense my whole body. I feel trapped. I don't hug them back.

Mya lets go and I breathe out in relief when Callie follows her lead.

"We're going back to my house tonight. Mya's sleeping over, if you want to come too?"

"Maybe another time, thanks. I'd like that one day."

They wave goodbye but just as I am about to close the door behind them, Mya pushes her way back in. "Wait, I'm busting! Give me two secs."

Mya rushes to the toilet while Callie and I wait for her in the hallway. Callie is keen to keep talking about Cane and admits that she thinks she has a crush on him. Mya emerges a couple of minutes later, dancing her way over to us.

"Hey, what's that room?" she wonders out loud, looking down to the end of the hallway.

My body stiffens. "Um, yeah, that's his bedroom. He always keeps the door closed."

Mya is intrigued. "Mysterious! Can we check it out?"

"No way. I don't go in there. No. Absolutely not."

Callie tugs at Mya's arm. "Come on, Mya, don't push it. Sadie doesn't want to go in there, it's time for us to go anyway."

"Please? Just a peak. I won't go in, I promise. We'll just open the door, have a quick look and then close it. Bam, never even happened."

I don't know why she wants to see in there so badly but there is a part of me that wants to, too. That is his world in there, the world where I don't exist. Just like he has always wanted. Deep down inside me, that hopeful, lonely 9-year-old girl craving acceptance and maybe even love from the person who constantly rejected her, still hopes. For my only family. Only now, I've got two best friends right alongside me.

I clench my fists instinctively at my sides. "We can't go in. But we can have a quick look."

Sloopy

I twirl Mum under my arm and she throws her head back laughing.

"You get your moves from me!" she beams.

Mum loves all these 60s songs. She couldn't wait to get out on the dance floor. It's not like Dad was ever going to ask her.

The band play the final note of Jailhouse Rock and Mum and I applaud them as they announce they are going to take a break whilst the main meal is served. Dad is heavily involved in a conversation with Adam's dad and doesn't seem to notice when we join the table. Mum gleefully tells Holly that she is having the most wonderful time. Holly says that she is disappointed with the entrees and means to take it up with the catering team tomorrow.

Adam tugs at the top button of his shirt, deciding he has had enough of being dressed up. "Fancy clothes are so damn itchy."

I unbutton mine as well. It's sweaty work keeping up with Mum on the dance floor. "I didn't know your mum knows Nikki's family."

"Yeah, she works with her dad at the accounting firm. Nice enough people, Nikki's a bit boring though. All she talks about is gymnastics. Oh, but she did ask if you and Sadie are together now. She said she heard some girls talking at school. Not sure how that got around, but it looks like people know. You guys are a thing."

"Good. She's the best thing that's ever happened to me. I want everyone to know."

Adam tilts his eyes across the table at Dad. "Even?"

The woman in the slinky emerald green dress is poised at the table next to us, staring longingly at my mother's husband. She sees me and quickly looks away.

"Yep. Even him. Especially him."

Sadie

The hallway between my room and his is narrow and dark, like the entrance to an abandoned mine.

Mya grips the rusted bronze handle, loosely affixed to the poorly painted cream door. "You've really never seen in here before?"

"No, he's a bit private. He likes his own space."

"We don't have to if you don't want to," Callie assures me.

"We'll just be quick," I affirm.

Mya gently pulls the handle down and apprehensively pushes the door open. It actually creaks and Mya's eyes widen. "Just like a horror movie."

The room revealed behind the permanently closed door is bigger than I assumed it was, much bigger than mine. I don't think it was built as a bedroom; it has the space purposed for a second lounge room. There are two windows, both on the back wall of the house, looking out into the garden. The curtains are always closed but if he opened them, he would be able to see down into the yard; like when I hang out the washing on Sundays.

A four-poster bed sits almost in the middle of the room, away from the walls. I've never seen a bed positioned that way. Towers of cardboard boxes are scattered around the room like a mock city landscape almost; as if he has been packing for years. There is an abundance of paperwork; piles stacked up sporadically around the room. A tv rests atop an old esky. There are empty cans of beer, VHS tapes and stacks of coins everywhere.

A Flinders University degree hangs on the wall adjacent to the door. Bachelor of Education. I'm stunned to see it has his name on it. A framed photograph hangs next to it that I actually recognise from an old photo album Mum used to show me. It is a family portrait, professionally taken in a studio. In the photo Mum used to show me, my teenaged mother stood in front of my grandparents, next to her slightly older brother. This is the exact same photo, only, hung up on the wall here, my teenaged mother is not visible. A rectangle of black paper has been glued on top of her, concealing my grandmother's hand as I have previously seen it resting on Mum's shoulder.

Mum had a uni degree, too. She was a primary school teacher. She told me once that her mum and dad always knew she would be a teacher when she grew up. Her graduation was one of the happiest days of their life. They both got cancer and died soon after, within three months of each other. I remember Mum showing me her wedding photos. Her brother wasn't in any of them.

Mum only ever mentioned her brother in brief, and only a handful of times. When I asked if I could have a brother or sister for Christmas one year, she told me, *Father Christmas could get it wrong and give you a bad person, someone who drinks and gambles.* I assured her that I didn't care; they would be my sibling and I would love them anyway. *Sometimes it's not that easy, Sadie. Sometimes even your own family can be bad for you.*

If Mya and Callie weren't here, I would light a match, throw it in and shut the door. I guess I was just hoping to find some sort of redemption behind the closed door; something that would make me sympathise with him, understand even. Maybe even find a bit of evidence that says he does love me, or did at some stage. Even if only for a little while. But he hated me before I even existed.

Callie loops her arm through mine, like that's just our thing these days. Her touch is comforting and reassuring. Dare I acknowledge that it feels like family.

Mya closes the door and sticks her middle finger up at it. "Wanker."

Within the walls of this house, I have never let myself think about my future because I didn't think I had much of one. I walk Mya and Callie to the door and hug them goodbye. *I* hug *them*. Neither of them seems to have any intention of letting go, so I do first.

I turn off all the lights in the house and make sure all the doors are locked. Even the back one. He has a key he can fumble around with. I want to be safe.

I don't deserve bad things to happen to me. I am not worthless. I am not in the way. I deserve to be loved. What a feeling when you start to care about yourself.

I sit in my bed, listening to the Top 30 and take out my Looney Tunes notebook. I have never used it before because once it's used, that's it. It's not the new thing that Mum bought me anymore. I smile at Tweety Bird on the cover and start writing a list of all the things I want to talk to Mrs Carrington about on Tuesday.

Sloopy

The waiter places Mum's plate in front of her. Chicken.

Her hand gently brushes his wrist. "So sorry, I actually ordered the zucchini omelette."

"Don't make a scene, Loretta," Dad whispers sternly, carving into his lamb. "Just eat the chicken."

"She's a vegetarian," I bite back, not even trying to hide my disdain.

Dad glares at me. "She eats fish, it's no different." He smiles at the waiter. "The chicken is just fine, no need to make a fuss."

The waiter waves his arm in the air, intentionally trying to sound unfazed. "Oh no, no trouble at all. It's my mistake, we have the omelette ready to be served." He picks up the plate of chicken and smiles warmly at Mum. "Won't be long, ma'am."

Dad sighs, wanting Mum to see his disapproval. She self-consciously looks over to the empty stage. Only minutes ago, she was dancing right in front of it with her son. She lowers her shoulders and hunches her back forwards, as if trying to make herself appear smaller. Like she wants to disappear because she's disappointed him.

Mum's omelette arrives and she eats it without raising her eyes from the table.

The band take to the stage again and incredibly, they kick off their second set with Hang on Sloopy. Mum smiles at me nostalgically.

"Mum, do you want to dance with your son?"

Sadie

I don't know how long I've been asleep for when the sound of him crashing through the back door abruptly wakes me. He's louder than usual tonight. I bet I angered him by locking up. I lay perfectly still, reminding myself that he never comes in here. I am safe.

An unmistakable ruckus resonates from the kitchen: the table scrapes along the floor and alerts me to the fact that he has fallen. I tense my body even more in the darkness and listen, waiting to hear him move. Minutes pass. The sound of my clock ticking fills the room. I can't hear anything else.

I creep out of my room and apprehensively slink across the hallway. I stand in the kitchen doorway, staring at his brown leather jacket. His whole torso is slumped forwards over the table; pushed from its usual spot in the middle of the kitchen from the momentum of his collapse. The corner street light shines through the missing slat of the venetian blind on the kitchen window, falling on his face like an actual ray of sunshine. One half of his face is exposed, the other half is squashed against the table. His eyes are closed. His mouth gapes open but there is no snore.

My voice croaks.

I am nine years old again.

"Hey, you should get into bed. You're in the kitchen."

His back does not rise and fall to indicate breathing but I listen intently for his breath. The house is deadly quiet. I can't even hear the traffic from the main road.

I swallow loudly and take a tiny step forward. He doesn't move. I take two larger steps into the room, bringing me to the edge of the table.

"Do you want me to help you get down to your room?"

His brown leather jacket looks new. I haven't seen him wear it before. And yet it already reeks of the pub. I turn to leave him here but the thought scares me. So close to my room. So out in the open, no protection from behind closed doors. I cautiously poke him on the back of the shoulder.

"Wake up, you're in the kitchen."

He doesn't move and I still can't hear him breathing.

Sloopy

Mum and I dance for five songs straight. She squeals, "this is my favourite song" at the start of every single song. I twirl her under my arm as often as I can, because it makes her giggle every time.

At the end of Mony Mony, Mum declares that she's thirsty so we head back to the table. Mum wipes her forehead and laughs to Holly that she hasn't danced this much since her wedding all those years ago.

"Ma, is it cool if Sloopy and I go for a look around outside?" Adam interrupts.

"Of course, dear. Just don't wander off too far."

Adam winks at me as we stand to leave. "Nikki's meeting me out back," he whispers in my ear.

It hits me that I'm his cover. I'm instantly awkward and fiddle with the end of my cuffs.

Out in the foyer, Nikki is leaning against a pillar and smiles smugly when she sees us coming.

"She's heaps hot hey?" Adam's voice is laced with enthusiasm.

Nikki has thick dark hair, swept up high into a pony tail that bothers me the more I look at it: it's off-centre, but not in a deliberate way. It's like she tried to centre it but just missed the mark. Her outfit is cute: white lace top with a navy satin skirt that hoops out above her knees like one of those dresses the women in the olden days wore. I guess Adam is right; Nikki is hot, but it never occurs to me to notice these things. I instantly wonder if there is something fundamentally wrong with me or if I'm just destined to always be two steps behind my friends. I walk with my hands in my pockets, pinching at my legs through my trousers.

I miss Sadie.

Sadie

I cautiously poke his still shoulder again. He grunts and I jump. I pray to the God my Mum believed in and ask Him to protect me.

"You're in the kitchen. D-do you need help getting to bed?"

He suddenly jerks his body upright and looks around the room, visibly becoming aware of his surroundings.

His stubble displays remnants of the day. His eyes are shadowed by his heavy eyebrows, perfectly matching the overgrown mane of greasy, greying curls clinging lifelessly to his head. I take a step back and then another, consciously trying to create distance between us without making it obvious how scared of him I am. Please God, I pray, make him go to his room now.

His hand connects with my chest and forcefully pushes me backwards. The pressure robs me of my strength and I fall to the floor. I don't attempt to stand.

"Fuck off!" he slurs.

I stare at the peeling vinyl flooring beneath my hands and say another prayer. Please protect me. I'm scared.

I apprehensively lift my eyes at the sound of his feet dragging his heavy body down to his bedroom. The back door was left ajar in his drunken entrance. The pitch-black night sky peeks through, beckoning me to lock up. I calculate that this will take precious extra seconds. Seconds I can't afford. His bedroom door slams shut and I bolt for my room. I shift my bookcase so it blocks my door; it's only three small shelves so not enough to block it from opening, but big enough to make a noise if it is pushed open.

I sleep with my arm under my pillow, gripping onto the knife. My fear instinctively wakes me up several times over night. But I am safe. For now, I am safe. Thank you, God.

I miss Sloopy.

Sloopy

Adam extends his arm and Nikki lunges for it eagerly.

"Finally, way to make a girl wait."

"Sorry babe, Sloopy was dancing up a storm with his mum."

Life has moved by without me again. I wasn't aware that we had started calling girls *babe*, yet Adam bands it around so effortlessly. I wonder how long his hook-ups with Nikki have been going on. The first term of Year 12 proves to me yet again that I just can't keep up with this whole growing-up thing.

We all try to get with the same girl now like it's some sort of game or competition. We hook up with them at our parent's 40th even though we're not dating them and don't even really like them. We call them babe. I spent my Christmas holidays reading passages from the Bible to the old folks in the nursing home. Everyone else spent them keeping up with the normal pace of puberty. Dear God, am I ever going to catch up?

Adam bumps me on the shoulder and leads Nikki off to the car park. "Thanks, man."

I nod my head in recognition and watch them as they disappear out of my sight.

It's not that I don't think about Sadie lunging for my arm like that; it's not that I don't wish that she was hungry and impatient for time with me, just like Nikki wanting to sneak off with Adam somewhere they can't be found. I do. All the time. But I also think about the band playing back at the party. The music is muffled but I can just make it out: it's the end of Dancing Queen. Does Mum like this song? Does she want to dance? I think about Sadie and being completely alone with her but I think about Mum being on her own, too: is she okay without me? It's Sunday tomorrow: is Dad expecting me to run the Kids Club again? Did I finally sound convincing enough in debate on Tuesday? Did I make Mum feel pretty tonight? Am I going to hell because I want to kiss Sadie? Because I want to feel underneath her clothes more than I want to do my homework? Because I want to dance in my room to Nirvana instead of writing out passages from the bible or volunteering at the nursing home? I got another application in the post last week for the seminary. Did I rip it up and throw away every single piece? Or did I inadvertently drop a bit near the bin for Dad to find? Will it be big enough for him to piece together what it was? Will they send out yet another one when I don't apply? Will Dad check the mail before I do?

The sky is black. Starless night. Nothing to wish on. Of course. How poetic. I lean against one of the white marble pillars in the foyer, overlooking the perfectly manicured grounds, the perfectly square hedges that line the gardens, the perfectly straight row of perfectly pruned roses. Perfectly presented. Perfectly poised. Perfectly maintained. Perfect. Perfect. Perfect. Such a perfect place. Dad must love it here.

The Monkees are playing now. Daydream Believer. I know Mum loves this song.

I smooth my thumb over every finger, feeling for my longest nail. They're all too short. I dig my index finger into my wrist anyway; pushing down hard on the Band-Aid. The evening breeze blows on my face as I focus on the blades of grass dimly lit by the old-fashioned light posts. The grass is too short to sway in the gentle wind: it is so perfect that it physically can't be affected by anything. I push down harder. The discomfort urges me to stop so I apply more force, twirling my finger into my skin as if trying to burrow through to the other side. Fresh blood seeps through the Band-Aid and my whole body tingles with relief.

A woman's voice breaks my trance. I freak out that Adam and Nikki might think I have been spying on them. My eyes trace the sound of laughter to the box hedge, to my father, curling his fingers through a mane of auburn hair. The woman has her back to me; her emerald green dress clinging to her round hips. She squeals, as if she really likes what Dad is doing to her and really wants him to know it. He tugs her head back and smooths his free hand over her backside as she lifts her leg up to cradle his thigh.

He feverishly grabs her lips with his own, gelling their faces together amidst a flurry of moans and frantic breaths.

"Cassandra," he sighs, "I need this. I need *you*."

His words echo across the garden, carried by the wind, as if he meant to announce it to the world.

Mum really does love this song. She will want to dance. I turn back to the party, intending to sweep her off her feet. I'm going to dance with her until her feet ache. Mum loves to dance.

But Mum is right behind me. Watching. Her eyes meet mine and she actually smiles. She smiles in the face of heartbreak. For me. Always for me.

I loop my arm through hers and we walk back to the absurdly lavish 40th birthday party; so burdened by the real truth of perfection that both our shoulders literally slump forwards.

"Hey Mum," I whisper, maybe for fear of being heard, "I really hate your dress."

Mum chuckles. "Thank you, so do I."

We head straight to the dance floor. It's only when the first few notes of Roy Orbison's Crying strums two whole songs later that Mum finally speaks, resting her head on my shoulder as I hold her close for the slow dance.

"I wish I had a superhero name, too, my Sloopy."

I spin her out and bring her back, cradling her against my chest. "You do, Loretta. Your superhero name is Mum."

Sadie

The sun shines through my curtains, colouring my bedroom with an orange hue. It is morning. Sunday. I relax my grip on the knife under my pillow; held tightly all night long. My palm aches. I sit on the edge of my bed and listen intently, trying to figure out if he is up yet. I wouldn't think so.

I tiptoe to the bathroom, wee and brush my teeth. The floorboards announce my presence as I retreat back to my room: the house is plotting against me. I change into my blue patterned shorts and cream-coloured tee.

My washing basket is close to overflowing. I visualise him waking from his slumber, instantly angry to see me hanging out the washing below his window, in his backyard.

Intuitively, I pick up my basketball and head off to the court.

Sloopy

In the solace of my room, Nirvana plays on repeat as I reach my target of fifteen sit-ups. Ten push-ups come easily next, before I get dressed for church and turn up the music a little louder.

Dad bangs on my door, furious that it's locked.

"I'll be ready in a minute!" I call out.

His voice is muffled against Drain You. "Turn that noise off!"

Not turn down the music.

Turn that *noise* off.

Too bad I can't hear him.

And even if I could, I wouldn't care.

Sadie

The local church is packed. Cars everywhere, people dressed in their Sunday best. Mum always used to dress in her best for the Sunday service, too. She wouldn't have particularly liked this church though; it's too big and cold and everyone is separated into groups, like they just stick with the people they came with.

Mum's old church was much smaller and seemed more personal somehow. It had its own little community, its own little family. Everyone knew each other's names. Everyone *knew* each other. I don't know how long it would take me to walk there but I might try one day. It was on a corner, I remember that. I think I'd like to see it again.

I almost expect this church to come with a red carpet: it's like the Oscars arrivals. It's not old, which seems unnatural. Churches should be old. This one is newly built; it's only been around for a few years. If it wasn't for the giant crucifix on the front, I doubt anyone would even recognise it as a church. It's just a grossly tall, square, grey building, like a factory or a warehouse. It's not the architecture I associate with a church. Sometimes the bigger something gets, the less meaning it retains.

A fancy car pulls in, driving straight past me. It is black and shiny with windows just as black and shiny, like those cars that escort important people like politicians. It parks in front of a 'reserved' sign and a man steps out of the driver's seat. Families rush up to greet him. Little kids jump at his feet. He's like a celebrity, only he wears a priest's collar.

A woman gets out the passenger side and I instantly recognise her as Sloopy's mum. This must be his dad's church. I don't know why that hasn't occurred to me before; there's not many other churches around here or in the adjoining suburbs.

Sloopy steps out of the back seat and his mother puts her arm around him lovingly, but not maternally. Their roles are reversed: she is the child seeking comfort and protection from him. My tummy flutters as he pushes his floppy hair off his forehead. I have missed him and I'm desperate to shout out to him from across the road but I stop myself. Something doesn't feel right. Sloopy doesn't seem right. And as much as it kills me to think it, he wouldn't want to see me now. Or for me to see him.

Sloopy

The congregation is out in force this morning. Or the fans, more like it. Julie from down the street is telling Dad all about the lamington cake she made for everyone to share at morning tea. Derek, who always sits in the front row with his wife, Eva and their 6-year-old daughter, Millie, wants Dad to come over for dinner one night during the week. *Bring your lovely Mrs, of course!* And a curvy woman not wearing a green dress today hangs at the back of the crowd, trying not to make it obvious that she is staring at Mum.

We leave Dad to revel in the adoration and make our way into the church. We take our usual place in the front row, directly in front of the pulpit.

Mum puts her hand on my knee. "Show time."

"Yeah," I utter under my breath, "it really is all just an act, isn't it?"

Sadie

The nerves in my stomach finally settle from last night, hearing only the glorious sounds of the basketball as it connects with the asphalt and the swish of the net. I remind myself that I can stay here all day if I want to.

I make five shots in a row and smile knowingly. Sloopy would like that. Five in a row.

I like being at school on a Sunday. It's like I'm the only person left in the world.

But then the door to my Homeroom swings open. Cameron, the bus driver, steps out into the fresh air and holds the door open for Mrs Carrington, who's cradling a large cardboard box. Cameron wedges the door back with his foot.

"Here, darling, let me carry it."

Darling.

Mrs Carrington passes him the box, leaning over it as she does, and kisses Cameron sweetly on his lips. "Thanks, darling."

Darling.

Darling?

I announce my presence by slamming the ball down aggressively. Mrs Carrington and Cameron instantly notice me in shocked surprise.

Sloopy

"And this is what we must constantly remember. Constantly remind ourselves!"

The lady sitting in the next pew utters *amen*, shaking her head as if Dad's words have touched her soul.

He slams his palm down onto the pulpit after each and every word.

"Constantly. Live. In. Honour. Of!"

The whole church erupts into applause.

Amen, Father Blean!

We hear you, Father!"

He continues his monologue amid the fading ruckus of the congregation.

"We are here to serve, both Him and each other. Every action we take, every day we live, we must remind ourselves of where we came from, so that we may live as righteously and as morally," he pauses and looks directly at me, "and as *good* as our Father intended us to."

The church roars with claps of approval. I feel nauseous and hold my breath to stop myself from throwing up right there and then.

This doesn't even look like a church. The walls are concrete grey. The windows aren't stained-glass like the ones at Dad's old church. They're just windows. It's the same with Father Blean's sermon: I'm not in awe like when I was a little kid. They're just words. Just windows. Soulless windows. Soulless words. Like what my faith has become. Like what my respect for my father has become.

Sadie

Cameron and Mrs Carrington cautiously walk over to the court, stopping directly in front of me. Cameron gently places the cardboard box down.

"I left everyone's essays here on Friday," Mrs Carrington explains as my eyes dart to the box. "I just wanted to pick them up so I could start marking them this evening."

I raise my eyebrows. I feel like a child. I try to stand tall and proud but all I want to do is stamp my feet and run away. My safe people aren't who I thought they were. Their secret marriage is an act of betrayal.

The sun shines from the side and I wince my eyes in annoyance. I'm pleased to think it probably makes me look tougher. "So, you're married then. Like, to each other." I don't say it as a question.

"Yes," they reply in unison.

My mind darts to the Tupperware containers. Friday's dinner. Cameron's lunch that he never seems to want on Fridays. That his wife makes for him. That Mrs Carrington makes for me.

"I guess I never made that connection."

Cameron wipes his frow and looks to his wife. "We, ah, we should have told you, I don't know why we didn't."

He shuffles his feet, physically trying to find a comfortable spot in the most uncomfortable moment.

"I just wanted to be able to keep an eye on you, even when I wasn't around. Please don't be mad at me, Sadie."

Mrs Carrington's voice is shaky and I can feel a lump rising in my throat.

I am mad at her, damn it. But hearing her voice, I don't want her to know that.

I scoop up my basketball and run away as fast as I can.

Sloopy

There are three separate kids' groups. The first one is for the littlest kids, under 6 years old. It starts just after the service. Everyone else goes to the shared morning tea. Dad spends the whole time basically signing autographs while Mum dutifully chats to the other women about how wonderful her husband is. That's the only reason I secretly like being the glorified babysitter; running the under 6s Sunday School for 45 minutes means I get to miss out on the after-party.

The under 12s group starts at 3pm and then the 12s plus straight after. Dad runs those ones. It's meant to be some sort of prize when he finally deems me capable of stepping up to the task.

Four little kids sit in a semi-circle at my feet and I read a passage from the children's bible. They all marvel when I talk about the donkey. They think 'Mer' is the funni-est word ever. Selling something I don't even know if I believe in...I may as well be in debate. Maybe that's why Dad makes me do it: practise.

Sadie

I have nowhere to go.

I can't be at home today. He was drunker than ever last night. He needs the day to recover. If I annoy him or set him off, he will kill me.

I reach Greener Side Estate and sit cross-legged on the opposite side of the road. The council must have only just mowed the strip next to the footpath; it doesn't make my thighs itch and the scent of freshly cut grass lingers in the air. I check my watch: 11:53. I can sit here and wait for Cameron and Mrs Carrington to definitely be gone, then head back to school. On Friday, when he dropped me home, Sloopy said he might come down to the court today. I hope he does.

A man with a neatly trimmed beard, wearing black leggings underneath grey cotton shorts, and a woman clothed head-to-toe in the latest Nike activewear, jog down the street, stopping to catch their breath at the estate entrance. I pull out a vegemite sandwich from my backpack and bite into it.

"Don't lie to me, Mason!" the woman unexpectedly screams at her companion. "I saw the way you were looking at her at the gym!"

I take another bite of my sandwich and watch on as Mason chases after the woman, whom I decide to christen Daniella, down the private roadway. I've fantasised about this estate since they started building it. Looks like the people who are lucky enough to live here still have problems, too.

Sloopy

"I wasn't very impressed with your attitude this morning, Noah. You don't actually like that trash band, there's no need to pretend you have something to rebel against. We are a respected family and I don't appreciate you trying to make my life difficult." Dad turns on the radio. 5AD plays a Wendy Matthews song. Mum rolls her window down in the front passenger seat and Dad loosens his grip on the wheel. "Dignity. Respect. Even in your music, son."

Mum stretches her arm back along the side of the car and wraps her hand around my leg. I reach down and cover her hand with my own.

Unexpectedly, Dad pulls over and unclicks his seatbelt. He takes my Ls out of the glove-box and passes one to Mum.

"Hop in the back, Noah needs the practice."

Sadie

A pile of fallen leaves lay beside me, offering a pillow for my head. I lay on my back and pick up a lone leaf, the largest of the bunch. It is round with a pointy tip; too green to have already left the branch. I peel the sides off, picking at the tiny remnants still clutching to the spine. All that remains is the needle. I find myself smiling and I wonder if Sloopy is smiling at this very moment too, because somehow, when I smile, I feel like no matter where he is or what he is doing, he is smiling too.

Sloopy

I fake a smile. "Thanks, Dad."

I've finally tallied up enough hours but my test is literally tomorrow so I'm grateful for the extra time on the road. I just wish he had let Mum stay in the front seat next to me.

"Do the checklist before you go," he instructs. "Brake, mirror, blind spot."

I do as he says and accelerate back onto the road. I maintain minimum speed, frustrating the car behind me.

"Stay below 40," Dad demands. "It's not a race. Speed kills. They can go around you."

A red Hyundai overtakes us and honks aggressively. Dad rolls his eyes. Light-heatedness swamps over me and I realise that I haven't taken a breath since I turned the keys in the ignition.

I drive all the way home in silence. Mum doesn't utter a word either. Dad says the occasional *good, nice and slow*, and *remember you are behind the wheel of a weapon, be careful*. I run my tongue over my teeth, feeling every groove.

When we reach home, Dad makes me pull over before we reach the driveway. "I'll take it in. You might scratch the sides of the car."

Sadie

I actually check for a bus in the school car park. *What an idiot, of course he doesn't drive the bus on the weekends.*

There are no cars parked in the street and the car park is empty. I think it's safe. They've gone.

I return to the court I stormed off from only a couple of hours ago. I'm not looking forward to school tomorrow. And forget the tutoring on Tuesdays. I don't have to go if I don't want to. Stuff that. Bloody liar.

And stuff their Friday Tupperware dinners, too.

I don't need them or their sneaky babysitting.

I had parents. And they are not them.

Sloopy

I watch a movie with Mum when we settle back at home. She needs the company. Dad went straight back to church to prepare for the afternoon Kids Clubs. He didn't even come inside. I wonder if a woman in a green dress has anything to do with that.

I let Mum pick the movie and she predictably chooses a lame, sappy romance. She cuddles into the couch with her legs tucked up beside her, smiling from her eyes as she becomes emotionally invested in the dramatic relationship of two people who don't even exist.

"This is so crap," I whinge an hour after I first wished it was over already.

Mum doesn't hear me. Or doesn't answer me. She is completely absorbed in the apparent loveliness of the scene.

"This is my favourite part," she sighs.

They kiss in front of the sunset just as an 80s ballad kicks off.

I roll my eyes. "How original. Why is it always a sunset?"

Mum squeezes the cushion tight. "It's the epitome of romance," she says softly, her voice croaking.

I'm relieved when the end credits finally roll. Mum heads straight to the kitchen, fills the sink with soapy water and starts washing the breakfast dishes that she didn't get around to this morning before church. She stares at the water with her head bowed, dunking the same bowl over and over again, like she's ready to curl up and go to sleep. She does this sometimes.

I switch on the radio on top of the fridge. Bob Dylan snaps Mum alive. She sings along to Just Like a Woman, suddenly happy. Suddenly *okay*. I smile to myself, fully aware that dancing in the kitchen really is her most favourite thing in the world.

"I'm going to walk down to school. I'll be back before dinner. Love you."

Mum sways her hips back and forth against the cupboards. "Love you more."

Sadie

I dribble slowly up and down the length of the court. I am livid. They betrayed me.

I stand on the three-point line and take a shot. I miss. Of course. Who cares though? Undercut is right, really: I don't have anyone to cheer for me. My family is gone. I don't have anyone. The world is full of drunks. Good people don't stand a chance.

I hate the world.

I hate my place in it.

I am about to let myself cry but repress the urge when I hear the school gates open behind me.

Sloopy

I see her before she sees me, but I always do.

She has a Daffy Duck scrunchie on today, holding her pony tail low against her neck, like she always wears it. It's so noticeable to me I guess because every single girl with long hair at school wears it in a high ponytail. Sadie is defiantly herself, never trying to fit in but not trying to stand out either. She just is who she is, without conscious effort or thought.

She inspires me like that.

I've never seen this scrunchie before. I calculate that this is the only one in her Loony Tunes collection that I haven't seen her wear yet. Given that this is the first time we've seen each other on a Sunday, she must save it specifically for this day. I want to ask her why but she'll think I'm a creep if she knows that I notice what scrunchie she is wearing and on what day. I drum my fingers on my basketball five times.

Sadie

He looks different.

Every time I see him.

Less...Noah. More...Sloopy.

He walks toward me with a confidence and reassurance that seems so rehearsed it almost looks silly. He holds my gaze and then drums his fingers on his basketball and adjusts the collar of his Indiana Jones t-shirt, as if it is suddenly too tight against his skin. *There he is.*

Sloopy

Dad has a mistress.

Mum pretends she doesn't know.

My whole life is a lie.

And the life waiting for me when I finish school is not one that I even want.

But Sadie is here. And maybe she is here because she knew I would be, too. I reach her and instantly push my mouth onto hers, forgetting to reign in my desperation to be close to her. I don't even look around to see if anybody can see us first. I need her. Our mouths move together naturally and effortlessly. I can't remember a time I ever felt this good. *That's what you should have done today when you said hello*, she told me once. Judging by the way she is kissing me back, I think I got it right this time.

Sadie lets her basketball fall to the ground and drapes her arms around my neck.

Sadie

He kissed me. First.

My smile dissolves into his lips.

Sloopy

I do actually try to win our one-on-one but Sadie is faster than me. Better than me. I'm okay with that. I kind of like it. We play for hours.

I fill her in on all the gossip from Adam's mum's party while she steals the ball right from under me. She tells me how much she loved having her friends over and how she wishes she had done it years ago, while I try in vain to block her shots. I tell her about the lady in the emerald green dress and about all the times I've found Mum crying in secret, and then kept it a secret myself. Mum pretends that she is okay for me and it would break her heart if she knew that I'm aware of how much she is hurting.

It's our court.

Our game.

Our life.

I can tell her anything.

But it's different for her. I always feel like there's something she holds back. Something she insists on keeping to herself. Fiercely secret. Hidden. Even from me.

Sadie

"I've never actually told anyone this, like I mean ever. Mya and Callie don't even know. But I want to tell you."

Sloopy misses his lay-up but he catches his own rebound and tries again. "Tell me. Tell me everything about everything."

"I don't know why it's so hard, but it is. I don't want to make you feel obligated or anything."

Sloopy finally scores. The side of his mouth curves up, like he's trying hard not to smile.

I steal the ball from him and dribble on the spot. "So, next Saturday is sort of, I mean it is, well, I mean it will be..." I shake my head, annoyed with my uncharacteristic stupor. "Yeah, so it will be my birthday."

When Sloopy's smile was for himself, he tried to hide it. But now that it is for me, it covers his whole face.

"Will you go out with me?" he asks.

Sloopy

I get home around 7.30pm. Mum is still in the kitchen, spring cleaning the cupboards. She has emptied the entire contents of the pantry. The radio is still on, so I tell myself that she has been okay on her own.

I help her set the table as I relay my excitement about my day with Sadie. She comes alive and bites her lip excitedly, begging me to tell her more. I ask if I can borrow the car next Saturday. Failing my driving test tomorrow is not an option. I gobble up the tuna mornay she has prepared, consciously making extra mention of how delicious it is.

"Aren't you eating, Ma?"

"I'm going to wait for your father to get home. He said he'll be straight home after the last Kids Club. We haven't had much time together lately."

The last Kids Club finished over two hours ago.

Mum prepares two plates for her and Dad and puts them in the oven, just as he bounces through the front door.

"Your father's home," she whispers, but not really to me.

Dad puts his keys on the table and kisses Mum. "Dinner smells amazing, darling. What are we having?"

Mum's whole face lights up. "Tuna mornay, if that's okay with you. I know the last one was a bit dry but I added more cheese this time."

"I'm famished, let's eat. Fancy a movie on the couch? Your pick."

Mum is so grateful for his affection and attention. I chew the inside of my cheek to stop myself from throwing my plate at his face.

Sadie

The house is in darkness when I get home. I tiptoe my way through the lounge and stand in front of my room, looking over into the kitchen. There are no dishes on the sink. Not even a glass. His door is closed, as always, and there is no light coming from underneath it. By the looks of it, he hasn't got up all day. His truck is in the driveway, I know he is here.

I make two vegemite sandwiches, carefully removing the lid of the vegemite so as not to make too much noise. I fill up my water bottle, only turning the tap just enough to let the water trickle out. A gush would be too loud.

I barricade my bedroom door with my chest of drawers and eat my tea sitting on my bed, reading my library books. I've read Tomorrow When the War Began already, but I love it and it's even better the second time.

I really needed to do some washing today. I spit on the grass stain on the hem of my school tunic, acquired from Thursday's biology class. Mr Webber thought we should have the class outside, being "such a lovely day and all." I rub the material between my fingers but the green smudge doesn't fade. I smell under the arms and spray them with Impulse. It's just going to have to do.

I get into bed and read my book until it's too dark to see anymore so I reluctantly close my eyes to go to sleep, hand under my pillow, holding my knife.

Sloopy

My driving instructor has a mullet. She introduces herself as Patricia. "But you can call me Trixie."

Trixie looks to be about my mum's age. She doesn't ask me what I'm doing when I grip and release the steering wheel five times before I even start the car but she does look at me strangely. She chews gum the entire duration of my test, ticking the assessment sheet on her clipboard often.

It's Monday, straight after school. I need to get my Ps. Failing is not an option. It's Sadie's birthday on Saturday.

I pass on my first try. Trixie hands me my completed test and swallows her gum. I suppress my anxiety and choose not to ask her why she isn't freaking out that it's going to be stuck in her stomach for 7 years now.

She sees right through me. "Try not to be too weird when you get behind the wheel, yeah?"

I get home just before dinner and head straight to my room. I retrieve my secret pile of posters, stashed on top of my wardrobe and plaster my favourites around my room.

After Mum's spaghetti, I play my CDs; loud enough to enjoy, soft enough to only just be heard outside my door. I remove my knife from the pages of the bible, lay on my back in the middle of the room and stare at my surroundings, blade resting against my side under my t-shirt. Baby Animals are hung up my door now. Garbage is next to my wardrobe. Silverchair and Nirvana take pride of place over by the window. The disassociation I normally feel in my own room has gone.

I breathe in and then out, puffing out my torso so it digs against the blade.

It's her birthday on Saturday.

She told me.

She wants to be with me on her birthday.

I got my Ps.

I can actually drive.

My bedroom looks like it's mine.

I relax my grip on the knife and don't press down as hard as I normally would.

Sadie

Mrs Carrington hands back our essays and I'm stunned to see the A- marked on the first page of mine. I have never received anything higher than a C+.

You write with passion for your argument, Sadie. I really felt your conviction. You made me see things from a different perspective. You love books the same way I do and I feel like Of Mice and Men will always stay with you. Keep up the great work. Believe in yourself like I believe in you.

There, in red pen. Her words on my page. I will keep them forever in my suitcase.

At the end of the day, I leave the washed Tupperware container on Mrs Carrington's desk. Returning it directly to her says what I just can't: thank you.

Sloopy

Cane, Leigh and Sam have started sitting with us at lunch, because they're friends with Josh now. I haven't quite sussed out how Adam feels about it, but I think it sucks. Josh is a jerk when they're around.

Cane squeezes the bottom of the plastic wrapper, pushing his sausage roll up so it pokes out the top. He blows on it before taking a bite. "I hate to break it to you boys, but I'm pretty sure I'm in with Callie. I called her up on the weekend and she's obviously got the hots for me. We're going to the movies on Saturday and I reckon she won't say no when I try it on after. We should have put a wager on it."

I pinch my wrist five times, squeezing the most prominent vein I can feel.

"Don't rule us out just yet." Sam has a vegemite sandwich. Just like Sadie always does. "We're still in the running. Now that Callie's lost all her weight, she'll be wanting to boost up her self-esteem. She knows she's got options. And I'm one of them."

Cane swats at a fly that attempts to land on his forehead. I wish he'd swat himself. "How about we actually make this a proper thing then, not just for Callie. We can get a tally going for the whole year. Two points a girl and one point each time you get them into bed. Or the backseat of the car in your case, Josh."

I imagine Sadie biting into her own vegemite sandwich, sitting with Mya and Callie. Her friends. I dig my thumb nail into the back of my index finger and play Nirvana's About a Girl in my head.

"Pass for me." The words rush out of my mouth before I have a chance to back out. "I don't want in on any of that."

Josh's bemused expression turns cold before he looks to Sam in panic. "Nah, Sloopy's just having a lend. Don't worry, he's in."

I return his icy glare. I'm pretty sure it's the first time I've mastered daggers. I try to tense my lips the way Sadie did when she first saw me looking at her. "No, actually, I'm not. I'm not having a lend and I'm not in. Stuff that and stuff you, Josh."

Josh starts to lunge for me and Adam blocks him, pushing him back by the chest. "Whoa, cool it! Sloopy's out. It's not his thing. And, and, well if I'm honest, it's not mine either. Betting on girls is a bit lame, yeah?"

Josh leaps to his feet. "You guys are such babies. You always think you're better than the rest of us just cos you go to church. You can take your high ground and shove it!"

I follow his lead and leap to my feet, too. I push my arms backwards and lean in towards him, puffing out my chest to give the impression that I'm tough.

"You're the one with the attitude problem, Josh! Church has got nothing to do with it. People decide for themselves whether or not they want to be arseholes in life and you've clearly made up your mind what you want to be."

Josh is stumped; I'm not sure if by my words or by my confidence. I don't back down. I hold his glare and he takes a step backwards.

"Forget it. Forget you, too, *friend*."

He storms off and Sam and Cane follow him.

Sadie

It's awkward today. The effortless ease of Mrs Carrington's company is now strained. I slump at my desk, stretching my legs out underneath. I feel like Lou Diamond Phillips in Stand and Deliver. He was tough. Like me.

Mrs Carrington starts talking about lowest common denominators and I look straight ahead, occasionally nodding or mumbling *yep*.

Mrs Carrington senses my disinterest and stands, lifting her hip so that she is half-sitting on the desk next to mine. She is wearing her usual fitted pencil skirt; dark grey with a peach-coloured chiffon blouse. She subtly hitches up her skirt when she sits, presumably to give the material more give. She just knows what to do with things like that. Intuitively. Being a woman is natural to her. She should write a handbook for girls like me.

She sighs, like in defeat and I feel bad that I can't just let it go. I know I need to get over it but I just don't know how to.

"I really am sorry, Sadie."

"It's fine. I'm just being a brat. Ignore me. Don't worry about it."

"It was never a deliberate decision to not tell you. It just came to be. I, um, I just wanted..."

Mrs Carrington loses her voice to her tears. I've made her cry and I hate myself for it.

"It's okay. I mean, I was just surprised, I guess. It's not like you lied or anything, you just didn't mention it. You guys are super right for each other. You're both good people."

"My husband and I care a lot about you, Sadie. We wanted to help and make sure you were okay. We weren't sure if your uncle was-"

I hastily push my chair back and it squeals against the laminate flooring. Mrs Carrington holds onto my desk in panic, as if really wanting to grab hold of me but probably thinking better of it.

"Please. Stay. I'm no threat to you, Sadie. I know your uncle drinks and I'm not going to force you to talk about it. When you ended up in my class, it was like God had brought you to me. I just want to be here for you."

"I don't have anywhere else to go. Please don't make a big thing of it. He's the only family I have. I would have ended up in and out of foster homes if it wasn't for him. And now I'm nearly 17, I'll just be on my own. I'm too old to be a child and I'm too young to be an adult. There's no place for me."

"You can live with Cameron and I. Any time. Any time you are ready. We can pick you up any time."

"It's not that bad, honestly, I'm okay. He just drinks a bit every now and again. He's my only connection to Mum."

Mrs Carrington bows her head, shaking it slowly. "I love you, Sadie. I want you to know that. I did what I could, I know it wasn't enough but I really did try."

Her words become incoherent and I don't know what she is talking about. Nothing makes sense to me anymore. I like my friends. I want to be safe. Mrs Carrington and Cameron have tried to parent me from afar. Nothing is what I thought it was.

I rest my head against her chest and she wraps her arms around me. The words fall out of my mouth without asking me for permission first. "I love you, too Mrs Carrington."

I check the letterbox when I get home. My birthday card has come. I have been expecting it. The postie always brings it the week of my birthday.

17, our Sadie. We are so proud of you and we are always here.

Two $50 notes and a few vouchers fall out of the card when I open it. I scoop them up, anxiously looking around the kitchen even though he's not home. I hold the money, the $40 CC Records, $30 Angus & Robertson and $100 Miss JM voucher in my hand and read the card over and over again. *We are so proud of you and we are always here.*

Mum and Dad's church friends must have been nice. I've got a card from them every single year since they died. I head into my room, put the money and vouchers in my backpack and add the card to my collection in the suitcase under my bed.

Sloopy

It's the right thing to do.

I grab the skin on the inside of my elbow and pinch hard. I do it once and exhale slowly, coaxing myself out of the need to do it four more times. I know this is right.

I see her before she sees me, but I always do. Mya and Callie sit with Sadie, overlooking the basketball court. Sadie is in the middle like always. Watching them now, I get why. It's just their way of protecting her. It always has been.

I don't know where Sam and Cane are. I look around anxiously but I can't see them. We don't have basketball training tonight because we've got a bye tomorrow. This is my only chance to talk to Sadie before the weekend. And her friends.

I take another breath and leave my skin alone. I tell Adam that I'll be right back, I just have to say hey to Sadie.

Mum put too much detergent in with the last cycle of washing. I have a white patch of hardened powder stuck to the inside of my pocket. I like it. It's Mum. I rest my hand in my pocket as I walk across the court, holding onto Mum's clump.

Mya puts her hand in Sadie's lap when she sees me, like she is blocking her. Keeping her safe. Sadie has good friends.

"Ladies," I nod.

Mya nods in reply. "Gentleman."

"I've, um, I've sort of borrowed my mum's car. Like, on Saturday. For Saturday, I mean. I got my Ps on Monday. Can I pick you up at 3? On Saturday, I mean?" *Get it together, Sloopy.* "Can I pick you up at 3 on Saturday? The Craft is playing at 4.30 on Hindley Street."

Sadie smiles with her lips together. "Sure."

I smooth my thumbs over every finger nail. Slowly, calmly. "Um, listen, I just thought you guys should know something. Especially you, Callie. You should know something."

Sadie

Callie lives about a ten-minute walk from me but I've never been to her house before. The driveway gates are open so I self-consciously sneak through. The front yard is barricaded by a tall fence that makes me feel like I'm stepping into another world. No matter where I go, I feel like I have a big red sign on my forehead, alerting every-one to the fact that I don't belong anywhere.

We have a bye today but I'm wearing my basketball uni-form anyway, because it's Saturday. It's basketball day and it's my birthday.

Would I Lie to You by Charles and Eddie plays across the spacious front yard, creating a mellow ambience; a secret Idaho hidden from the main road. There is an abundance of gum trees; maybe six, all scattered around. A tyre swing dangles from one. The grass is exactly the right height to tickle your ears when you lay on it. I imagine Callie's dad mows it on the last Sunday of the month. There is a trampoline in the far corner, adjacent to a well-used fire pit with four chairs situated around it.

The front of the house is dominated by a single window. An old roller shutter clings to the bricks above it. It seems redundant to me. They have enough trees; the house must be in permanent shade anyway.

I tread slowly down the long, pebbled driveway, taking in everything. You can tell a family live here. There is an element of mess and chaos, shrouded in contentment. Some houses merely look like a house. This is undeniably a home: a family home.

I trace the music to a small silver radio, sitting atop a blue Datsun, parked right in the middle of the driveway. A man wearing baggy, grey coveralls sticks his head out from under the raised bonnet.

"You must be Sadie!"

I shyly wave.

He resumes tinkering around in the bonnet. "Head on out the back, love. Mya's already out there with Bianca. Callie's in the house. Mya will show you the way in."

I cautiously slide past the car.

"Glad you finally popped around, love," he winks at me.

Sloopy

There is a sadness hanging over Mum today. I drive us to the shops and she stares out the window, blankly, barely even blinking. I put one of her cassettes into the tape deck. Some crooner starts singing about being a teenager in love and it brings Mum back to me, from wherever her mind had escaped to.

"Your father used to sing this one to me, in another lifetime."

Mum rests her head back, closing her eyes. She's sad again. Or still.

I crank the volume and sing along, deliberately badly. Really badly. Mum tries to join in but the words are lost to her laughter, which is my whole goal in life, really. She's not sad now.

We pull into the carpark at Arndale and it's packed. Mum moves her hand to the buckle, readying herself to unplug. "Do you want me to park?"

I shake my head and grip the wheel tighter. "Nope, I got it."

Mum returns her hand to her lap. "Yes, you do, son," she says softly. "You've got your Ps. You can handle it. You are perfectly capable."

I creep the car forwards, barely even moving. I glance in the rear-view mirror: the elderly lady driving behind me sticks her hand out the window and raises her middle finger. She must be about 80 years old.

"You drive slower than an old lady!" she shouts as she over-takes us.

Mum cups her mouth with both hands, banishing her laughter.

I find a spot with only one car to the left of it. My side is clear. I ease the car between the parallel lines, biting the side of my tongue five times over and over again. I edge slowly forwards, not taking my eyes off the parked car on Mum's side. Miraculously, I don't scrape it.

I turn off the engine and leave the keys dangling in the ignition. Mum and I stare ahead in a stupor. My palms ache. I've been gripping on to the wheel pretty tight.

Mum breaks the silence. "Well. Thank you, Sadie," she says and I can only nod my head to agree.

Sadie

Mya lays on her back on the cement path that runs through the backyard, leading to a Hills Hoist right in the centre. She is wearing denim shorts and a red bikini top; the straps rest loosely off her arms. Her arms shield her eyes from the sun, which is very clearly welcome all over the rest of her body.

"She's baking!" a girl who looks like a mini-Callie giggles. She even has the same blunt fringe and the same long plat. She is collecting ants; fossicking for them amongst the blades of grass. She scoops some up on the edge of a piece of cardboard and tips them into a small aquarium with sand in it. How is this not kidnapping, I wonder to myself.

Callie talks a lot about her sister, so I know Bianca must be around 10 these days. I feel bad that I'm not exactly sure though.

Mya peels herself off the ground and rushes up to Bianca, tackling her. "I'll bake *you* in a minute!"

Bianca's giggle resonates all around the backyard, all around me. She and Mya seem to be really close, just like sisters. I don't know why I'm surprised: Mya has been a much better friend to Callie than I have ever been. I watch them joyfully muck around; ashamed of my shortcomings as a friend.

Back when we were in year nine, Bianca got chicken pox. Mya asked Callie how her sister was doing every single day and even bought a block of chocolate for Callie to take home to her. I didn't even pass on a hello. When

Callie told us that her little sister won a colouring-in competition, Mya could barely contain her excitement. In my mind, Callie was merely full of herself, gloating about how wonderful she was just because she had a sister. It made me hate her.

Mya ruffles Bianca's hair and opens the back door, motioning for me to follow her. "Keep kidnapping those little fellas, B. I'll be back out later."

Sloopy

Mum and I frequent every single shop in Arndale, looking for Bugs Bunny scrunchies. Harris Scarfe has every single item of Looney Tunes merchandise out, except the one thing that I am actually looking for. It's hopeless.

We finish up in Eliza's. Mum grabs a tray and slides it along the bar, picking two salad sandwiches. She moves up to the dessert fridge and puts two frog cakes on the tray, then slides it along to the cash register.

The woman behind the till presses some buttons and the register pings open. "$11, love."

Mum pays and carries our tray over to a booth.

"I just wanted to complete the set for her," I grumble, taking my seat. "She was devastated when she lost one of them. I thought I could replace it for her."

Mum sits opposite me and bites into her sandwich. "She just wants to spend time with you on her birthday, that's what she really wants. Not a scrunchie, even if it does hold significance. Whatever present you buy for her, she will love it just because it's from you."

"What's been your favourite present, I mean, from Dad?"

"Well, the last couple of years he's just sort of left a Lloyd's $20 voucher on the table." She looks past me, as if looking back through the years. "When he was courting me, he bought me a necklace with a rose on it. I've always loved my flowers."

"That's more like it! What happened to the necklace? I don't think I've ever seen you wear it."

"Oh, I did, for a long time. But then life, you know, I mean I guess a lot of things happened over the years. Experiences, decisions, regrets."

Mum bows her head and takes a bite of her sandwich. I am hearing her speak for the first time and I don't want her to stop now.

"Tell me more, Mum. We don't talk about things that we should."

Mum smooths her finger over her bottom lip. "Our life didn't turn out the way your father had planned. I know he feels that. It shamed him to have to start over again in a new church, new congregation. And then when he did, I think he just lost his way a bit, like he's constantly trying to prove something. To who, I don't know. The wrong things to the wrong people."

"Why don't you wear the necklace anymore?"

Mum swipes a bit of cream off her frog cake and licks her finger. "I flushed it down the toilet, the same as he flushed our marriage down the toilet."

Mum looks to me, visibly apprehensive about how I will react. I just nod and let my smile come. Mum smiles back, rampant with relief.

Sadie

We pass through the kitchen on the way to Callie's room. The radio is muffled but it can still be heard from outside. Sonia Dada's, You Don't Treat Me No Good No More is on now. It relaxes me to hear songs I am familiar with in an environment that seems so foreign to me.

Callie's mum is baking scones. If Bianca looked like a mini-Callie, her mum must be the original. All the females in the family have the same blunt fringe. She puts the bowl down on the sink and holds the wooden spoon in the air, rushing up to greet us.

"Sadie, darling! Welcome!"

She stretches out her arms but all I can see is the wooden spoon aimed at me. I instinctively step backwards and bring my hands up to protect my face.

An *oh* escapes her lips. She is visibly uncomfortable and maybe even insulted.

I realise what I have done and laugh awkwardly. "Um, gosh, I must be in basketball mode. So used to balls coming at me." I scan the kitchen looking for something, anything, to lighten the mood. "I really like your fridge. It's heaps...white."

"There you guys are," Callie thankfully cheers from the hallway. "Come on, come help me choose my outfit for tonight."

Sloopy

Mum wanders off to look at handbags while I head back to the disappointing collection of Looney Tunes merchandise in Harris Scarfe. I pick out a silver-chained Sylvester necklace. I look for scrunchies again but there are none. The Sylvester pendant is black, of course, but the back is smooth and silver. It's perfect for what I plan to do.

I pay for the necklace and take it to a Mister Minit at the other end of the mall.

"Do you think there's enough room on the back to get 'Sloopy and Sadie' engraved?"

The gentleman behind the counter is old, maybe 70. I get the feeling he's worked here his whole life. His blue apron is frayed around the edges.

"Ah, geez, lad, you'd be lucky. I could probably get S and S. Ten dollars, give me twenty minutes."

I take my receipt and head off to get my hair cut while the Mister Minit man completes my order. I walk past Mum in Katies, eyeing off a dress that's completely her style: long, flowy, flowery. Her. She picks up the hem, longingly rubs the material between her fingers and then lets it fall back down. She moves over to the rack at the back; a row of black dresses before her.

My birthday was at the beginning of January, so I'm just that little bit older than Sadie. Everyone knows when it's my birthday, like it's just common knowledge. But Sadie told me it was hers as if no one else in the world knew. I think about all the years that have likely gone by and no one ever knew to wish her a happy birthday.

I'm realistic enough to know that not everyone's first love is forever. But Sadie helps me be who I *want* to be, and that's a power I will keep, come what may. And no matter what happens in our lives, she will never feel compelled to flush her necklace down the toilet because of me.

Sadie

Mya and Callie rummage through Callie's wardrobe. I sit at her desk, half-spinning back and forth on her wheelie chair. They are gossiping about boys. Josh finally rang Mya and asked her out tonight. I want to tell her that this is not something worthy of her excitement: he should have called her right after they hooked up, not ignored her basically all term. She deserves better. I want to tell her this, but I don't.

"I had almost given up on him," she sighs, holding up one of Callie's maxi skirts against her waist. She hangs it back in the wardrobe and continues to fossick. "Like, yeah okay, he was a dick to blow me off right after we did it. But he explained all that. He said he really likes me and it scared him."

I roll my eyes and accidentally utter *oh, please* out loud. Callie looks to Mya apprehensively, no doubt expecting her to explode. Mya laughs, which is not the reaction either one of us expected.

"Yeah, I know, sounds like a line, right? But I really like him. And plus, I don't want the memory of my first time to be that I was dumped right after."

Callie picks out a red summer dress and holds it in the air, studying it. "Sadie, you got the only good guy at school. Hey, I thought you had a bye today? Why are you wearing your basketball top?"

I could scowl or brush her off like I would normally do, or I could just be real with my friends. "My mum never missed a game back when I played at my old school. Every Saturday she would be there, setting up the drinks stall, slicing the oranges. She'd take everyone's bibs home at the end and wash them. It took me a while to be able to play again but when I did, I felt close to her. So, I guess Saturday is just my basketball day, whether I play or not."

I don't tell them that it's my birthday.

Mya sits on the cream-coloured carpet and tries to stuff her foot into a pair of Callie's boots. "We'd love to come watch you one day, if you want us to."

I wonder if my smile looks as big as it feels. "I normally just sit on the bench but that'd be heaps nice."

She gives up on the boots and reaches for another pair. "Then we will. Okay, time to start wrapping up. I need to get home to pick my outfit for tonight, too! How cool that the three of us all have dates tonight. Definitely a first!"

"Hey Mya," I hesitate, "remember what Sloopy told us. I mean if Cane is in on all that stupid stuff, Josh might be too. Just be careful."

"I know Josh has been a jerk. I just want him to like me. Is that so bad? I know we won't be together forever, but if it's not for at least a little while, the memory of my first time will always make me feel like shit. And that red dress is the one, Callie. You'll drive Cane crazy in that. Too bad the night's not going to go like he plans."

Callie smirks to herself. "Well, he did invite me to watch a movie and that's exactly what we're gonna do. Here, at my house. With my little sister. And my parents."

Sloopy

The barber took more off the sides than he usually does. I'm very aware of my ears as I dry myself from my afternoon shower. I study my face in the mirror, running the towel over my arms. I wonder if Sadie thinks I'm okay to look at.

I tie the towel around my waist and smooth both my ear lobes down against my face. I consider dabbing on some glue to hold them there. My ears stick out too much now with this stupid buzzcut. I try to fluff out the sides with increasingly frustrated vigour but it doesn't make a difference.

I rush into my room and open up my bible for relief. The light of my room catches the blade's shine; magnifying the appeal. The panic gushing through my veins begins to calm. I hold the knife against my tummy, breathing in and out five times. It's the slow, deep breaths out that feel the most incredible: they push harder against the blade.

Sadie

I tilt my head to the left and snip the ends off. Chunky strands of my hair fall into the bathroom sink. I do the same on the other side then shake my head so my hair falls over my shoulders. It looks even enough. I guess.

I brush off the clippings that have stuck to my shoulders. I probably should have cut my hair before I got changed. I'm wearing the same dress I wore when I went to Sloopy's house but with a black top underneath this time. I hope that's enough to make it look like a different outfit.

I can't wait to spend my vouchers. They always get me enough clothes to get through. I really need some. I've had a growth spurt since last year and most of my clothes are too small for me now. Hence the recycled outfit tonight.

He used to bring the letters in back when I first came to live with him. He opened my birthday cards before I had a chance. They were clearly addressed to me but he took the money that came with them, even the vouchers. Then he'd either fling the card at me or chuck it in the bin.

"Fuckin church do-gooders."

My 12th birthday card was wet with soy sauce stains by the time I was brave enough to secretly retrieve it from the bin, but I cleaned it as best as I could and put it in my suitcase with my growing collection regardless. Somewhere, somewhere out there, somebody cared about me. I kept every single card, and read them often.

On the week of my 13th birthday, I noticed the pile of letters on the table. I saw the envelope with my name and without thinking, I excitedly picked it up and opened it. He was stirring something on the stove. He heard the envelope rip open and lunged across the room, whacking my arm with the wooden spoon. Hot pasta sauce seeped through my sleeve.

I started checking the letterbox every day soon after, leaving them on the table for him. He didn't seem to mind; one less thing he needed to do, I guess. He started staying in his room on Sundays. He probably assumed that since I was a teenager now, the cards had stopped.

But they never did.

Every year, without fail, somebody out there cared about me.

Sloopy

I stand in front of Sadie's door, readying myself to knock. I smell under my left arm and then my right and then quickly repeat four times. I rub my hand over my torso where the blade rested only an hour before.

Dear God, I'm so nervous I could puke.

Sadie

His hands fidget constantly as we walk over to his car. It's not the same one I saw him get out of at church. It's much less intimidating; a Mitsubishi Lancer. Maybe it's his mum's car. I don't know anyone who has two cars.

He's had a haircut. He is nervous. Like, Noah-level nervous. I don't want him to be. I want him to feel like Sloopy.

"Your hair looks good, did you cut it?"

He fluffs the ends on his neck. "Yeah, they did it a bit too short this time. I look like a dweeb."

"I like it, you look really pretty." I get in the passenger side and he closes my door as I click in my seatbelt. "Idiot," I mumble to myself. *"Pretty?"*

Sloopy gets in the driver's seat and puts the keys in the ignition. "I like your hair, too. You look really handsome."

That's all it takes for the awkwardness to lift. We talk and laugh the whole drive into town. I'm not perfect and neither is Sloopy but together, we kind of are.

Sloopy

Why was I so nervous? Being with Sadie is the most effortless thing in the world. It's like I hold my breath all day, every day and when I'm with Sadie, I can finally let it go.

We park in a side street a short walk from the cinema. She holds my hand as we make our way down and I hold it tighter than most people probably would.

I buy two tickets to the 4.30pm session. Sadie insists on buying the popcorn but lets me buy two cokes. The cinema is packed; we can only find two spare seats in the front row.

"I hate sitting in the front row," I tell her. "No one better throw popcorn at my head."

Sadie throws a piece of popcorn at my face.

Sadie

I'm uncertain if I enjoy the movie as much as I do because it's actually good, or because this is my first date, on the first birthday I've celebrated since losing Mum and Dad. The end credits roll and I already want to watch it again.

"That was so good. It's probably my favourite movie now."

"It was awesome. I didn't like the way it ended with Nancy, though."

We sit low in our seats, waiting for everyone to make their way out. We don't say it, but neither one of us want to be stuck in the middle of that crowd. We both get more comfortable in our seats the same time as we should be standing up to leave.

"Sadie?"

"Yeah?"

"Happy Birthday."

I can't recall the last time those words were spoken to me. "Thank you."

Sloopy looks at his watch and clears his throat. "So, um, it's not even seven yet. Do you maybe want to drive through Maccas and get some ice creams and go park somewhere? That sounded bad. I didn't mean it like that. I mean, like, just so we can sit and talk."

I don't care if he did mean it like that. "I'd love to. As long as I can be home before 9."

Sloopy

Sadie cradles the chocolate sundaes in her lap while I drive. I was going to park near the River Torrens but I know she is conscious of the time and she will be less anxious if we are closer to her home. I want to kiss her so badly.

She holds a spoonful of my ice cream in front of me and I take it in my mouth at the red light, scooping up a bit of the chocolate syrup as it drips on my bottom lip. She has a mouthful of her own and then gets my spoon ready again. By the time I get to the railway tracks near her home, she has fed me my whole ice cream.

I park on an angle across three spots, facing the railway, intending to look like a cool rebel (even though no other cars are around and the railway station is closed). A lone street light attempts to illuminate the isolated car park but it just creates a tinted yellow glow, like we're in a photograph from the 1970s.

I turn the engine off, leaving the radio and the head lights on. I put in one of my mix tapes. Paula Abdul's Rush, Rush burgeons my desire to kiss her.

Sadie puts the empty plastic ice cream cups on the floor by her feet. "You can kiss me, if you- "

My mouth is on hers before she can even finish her sentence.

I am desperate. I am addicted to the confidence she gives me and I want more and more of it every time we are together. Now that we are finally truly alone, I can't get enough of her or the way she makes me feel.

Sadie

Sloopy's enthusiasm doesn't startle me. I feel it just as much. We kiss hard, feverishly at first, then settle into a rhythm, as if we are making out in time to the song. I've never heard it before but it makes me feel like we're auditioning for a scene in an American high school movie.

He leans across the handbrake, pushing his whole body onto mine. I am pressed back against my window. I sense his desperation and it spurs my own. I drape my arms around his neck and hold him close to me.

His hand grips my hip. His tongue cradles mine. I open my eyes for a brief second, shocked at the sensation. His fingers ever so slightly pick up the hem of my dress and he slides his hand up my thigh. Visions of Mya flash through my mind. I wonder how Cane reacted when he found out he would be having a night in with Callie's family. Then without realising what I'm doing, I forcefully push Sloopy off of me and jolt my leg, kicking him back to his side of the car.

"Am I part of that stupid tally, too?" I rage.

Hurt splashes across his face. I can't take my accusation back. A sickness churns in my stomach and I wish that I could. But I just sit there scowling and cross my arms on my chest, hiding my fists.

Sloopy

She thinks I'm using her. "I don't know what to say to that."

Sadie is lost to her anger, like she is suddenly back to hating me like she did at the beginning of the term.

"Well, that's a yes! Thanks a lot."

I feel like I could throw up. I can't believe she thinks I would do something like that to her. I'm not compelled to pick at the skin around my fingers or press one of my scabs to flare up the pain. I don't feel anything, I'm just numb.

We stare at one another, dead quiet. And that's exactly what it feels like inside me: dead quiet. Everything is silence. Apart from Paula Abdul.

"I would never do that to you. I would never do any-thing to hurt you; physically, emotionally, anything. I just wouldn't. I thought you knew that."

"Why are you moving so fast then, if it's not because of that stupid tally thing?"

"I'm sorry. I didn't mean to rush you. You can tell me to stop or slow down and I will of course, without hesita-tion. I'm sorry." I swallow against the deafening silence. Sadie glares at me, poised for a fight. "I promise. I would never make a bet about that, let alone about you, and I wouldn't let anyone else either. My head is a constant battleground of thoughts but you make all of the nonsense quiet down. You're it. You're the thing for me. You're my girl. I-I love you."

Sadie

I have to get out of here.

I jerk the door open and storm off to front of the car. I don't know where to go. I'm crying and I don't know how to stop it. I ruin everything.

Two minutes ago, Sloopy put his tongue in my mouth and I was starving for more of his touch. Now I'm out here crying in front of the railway lines on a Saturday night because he loves me. There was no issue. But I made one. Because I just expect that everyone wants to hurt me.

Sloopy's door opens. I hastily wipe my face. *Tears don't work on me.*

Sloopy

I lean with my back against the bonnet of the car, next to Sadie and stare out across the empty railway station. It looks haunting at this time of night.

Sadie won't look at me.

"I didn't mean to upset you. I'm sorry." My stomach is in knots. I put my hands in my pockets and pinch my thighs through my jeans five times. "I can't fight with you, Sadie. I can't upset you. It tears me apart. Like seriously, I feel physically sick. Please, can we be okay now?"

She still won't look at me.

She sniffs loudly. "I'm sorry I jumped to conclusions."

"Hey, I mean, it's fair enough given what's going on with all the other guys at the moment. I would never get involved in stuff like that but I understand why you wondered if I was. I know I'm a sheep. I've been one my whole life. I'm trying to think for myself more, because of you. Let's just forget about all this, yeah?"

"I'm sorry."

"Me too. So can I give you your birthday present now?"

Sadie laughs and finally looks at me. Her eyes are hazy.

I pass her a small gift bag. "Happy Birthday, Sadie."

She delicately pulls out the necklace. "Is this- did you get me a Sylvester necklace?"

I turn the pendant over to the engraved side and she gasps. Her reaction is everything I was hoping it would be.

Sadie

"S and S." It reads like poetry to me. I run my fingers over the engraving like it's braille. "How did you do this? Like did you have this made or something? I just, I mean this is the just the most- I'm sorry, I don't even know what to say. Thank you."

I rush my kiss onto his cheek, keeping the necklace safe in my fist. "Can you put it on me?"

Sloopy puts his hand where my lips touched and smiles shyly.

Sloopy

My mix tape is the ultimate wingman. I left my door open and now INXS, Not Enough Time floats over to us at just the right volume. Sadie holds her hair up and I place the necklace around her neck. She has fine hairs on the back of her neck, blonder than the rest of her hair.

"Thank you, I really love it. So much."

Her eyes are almost black in the evening sky and I'm mesmerised by them. And by the way she looks at me.

"Will you dance with me, Sadie?"

Her smile replies a hesitant yet intrigued *yes* as I lead us a few steps away from the car. We fumble with our arms and wrestle with our nerves in the beam of the headlights.

"I think mine goes here," she guesses, putting her hand on my shoulder.

I wrap one arm around her back. "I think mine goes here."

Our fingers weave together on our free hand and we begin to dance, only barely swaying side to side. For the first time, maybe in my entire life, my mind is perfectly still. All I think about is this moment, with her. And INXS.

Sadie

I am still on a high come the next day. I tiptoe into the kitchen, make myself two vegemite sandwiches and pack them with my water bottle and discman. It's six thirty in the morning.

I brush my hair at my mirror and tie it up with my Daffy Duck scrunchie. I only wear it on Sundays. Mum always did my hair with that one on Sundays. It's warm today so I put my Sportsgirl cap on, smudge some sunscreen across my cheeks and roll up the ends of my black tracksuit pants so they come up to my knees. I put three CDs in my bag and one in my discman, as well as some spare batteries. I don't know how long it will take to walk to Klemzig but I'm guessing that it's not a quick trip. I'm expecting maybe three hours, unless I can find a bus actually going my way. On a Sunday, it's doubtful.

I leave by the front door, barely even closing it. It needs a decent shove to be able to close properly: a noise I have no intention of making.

I don't remember the name of the street we lived on and I don't remember exactly where Mum's church is. But I do remember the old mechanic on the corner. I remember the road that felt like we were on a rollercoaster every time Dad drove us home on it. I remember the fish and chip shop. I know that I will find it.

If I can just get there, I will find my home again.

Sloopy

The adrenaline pumping through my body has yet to slow. Come six thirty the next morning, I have already done fifty sit ups in ten groups of five, showered and got ready for the day. I tiptoe into the kitchen, expecting Mum and Dad to still be asleep but to my surprise, Dad is snoring on the couch, fully dressed and Mum is reading the Sunday Mail in the kitchen with her morning coffee. Hair and make-up done, fresh flowers picked from her garden on the table. The house and her are presented for the day.

Her whole face lights up when she sees me. "You're up early, Sloopy. Not like you on a Sunday. Excited for the service this morning, are you?"

"Very funny. I'm sure I enjoy church just as much as you do these days, Mum."

Mum fetches me a glass of orange juice and pops some bread in the toaster.

"You don't have to do that, Mum. I can get my breakfast."

"I'm sure you can. I like looking after you. I don't know what I'd do if I didn't have-" Mum stops herself and gets the peanut butter out of the pantry. She puts a knife and plate in front of me, retrieves the two pieces of toast when they pop from the toaster and brings them over to me. "Eat up."

She smooths her hands over her fitted, dark navy dress and sits back down at the table, resuming her morning coffee.

"How's the Avon going, Mum? Did you get many orders this month?"

"Oh, I'm, uh, I gave that up. Your father thought it might look better for us. He was worried some of the women in the congregation might feel hassled or pressured to get something just because I'm the priest's wife. Which makes a lot of sense really when you think about it. We have to support your father; it hasn't been easy on him."

"Yeah, by losing our own identities."

Mum brings her finger up to her lips and holds it there. "Ssh, your father's asleep on the couch. He got in late last night from the bingo fundraiser. I was asleep when he got home, he must have decided to sleep on the couch so he didn't disturb me."

"Bingo fundraiser, huh? Why didn't you go?"

"He forgot to tell me about it. We were just about to have dinner when he remembered and had to rush off.

It's okay, I got into bed nice and early and worked on my cross stitches for the Easter market. Anyway, please tell me all about last night!"

I eat my breakfast while Mum hangs on my every word. She insists on washing my dishes when I'm finished eating. I reach up to the top of the fridge and turn the radio on for her.

I pass through the lounge and carefully lower myself onto the rectangular coffee table; Dad's breaths peacefully exiting his open mouth as he lays on his side facing me. I stare down at him in his state of slumber, wondering how he can even sleep. Does he really like who he is? He doesn't like me, even when I try to be the person he wants me to be. Surely, he's not the person he wants to be either.

My thoughts escape my mouth in a delicate whisper.

"Dad, I'm going to quit debate. I won't be on the team next term. I hate it. The seminary application has already come twice, maybe three times now. I just keep putting them in the bin. Nirvana's the best band in the world and you ripping a sticker off a desk doesn't change that for me. I have a girlfriend and I'd rather make out with her than tell little kids what they should and shouldn't believe in. Especially when I don't even know what I believe in myself. I'm not saying I don't believe in what you do, but I'd like to think about it. I'd like to be allowed to think about it. Decide for myself. I don't automatically want everything that you want for me. I want to be Sadie's boyfriend and figure out who I am, for myself."

I catch my breath and let the words linger in the air. I can almost see them floating; big, bold flash words. *Quit. Nirvana. Girlfriend.* They have been suppressed, sucked in for so long and now they are out. I grip the edge of the coffee table and squeeze down hard five times.

Every single thought, every single anxiety: out.

I run up the stairs, two at a time. I lock my bedroom door, press play on my Nirvana CD and get ready for Church.

Sadie

I take a break on the overpass on Regency Road, sitting cross-legged on the pedestrian walkway with my back to the traffic. The huge space of land underneath the overpass is wasted; occupied only by dead grass and the occasional abandoned shopping trolley. I count how many pieces of rubbish I can spot down there, wondering if they'll turn it into another housing estate one day. They are popping up everywhere.

My feet are sore, although I have only been walking for just over an hour. I take a few small sips from my drink bottle; consciously stopping myself from guzzling it because then I'll need to pee.

There are a lot of cars out for a Sunday. The shops aren't open today so I don't get where they'd be heading. Surely this many people don't all have places that they can go. I haven't seen a bus yet. Just as I suspected, not that many seem to run on Sundays. I smile to myself, realising that Cameron would probably be sad if he knew I could have done with a ride today.

I take out one half of a sandwich and resume walking down towards the traffic lights. Max Sharam's Coma blares right into my ear drums. If I could turn it up past full volume, I would. On repeat, the song keeps me company through half the streets in Adelaide.

Sloopy

I sit cross-legged in the middle of my room, cradling my bible against my chest.

I need to open it.

What if Dad was actually awake?

I need to open it.

What if he heard everything?

I need to open it.

What if-

I open it, grabbing the knife like a junkie about to get his first hit in weeks.

Shame washes over me and suddenly I am drowning. The light touch of the blade doesn't relieve me like it normally does; it terrifies me. It terrifies me that this is who I am. I have only just kind of figured out that we can choose who we want to be. I don't think I want to be this person.

I will myself to return the knife to its page in the bible, before I inevitably weaken and press it down hard on myself. I really am drowning.

Swim, Sloopy. Swim.

My hands tremble. I concentrate hard on Nirvana. Floyd the Barber ends and miraculously, About a Girl starts to play. I exhale.

I put the bible back in the drawer, making sure it sits flush in the corner. It's there when I need it. I don't need it today.

I have Sadie. I don't need the knife. I need her.

I lay in the middle of my room, watching my posters like I would TV. I tap my fingers against the carpet five times and let my thoughts drift to Sadie.

She's with me even when she's not.

Sadie

I have no idea where I am.

I reach an old pub and three men stumble out; I can't tell if they are hungover or still drunk. They loiter by the entrance and gesture at me as I near them. I step onto the road and walk in the gutter as I pass them: a natural instinct it seems to create distance between me and a drunk. I pick up my pace, constantly looking back for reassurance that they are merely stumbling about on the side of the road and not coming after me; looking for a fight because I ruined their life.

I pause my CD so I can be totally aware of my surroundings. I don't press play again until long after they have left my sight.

Every step is one step closer to home. I can feel it. I am heading in the right direction. I know I will recognise it when I see it.

Nearing Our Lady of the Sacred Heart College refuels my hope. That's the high school that Mum wanted me to go to. I remember her talking to Dad about it. That two-storey pebble-coloured brick building could have been my life.

My heart aches for it. I mourn for a life I never got to know.

And walk straight past it.

Sloopy

Dad's voice is at my door. "Are you in there, Noah?"

The blood drains from my face. He heard me.

I yank the cord out of the wall; Nirvana comes to an abrupt halt.

There is no time to take down my posters. I don't know what I was thinking putting them up. This is going to cost me. Maybe he'll refuse to ever let me borrow the car. Maybe I'll have to do bible study every single night before bed. Maybe he'll send off the Seminary School application his damn self, now that he knows that I've been ripping them up.

I unlock my door and open it up the width of my body. That white collar stands there, waiting to tell me everything that is wrong with me and everything that I am expected to do with my own life.

"Took your time, what are you doing in here? We're leaving in a half an hour."

"I'm ready, Dad. I've just got to put on my shoes."

Dad gently pushes the door all the way open. "I see you've been doing some re-decorating in here."

I stutter half a word that doesn't even exist. The white collar steps into my room, looking around at the walls laden with posters of my favourite bands. I bow my head, awaiting the wrath of Dad's disappointment.

I am suspended in time, afraid to move. Afraid to speak.

Dad leans in and takes a closer look at the Silverchair poster. "They're local, I hear."

I cautiously watch as he studies each individual poster, as if strolling through an art gallery. Then he sits down on my bed and sighs to himself.

My feet dig into the carpet and my knees tense stiff. This man I call Dad feels like a total stranger to me. No doubt I feel like one to him as well.

"I let you and your mother down. Years ago. I made decisions that I regret and I have been trying to make up for it ever since. But I've failed. I made you both feel as if it was our whole family that wasn't up to scratch, but it was me who wasn't. It was just me."

"Do you mean when you had to move churches? You think that let us down?"

"They all left. Every single one of them. No one turned up for the service, not one person. Can you imagine how that felt? That level of rejection? I cost the church a lot of money. I ruined its reputation because I ruined my own. I tried too hard to be almighty and I got involved in business that wasn't mine."

I relax my frown and apprehensively sit next to him. "Can you tell me more about it? Or Mum? Maybe you should talk to Mum?"

"Your mother knows. She knows. She stays when all I do is push her away. I am a good priest, but I am a terrible father and an even worse husband. I've focussed on all the wrong things, out of my own shame. All I cared about was looking good in everyone else's eyes, because in my own, I had failed my family. I sought validation from everyone else because I didn't feel worthy of you or your mother. I'm sorry, son." He pats my knee as he stands. "Time for church."

When Dad found a Nirvana sticker on my desk, he ripped it off. He heads to my door now, walking straight past the Nirvana poster on the wall. Before he closes the door behind him, he looks back at it for a second. "It's okay if you quit the debate team. You have my blessing."

Sadie

The clouds are doing a poor job of shielding the sun. My cheeks are cooking. I squeeze water from my drink bottle into my cupped hand and splash my face for cool relief.

My feet have developed a mind of their own. They quicken their pace, carrying me closer and closer. I recognise buildings unseen for years. I can *feel* where I am. A succession of cars up ahead all turn into the same side street. I run like crazy to catch up to them. I know where they are going.

It's still there and I recognise it straight away by the steeply pitched roof. Who knew a mere roof could evoke such a strong feeling of nostalgia? This roof is my childhood.

I did a puzzle with my parents once. The picture was a Swiss Alps village. I asked Dad why all the houses had triangular roofs and he explained that it was so the snow wouldn't stick. I said he must be wrong because Mum's church had a huge triangular roof and it never snows in Adelaide. Mum and Dad both laughed.

This is my mum's church.

It stands exactly as I recall, right on the corner. I hide next to a tree on the other side of the road, trying to catch my breath. I lovingly watch from afar as families with little kids skip through the car park and head into the Sunday sermon. They are all dressed in their best, brimming with contentment. Happy to be together, as one congregation, one big family.

Even Cameron and Mrs Carrington.

They stroll hand in hand, warmly greeted by another couple as they reach the wrought iron gates. I literally shake my head, dumbfounded.

Cameron and Mrs Carrington go to my mum's church.

I remember now.

They did back then, too.

I remember *them*.

I remember.

Sloopy

Mum loops her arm through mine as we sit in the front pew of Father Blean's church. The chatter quietens down and Dad welcomes the congregation. I stare up at the flat concrete ceiling, already bored. We sing a hymn, one of the ladies reads a verse, and then Dad starts his sermon ahead of the communion.

"I want to talk to you all today about family. About life. About mistakes, decisions, regret."

Mum's grip on my arm tightens. The woman next to me nods her head in slow motion, absorbing his words.

"But most importantly, I want to talk to you about recovery. About growth."

Mum's grip tightens more. I'm scared to look at her in case she is trying not to cry.

"I have made mistakes and tried so hard to hide that truth from you, so that you would think I was worthy of standing up here. I lost my way and neglected to follow the path of the Lord. I shut my family out and made them feel as if they needed to change, when really, it was me who needed to. I have been struggling and I hurt them because of that. Love is an emotion purely created through God." The congregation has fallen silent. "If someone gives you that love, that unconditional, supportive, unwavering love, cherish it. Don't disrespect it. Don't choose anything or *anyone* over it."

I turn my head to the back of the church. Green dress woman isn't here today. The older woman she normally accompanies sits on her own.

"Love truly is a gift from God. We are each other's gifts from God. To my family, I am sorry. To my wife, Loretta, I am sorry. I lost my way. I will spend the rest of my life trying to be a better man, worthy of the love you give me. To my son, I will cheer for you no matter what you decide to do. No matter who you are, is who I'll love. My family, my Loretta and my Noah- no, my Sloopy. Thank you for standing by me. To my congregation, I am not perfect and I am not going to stand up here anymore pretending that I am. I come with mistakes and poor judgement and guilt, but I have the power to be better. That is my journey. I would love to hear about yours sometime. We are all a little bit messed up, adults and children alike. Even priests. Let's lay our problems out. Let's offer them to the church, ask for help, give advice, let's be there for each other. Let's support each other's journeys. Let's do this, my dear friends. Let's all be the most perfectly imperfect congregation there ever was."

A little boy leaps from his seat and fist pumps the air. "Yeah!"

A split second later, the entire church is on their feet, applauding. Dad leaves the pulpit and stands in front of Mum. He waits, as if seeking her permission, or forgiveness, then pulls her to stand, kissing her with a passion and love reserved only for her. I've never seen two people hold each other like that before. They are one body. Tears flow down her cheeks and I cheer louder than anyone else.

Sadie

Mum's church leaves its doors open, even after everyone has disappeared inside. Like an open invitation. The muffled sounds of the sermon echo across the road, as if attempting to lure me over. I wait for a little while and then cautiously make my way into the church.

I slip into the back row next to an elderly couple. A Pomeranian sits on the lap of the lady. It looks to be about as old as she is.

The priest or pastor or whatever they are supposed to be called is not who I remember, although in truth I don't remember who it was back then anyway. I recall him being younger, like my parents age. This man must be about 70. He is tall and slender with grey patches of hair on either side of his head. I'm not sure what Mum would have thought about him.

Everyone is dressed in beautiful summer dresses and smart shirts and their hair is neat. I look down at my tracksuit pants, rolled up to my knees as if I've been jumping puddles. I tug at my baggy t-shirt and feel my flushed cheeks. I have no place being here. I don't belong.

I quietly stand to leave. Mrs Carrington is sitting a few rows in front and turns back, capturing my eye contact. I quickly look at my feet and rush out to my tree on the other side of the road, trying to convince myself that maybe she didn't see me.

But she is already half-way across the street.

Sloopy

Dad doesn't ignore Mum and I after the service like he normally does. He wants us with him when the congregation swarm on him in the car park. We stand right next to him while all the families gush over his 'revolutionary' sermon. He says he doesn't have long to mingle today: he won't be at morning tea because he has to run the first Sunday School session. I guess I get out of it today.

Mum is quiet. She smiles and nods, but she doesn't say anything. And she doesn't look at anyone. She looks past them.

A nice speech isn't enough. The emotional damage is still there. I know that. Mum knows it, too. Maybe she thinks he is just using us yet again to make himself look good. Maybe Mum doesn't even love him anymore. Maybe if he wasn't a priest, she would have asked for a divorce years ago. Maybe now that he is trying to let go of his obsession to prove how perfect we are, she will tell him that she wants one.

The clouds are greying in anticipation of the expected rain this afternoon. The sun still shines through, illuminating the fluffy edges. There is a light that shines in all of us. It's time for Mum to find hers.

It's time for Mum to be Loretta.

Sadie

Mrs Carrington sits herself down and I follow her lead. We both sit with our knees raised and our arms stretched out over them.

"I thought I saw you come into the church. I wasn't sure if I was dreaming."

I already know the answer but I ask anyway. "Did you know my parents? Did you know my mum?"

"Yes. I did."

I just nod. "Okay."

A flock of birds fly over our head, squawking amongst themselves. The clouds are greying. A summer storm must be coming.

"We didn't really know each other outside of church. I only met your dad a handful of times, when your mum used to drag him along. I loved the Christmas services, because she always bought you two, and then your sister when she was born. Sweet little Willa. Vivian called her a koala baby because she couldn't go anywhere without her clinging onto her. Willa was only four weeks old when your mum first brought her to church. She never cried."

No one has spoken Willa's name since the drunk driver took her and my whole family away.

"Okay." I suck on my bottom lip, coaxing myself out of crying.

She was five the year that it happened. Mum dressed us up in matching dresses to go to the Christmas service. Patchwork brown with white lace collars. She died wearing the same dress as me.

"Back then, the church ran a foster system. Cameron and I were the main volunteers. We fostered lots of children whose parents needed time to get back on their feet and the like. When your parents passed, we applied to foster you. We wanted, um, we tried to adopt you." Tears pool at the bottom of her eyes. She blinks and they gush out. "I wanted to give you a good life. But times were changing and the priest we had back then had just revoked the church's involvement with the foster system, unbeknownst to any of us. We tried to get it reinstated but it was already final. I think it really hit home for the priest, losing someone so young from his congregation. It was too close to home. He had a child your age. Everyone protested, insisting that we get the church involved again but the funding had already been reallocated. Rumours circulated for a while, a few people said that your uncle was a drinker and a gambler and they turned against our priest. He lost a lot of respect. People stopped coming, like altogether. The board stepped in and relocated him."

The birds quieten down. There is a still in the air. The calm before the storm.

"And then one day, like a miracle, Cameron came home and said a girl boarded his bus and he could have sworn it was Vivian's daughter. Then I heard about some trouble one of the teachers was having with a girl he described as *mad as hell with the world*. I knew it was you. God brought you to my school. He brought us together again."

"The cards were from you, weren't they?"

"And Cameron, of course. He cares about you so much."

"How did you know my uncle's address?"

"It wasn't easy. I found it in an old receipt book from the hamper drive we did one year. Your mother added him to the list of recipients because he had just lost his job again."

"Was the priest back then, was it- was it Sloopy's Dad?"

Mrs Carrington looks up at the sky. "He is not a bad man, Sadie. He did what he thought was right at the time. He believed there should be a clear distinction between the church, home and family. He will realise one day that they are all connected, if you choose for them to be. He didn't knowingly send you to an unstable home."

I want to tell her that it's not unstable. It's terrifying. "Does Sloopy know that you knew his dad?"

"No, that poor boy has enough going on with his nervous system. I'm sure he'll figure everything out in his own time."

"Mrs Carrington?"

"Yes, Sadie?"

"Can you and Cameron please drive me home? It took me hours to walk here."

"You could come home with us? Any time you want to."

"M-maybe next Sunday morning you could pick me up and I could come to church with you?"

"We would like that very much."

Sloopy

Dad heads off to run the first Kids Club of the day. I'm still shocked that he didn't make me do it. Mum lets me drive us home. The P plate fuels my confidence. I grip the wheel five times in fast succession.

I have to know.

"Why did everyone leave his old congregation, Mum?"

"It was a small church. Only about 30 people back then. We had a contract with a foster company. The church compensated the families who were involved. But your father believed it would be more economical to allocate the funding to other areas. The board supported his decision to terminate our agreement with the agency. Only a few weeks later, one of the ladies from our congregation died in a car accident, along with her husband and one of her children. Her nine-year old daughter survived. One of the couples in church realised that they couldn't step in now. Everyone blamed your father."

"Was it Sadie's parents?"

Mum's bottom lip quivers. "I believe so. I couldn't quite tell when you brought her home, but yes, I think it was."

"She never told me she had a sister. She doesn't talk about that. She really did lose her whole family."

And our lives have always been connected. Even before we knew each other. All this time.

"Mum?"

"Yes, Sloopy?"

"Are you going to leave Dad?"

Mum chuckles to herself. "Maybe, Sloopy. Maybe. Just maybe. I don't know right now. But it's nice to realise that I have that choice. To feel I have an option."

I wish Mum knew how much I really do get it.

She continues warily. "I've used up every ounce of mental energy I have to keep it all together. I wanted you to think that you had a perfect father, the same way that he wanted everyone to think that he had a perfect family. We just had a different target audience, that's all. But it's okay if things aren't perfect. Anyway, I actually think you cope better when things aren't perfect."

We both smile.

"I'll be okay no matter what you decide, Mum."

"I know. You saw me, and that helped me see myself, too. I've applied to do a floristry course."

"That's the best news ever, Mum. I can't wait to hear how much Loretta loves it."

And for the first time since I can remember, Mum switches on the radio.

I don't turn it on for her.

Sadie

The world looks different come Monday morning. I feel different. I don't know if it's called closure, or maybe just acceptance. *Hope*. Hope seems like the best word.

There's only two weeks left of term.

Recess takes forever to arrive. I rush to our spot, diving in-between Mya and Callie. I want to hear all about their weekend. "Updates, please!"

Mya and Callie's laughter is laced with warmth.

I bite into my apple. Callie chomps on her carrot sticks and Mya struggles with her oversized mouthful of barbecue chips, as obnoxious as ever. She really can't figure out the right amount of food to put in her mouth at once.

"Cane was like a stunned mullet," Callie laughs, accidentally spitting a fleck of carrot onto her tunic. She brushes it off self-consciously. "When we sat on the couch and he started to figure out what was going on, he whispered, 'please tell me we're actually going out to the movies and not staying here to watch The Boy Who Could Fly with your parents and little sister."

My usual resentment towards Callie rises up my throat when she mentions her little sister, but I swallow it down.

Mya kicks her legs about gleefully. "Yes! I wish I could have seen his face! Did he stay for the whole movie?"

"Nah, about half-way through he suddenly remembered that he had to get up early for church. Pretty sure that boy doesn't go to church! So clearly *my* first date was romantic as. What happened with you and Josh, Mya?"

"We went to the drive-in and he tried it on. I told him I wanted to take it slow and just date for a while. He got shitty and said we've already done it once so what's the big deal now? He's not interested in having a girlfriend. So, it's over, I guess. Not that it even started for him, really. But it did for me."

"He's a jerk, you deserve so much better than that." It's the first time I've ever been supportive and I want to do more. "You don't get how incredible you are. I mean you're obviously gorgeous. But you are also a good person. You are witty, confident, caring and I am very lucky to have you as a friend."

Mya stuffs another oversized handful of chips in her mouth. "Yeah. I am pretty amazing, hey?"

I made her feel better.

I think I'm really starting to get a grip on this whole friendship thing.

Sloopy

Cane's punch lands right in my gut and I collapse onto the oval, right next to the footy post.

"You little suck-up! You told her, didn't ya? Fucking snitch!"

Bile rises up my throat. I gasp for air then spit onto the grass, expecting to vomit profusely. Cane grabs me by my shirt and pulls me back up onto my feet. "I know you told. That was a piss poor move, mate."

His swing connects with my cheek and vibrates across my whole face. I stumble backwards, tripping over my own feet. I feel confused, as if he has knocked some of my brain cells right out of my body. I hunch down on the grass and cradle my head.

Josh wraps his arms around Cane as he lunges towards me again. "Just leave it, Cane! He's not worth it."

Cane is stronger than Josh and before I can regain my sense, he is physically on top of me, punching me in the ribs.

Adam tries to push Cane back by his shoulders. "Get off him, you prick!"

Cane shoves Adam hard, knocking the wind out of him. It gives me a second to free myself. I jump to my feet and raise my fists in the air, ready to fight.

He merely smirks at me. "This will be fun. I might go to hell for beating up the son of a priest."

I take a swing but Cane ducks and punches me in the stomach again. I straighten up and take another shot at him. My fist collides with the side of his head. My knuckles throb and I pray I don't have to hit him again.

Cane lunges at me but I swoop to the side, pushing him on his shoulder. He stumbles then resumes his stance with refuelled hatred and anger.

"Josh is right: you really do think you're better than the rest of us just because you go to church."

His fist plummets into my chin, slamming my teeth together.

I retaliate and punch his shoulder hard. "I'm just as fucked up as we all are actually."

We tackle each other to the ground. I try to push him off but he is much bigger and stronger than me. His fists attack my sides repeatedly like I'm his own personal punching bag.

Adam grabs Cane around the waist and tries to pull him back but Sam gets him in a headlock.

"Come on, four-eyes, you're not a fighter. Just let them do their thing."

I am on the verge of passing out from the pain. I try to kick but Cane's knees have me pinned. Everything is getting blurry.

"Cane, teachers are coming!" I hear Josh hastily announce. The punching doesn't stop. Josh tugs on the back of Cane's shirt. "Did you hear me? The teachers are coming!"

I feel Cane's body shift off of mine and I roll to my side, coughing and spluttering.

Cane and Sam rush off, Josh trailing behind them. My right hand is throbbing; the knuckles grazed red raw from the one or two hits I managed to get in. I dab at the blood on my lip. My ribs ache. My skin is prickled with dirt.

I lean all my weight against the goal post, too weak to support myself. We watch as the three of them disappear into the chaos of recess.

Adam rubs the base of his neck, no doubt sore from Sam's headlock. "Bye, Josh."

We scan our eyes around the oval.

There are no teachers coming.

Sadie

It is nearly the end of term, so there is not much to go over in my tutoring class after school on Tuesday. We do trigonometry for twenty minutes and then talk about boys for forty. Mrs Carrington hangs on my every word about my first official date with Sloopy, just like my mum would have.

I say hello to Cameron as I step onto the bus, actually saying his name. I can't think if I ever have before.

"Thanks for waiting, Cameron. Sorry I'm a bit late, again."

"You know I'll always wait for you, Sadie."

Cameron Carrington. I nod to myself, practising his name in my head. It's a good name.

Sloopy is sitting right down the back. He sees me before I see him but I feel like he always does. I like the way he watches me as I make my way down the aisle. Even though he is covered in cuts and bruises from yesterday's fight, he still gives me butterflies.

Sloopy

My bottom lip stings. "Wanna hear what I did after school today?"

"It's Tuesday, don't you just have debate?"

"Ordinarily, yep and I did today, too. Only, I quit. Right at the start. I told Mr Gates that I had my father's blessing to quit."

"For real? You actually quit?"

"I actually quit."

"And your dad actually said you could?"

"He actually said I could."

"You actually told your dad that you wanted to quit?"

"I actually told him." Granted, I thought he was asleep, but that pivotal detail kind of ruins the tough-guy image I'm trying to sell her.

"I'm heaps proud of you." She traces her thumb over the bruising on my knuckles. "Is it still sore?"

"Killing me."

Sadie pouts her lip and gently touches my face. "I want to kiss you but you look so sore! What did your parents say?"

"Mum and Dad were out when I got home yesterday. I think they're going to counselling. Mum saw me this morning and nearly cried but when I told her what the guys were doing and stuff, she was proud of me. Ordinarily she'd wait to see what Dad said first but she is starting to come back to herself, say what she wants to say, think what she wants to think, like without checking for his approval first."

"Just like you."

Yeah, just like me. "They went out to tea together, too."

"That's promising."

"Yeah, I guess. I kind of think Mum should just leave him."

"Don't say that. He's your dad. And he knew my parents, well, my mum. So, he's a good person in my book."

"We probably saw each other once or twice when we were little."

"Probably."

I bump shoulders with her, playfully, shyly.

"I love you, Sadie. I'm just going to keep telling you until you say it back one day. You should probably hurry up though. Dad will kill me when he sees the bruises and I'd like to hear you say it before I die."

Sadie

My heart jumps into my throat when I walk into the kitchen to see him sitting at the table. He is home before me. I came in through the front door: I didn't see his truck parked around the back.

He slurps what smells to be mushroom soup, in between chugs of his beer. There are nine empty bottles sitting on the sink. I stand in the kitchen doorway, frozen. My body stiffens and I clench my teeth.

"I got fired. Fucking pricks. Sent me home at lunch time."

An intense tension radiates through me; as if someone has lassoed all of my organs in a tight noose. "I'm sorry about your job."

"Yeah, I bet you are. I bet you're really sorry."

His bloodshot eyes glare at me, seeming to wish me dead. My mouth is drained of saliva and I feel compelled to swallow but I'm terrified of making a noise that could set him off. Fear holds my body hostage. I am completely alone with him. I have no one to protect me and I don't know how I can protect myself.

I hear my mum's voice, egging me to get out of here and I'm suddenly made aware of the weight of my backpack, as if it is forcefully pushed against my back.

"I better go put my bag away, it's heaps heavy today."

I take a step backward, giving my other foot the confidence to turn my body away from him and walk over to my room.

He is smirking at me when I turn around again to close my door.

"Sleep well, Sadie."

I shift every single piece of furniture I own up against the closed door. My wardrobe, desk, chest of drawers and even my bed form a barricade. I put my suitcase in front of it all, as if the birthday cards, CDs and photos of my family will lock everything in place and keep me safe.

I roll up a jumper and press it between my legs, letting the urine flow. I wrap it up in a pair of jeans and put them in my washing basket. I fall asleep hours later, only after I hear his door slam. I curl up in the corner furthest away from the door, on the floor, cuddling my knife.

Sloopy

Sadie isn't at school on Wednesday. Mrs Carrington asks me if I know why but I'm just as surprised as she is that Sadie isn't here. All I see in class is her empty desk. It's the first time this year that I don't have her Looney Tunes scrunchie in front of me to shut out all the noise in my head.

I run my fingers over my bruised knuckles, yearning for Sadie's touch. She'll be back tomorrow, I motivate myself.

But she isn't at school on Thursday either. Mya and Callie sit on their own. No empty space purposely saved for Sadie in between them. I ask if they have heard from her but they haven't. They say they don't want to ring in case her uncle answers and they unintentionally create trouble for her.

"I mean she does miss school sometimes. She was away for like two or three days last year. We asked her what was up when she got back but she got annoyed and told us to mind our own business. We were just now saying that maybe we could go around later but if her uncle is home, she would really hate us being there."

Sadie isn't at school on Friday either. Mrs Carrington said she got the office to ring her home yesterday and her uncle said she had gastro. She is going to drive past on the weekend with her husband anyway.

We've got basketball training today. She's going to miss basketball.

She would never miss basketball.

But I will.

Sadie

It's not the first time I've made myself a prisoner in my room. Last year he got a speeding fine and started smashing up the house. I hid in my wardrobe, afraid to come out. I would have stayed in there forever but my period came on the second day. I had pads in my room but nothing to clean myself with. By the fourth day, dry blood was stuck to my skin and it felt disgusting.

This is my third day in my room. If it was winter, I could last longer but the lingering summer heat is against me. My school drink bottle ran out yesterday. I am hungry. I am thirsty. I am so scared.

My watch tells me it's 11.16am. It will take me ages to shift everything away from the door, especially without making a noise.

I make just enough room to be able to pry my door ajar, and peep out into the seemingly abandoned house. A ray of sunshine breaks through the kitchen blind, capturing the dust particles floating in the air. They hover to his room.

There is no light underneath his door. His curtains must be closed. I can't hear a tv or bottles clinking. He never sits in the lounge. If he is not in his room, he would be in the kitchen but my room is right opposite so I know he isn't there.

I close my eyes and say a silent prayer. I tiptoe down to the bathroom and use the toilet with the door open, gripping my knife as it rests on my knees. I have been busting for days and my tummy squirms as I finally relieve myself. I can't control the volume of the flush. I ready myself with the knife held out in front of me until it quietens. I let the tap drip onto my soapy hands and then slide down to the kitchen to grab a few slices of bread.

I sense his presence before I actually see him.

He is here. He is watching me.

I take out four slices of bread, close the bag and inhale deeply, preparing myself. Or maybe even subconsciously sucking in as much air as I can, for fear that it could very well be my last opportunity. I turn to face him, bracing myself against the cupboard. He stands in the doorway, blocking the exit to the hallway. And to my room.

His feet shuffle on the spot, like a baseball player readying himself to run from second base. The taste of blood in my mouth makes me realise I've been biting my tongue.

He looks around the room, unnaturally pensive. "She could do with a bit of a paint job. I might get some paint out the shed while I've got some time between jobs."

I'm a mere shell. I can't speak or move. His abnormal attempt at conversation heightens all my senses. I feel like I'm being hunted, lured into a false sense of safety.

He looks at the bread in my hands. "I'm getting groceries later; you can finish the loaf."

I nod once, raising the four slices of bread up to my heart. "This will do me, I'm not that hungry."

He walks past me, deliberately knocking into me. The knife falls from my grip and my breath falters. He takes a family sized packet of Chicken Twisties out of the cupboard, rips them open and shoves a fistful in his mouth.

"Fucking teenagers, trying to talk to you is like trying to get blood from a stone."

I am paralysed with fear, my knife now out of reach. "I'll-I'll hop out of your way. I was just grabbing some food."

He slams the Twisties onto the table; his fist colliding with the surface so forcefully that the legs bounce off the ground. "So much better than me, aren't ya? Self-righteous little bitch. Just like she was. Always so much better than me."

He waits for my response, egging me with his eyes to fight with him.

My voice is shaky. "I'll go back to my room now."

He motions to the knife on the floor. "Pretty fucking sharp knife just to spread vegemite."

I take a step backwards, too afraid, too smart to turn my back on him. He lunges at me, grabbing me around my neck and pinning up against the fridge. My head aches instantly from the impact. His hands squeeze harder. Tears stream from my eyes. I clutch onto his hairy arms and claw at his dry skin, pathetically trying to loosen his hold.

"You're hurting me," I whimper.

In this moment of sheer desperation and defeat, I realise: I have never told him that. I have never said these words. You're hurting me. You. Hurt. Me. Have I told *anyone*? I want to shout it to the universe. I. Am. Hurting. Some-one, please help me. It shouldn't have been so hard to ask for help. I am asking now.

His grip tightens and he grinds his teeth, as if trying to summon more power within himself. He is hurting me. I am saying it, Mrs Carrington. I am saying it, Cameron. I am saying it, Sloopy. I am saying it, Mya and Callie. He hurts me. I am asking for help. I'm asking. I need help. Help me, please help me. You have been listening for years, unsure if I needed to ask. I'm asking now. I'm saying it now.

I scratch helplessly at his hands as they purposefully attempt to squeeze the life out of me.

I choke on my own voice, on my own words. "You're hurting me, Uncle Peter."

Sloopy

It is the slowest day ever. It is 11.42am, only two minutes since I last checked the clock. I've got double maths straight after lunch, on a Friday. I have the worst timetable in the world.

I told Adam not to wait for me for basketball after school. The second the bell goes, I'm out of here.

Mrs Carrington said she will drive me.

Sadie

He raises his arm, hoisting me up under my chin. My toenails scratch at the floor, desperately trying to get my feet back down. He grits his teeth and burns his gaze into my neck, relishing the sight of his hands finally getting rid of me. I can't get the air down into my lungs. I can feel it, blocked at the base of his hands: piling up at the top of my throat, spilling into my cheeks. I cry uncontrollably. I always knew he would kill me.

His hold on me relaxes abruptly. I cough violently, clasping my hands around my throat.

He raises his fist, gearing up to deliver it onto me. "Tears don't work on me."

But then his expression changes.

He takes a step back, and then another.

His eyebrows tense.

Evident pain takes over his face.

He frantically clutches at his chest.

I freeze.

If I blink or move in the slightest way, I may realise I am dreaming. His hands will still be on me, not grasping at his own body in desperation. *Don't move, Sadie. Don't move.*

He crashes onto the side of the sink, trying to grab onto it before collapsing to the floor. Fear saturates his eyes. They burn into me, furious that I am privy to his pain. Even now, when his heart is under attack, he is still overcome with resentment for my mere presence.

"C-call an ambulance, you bitch," he splutters. "Fuck."

I nod, sliding over to the phone on the adjacent wall. I keep my eyes fixated on him and pick up the receiver. I rest it on my shoulder and tilt my head to hold it in place. My fingers slowly press the 0 three times. I wonder if Sloopy would feel compelled to press it two more times.

"Yes, operator, I need an ambulance." I pause for authenticity, imagining someone actually speaking at the other end so the timing sounds right. But of course, my finger is holding down the dial-tone button. "Please hurry."

I give my address, hang up the receiver and sit down at the table. "They're on their way."

He doesn't answer me. I look at the clock hanging above the kitchen window. It is 11.58am. The ticks of the second hand are louder than usual. I sit perfectly still, watching him. He doesn't move and neither do I.

At 12.45pm I remind him, "They're on their way." I absorb the sound of the clock ticking. Minutes. Hours.

At 2.58pm I have yet to see his chest rise. "They're on their way."

The silence evokes a physical warmth within me, as if the universe gives me a reassuring embrace. It bestows me with a sense of safety. I stand carefully. When he still doesn't move, I tiptoe to the cupboard, take out a glass and pour myself a red cordial.

I sit down on the kitchen floor, right next to him. My drink is too strong and the flavour makes me squint, but I skull it anyway. *Cheers, Uncle Peter.*

His chin is squashed against his neck, as if he was trying to see what was happening to him. I study his face. I count his wrinkles. His hair hasn't been brushed in days. His skin is grey. I wonder how old he is. He looks older than he should.

I summon enough bravery to hold my hand under his nose. I can't feel any air.

I wash my glass and then pick up the phone to dial triple 0. I let it ring this time.

"Triple 0, what is your emergency?" the man on the other end answers.

"I think my uncle is having a heart attack."

Sloopy

Mrs Carrington speeds away from school like she's the getaway driver in a bank robbery. She doesn't even slow down when she goes around corners and she seems to think red lights are just a casual suggestion.

"Do you want to get there or not?" she laughs as I hold onto my seatbelt just to reassure myself that I'm theoretically safe. "It's funny, my husband drives for a living. Maybe we should swap jobs?"

"Is your husband a courier or something?"

"Bus driver, actually. You might know him. He gets a lot of school kids on some of his trips."

I jerk my head. "Oh my god. Are you married to that Cameron man?"

"Yes, isn't life funny the way it connects us all."

"I didn't picture you with someone like him. He's a bit grumpy."

"He's a teddy bear, really. He cares a lot about people."

"Yeah, I noticed he always looks out for Sadie."

"We went to church with her mum."

I suddenly feel like a child. Just when I think I'm starting to figure things out, I realise how very little I actually know about anything.

"Does Sadie know that?"

"Yes. Cameron and I had plans to adopt her once upon a time. I'm sure you've heard that story by now."

I touch the graze on my chin. For the first time in my life, I am covered in bruises, cuts and scabs that I didn't inflict on myself. "I guess so."

Sadie

I bounce my basketball along the footpath. I rushed out the door, I didn't put any socks on. My sneakers rub against my heels but I don't mind.

I wonder if the ambulance will be there yet. Will they send the police, too? What if they can revive him?

I concentrate on the sound of the basketball bouncing. It calms me. My mum used to love watching my games. She screamed so loud every time I scored. At 8 years of age, I was hardly any good. I basically just ran back and forth the whole game. But any time I got my hands on the ball, all I could hear was Mum cheering. Even if I just got to dribble it for a few seconds, Mum thought it was the best thing ever.

I lost myself when I lost her.

Basketball brings me back. To her, to myself.

It is 3.30pm.

I walk slowly, up and down all the side streets. I can't get there too early.

Basketball training will still be on.

Sloopy

Mrs Carrington's voice shakes as we pull up a few houses down from Sadie's. "Oh my god." There is an ambulance parked out the front and two police cars. "Oh my god."

The hairs on my arms prickle. I jump out of the car before Mrs Carrington even turns off the engine. I run towards Sadie's house but a policewoman stops me as I get to the gate.

"Let me through! My girlfriend is in there!"

She holds me back. "Sir, you can't go in there. Please kindly return to your vehicle."

Mrs Carrington rushes up behind me. "What's happening? Please tell us what's happening?"

The desperation in her voice is heartbreaking.

"I'm going to have to ask you to return to your vehicle at this point in time," the officer repeats.

I scream from my lungs; louder than I knew I was capable. "Where's Sadie?"

Mrs Carrington pulls my arm back, and that's when I see it. Two men navigate a stretcher out through the front door of Sadie's house. A white sheet covers the whole body; strapped in place across the legs and torso.

My heart sinks. Tears pool at the bottom of my eyes. They sting and I am forced to blink, pushing the water down onto my cheeks. Mrs Carrington's fingers dig into my arms. She is using me to brace herself. To stop herself from completely collapsing.

I close my eyes. I breathe. I swallow the vomit that is rising up my throat. When I open my eyes, the stretcher is closer.

The officer is more forceful this time. "Please, return to your vehicle immediately or move to the street."

Mrs Carrington pulls me back. We wait by the fence, just back from the ambulance. We don't speak. Oh my god. This can't be happening.

Sadie

I stare at my reflection in the corner shop window. I see all the little kids come here on Sundays with their dads. They go in empty-handed and come out with candy necklaces and mini white paper bags filled with 20 cents worth of mixed lollies.

My neck is red. His grip is etched onto my skin. I can still feel his hands on me. What if they can revive him?

Am I evil for praying that they won't be able to? Am I psychotic because I am not sorry? Not one little bit. I would watch him collapse to the ground, clutching at his heart, over and over again if I could.

If Sloopy and I ever have a son one day, I'm going to name him George.

Sloopy

The body is big; the stomach is convex. It can't be her.

They load the stretcher into the back of the ambulance.

"C-can you just tell us if that is a man, or is it, is it a girl?"

The ambulance crew take pity. "It's a man, kid. Maybe about 40 or 50. It's hard to tell."

They pull the doors closed and drive off, without the siren. I thought they always put the siren on. If he's dead, I guess there's no real urgency to get him anywhere.

I look back to Sadie's house.

Where are you?

Sadie

I get to school just as basketball training is finishing up. I sit on the far side of the oval, concealed from view by the biggest tree. I wait until I see the last person leave and then walk over to the court.

Sitting on our bench, I roll my basketball in my lap, look up to the sky and laugh, kind of hysterically. Or maybe I cry. I can't tell the difference right now.

I am here.

I am finally safe.

The afternoon breeze caresses my face and I know, I know, I am safe.

I throw my basketball high up to the sky, catapulting it right above me.

I admire it soar.

I am free.

He is gone.

He really is gone.

Sloopy

Mrs Carrington is flustered. We sit in Sadie's kitchen; at the same table I guess she eats her dinner at every night. The police are asking us a whole bunch of questions that we don't know the answers to. No one knows where Sadie is. Or if she is okay.

The house is dim for the time of day but somehow it doesn't feel atypical, like this is just the way it normally is inside these walls. I can't put my finger on why, put there's an underlying sadness, like just attached to everything here. Maybe it's just so different to my own home.

The door of the room across from the kitchen is ajar. I can see a pile of furniture pushed to the side. He really was a hoarder.

The police must have called my parents. Mum and Dad come rushing into the kitchen, together, frantic. Dad talks to the police. Mum hugs Mrs Carrington. There is history there, I can tell.

Cameron enters shortly after, tipping his cap to Mum. He stands by his wife. He doesn't look at Dad.

Everyone talks all at once. A police officer motions with his hands for silence.

"Look, our main intention at the moment is to find Sadie and make sure she is okay. We have a patrol car out there looking for her now. Does anybody know where she might go?"

They all look to me. I suddenly wish I wasn't the only one sitting. "No." I press my fingers down onto the chipped laminate surface of the table. Five times.

Mrs Carrington and Cameron decide to drive around the neighbourhood to look for her. The police start writing things down on a clipboard.

Dad pulls up the chair adjacent to me at the table. He cups his hand over the bruising on my cheek. I'm overwhelmed with a sense of trust. I don't recall ever feeling this way in his presence.

"I do, Dad," I faintly whisper, "I know where Sadie would go."

"I'm going to take Noah home," Dad announces to the room before whispering to me; "I'll drive you to her, Sloopy."

Sadie

Every shot goes in. I can't miss. I dribble from one end of the court to the other, cathartic tears flowing. I haven't cried for my family in so long. I wasn't allowed to. I was thrust into survival mode. I cry for them now. I cry for my parents. I cry for my sister.

I navigate the ball between my legs. I spin it on one finger. I try to, anyway. Basketball is my connection to Mum. It is my connection to who I was before I lost everything.

When I was a daughter.

And a sister.

I let my tears flow freely. I don't even wipe them, no matter how saturated my cheeks get.

It's okay to cry. I'm allowed to cry.

The sky is dimming but I feel brighter than ever.

Sloopy

I see her before she sees me, but I always do.

Her hair is a bit matted, as if she hasn't brushed it in a few days. Her pony tail is trying to hang on but half the hairs have escaped. Her laces are untied. Her oversized t-shirt slips off one shoulder.

She is such a mess.

And so beautiful.

I am apprehensive as I sit down on our bench. I don't know what has happened. I don't know what she knows. Is she aware that her uncle has died? I don't know what to say or what to do. I clear my throat and tug at the collar of my school shirt five times.

Sadie abandons her basketball, letting it fall onto the court. She comes over and sits down next to me. Neither one of us seem to know what to say.

She looks straight ahead. I look straight down. Her feet are pointed together at the toes, her hands rest in her lap. Clenched fists. Always ready to fight with the world.

There is a gap between us and it feels wrong. I wiggle over so our hips touch. She grabs my arm, pretty aggressively, and dumps it in her lap. Just like Sadie.

"That's better," she affirms, smiling to herself.

Her cheeks are flushed and her eyes are puffy. She doesn't try to hide her face: she has been crying and she is okay with me knowing it.

It is warm but the subtle afternoon breeze takes the edge off the heat. My shaggy hair blows off my face, reminding me that the seasons are about to change, along with everything else in life now, it seems.

I hold her hand tighter, feeling overwhelmed by it all. I am so aware of my surroundings. This bench is where I first summoned the nerve to talk to the girl with the Looney Tunes scrunchies who hated me and everyone else who tried to care about her. Next week is the end of term already.

Everything is different.

We are different.

I bite the insides of my cheeks. "Were you there? I mean, do you know?"

"Yep. He's dead."

"Yeah."

"Do you want to ask me if I'm okay?"

"No, I get the feeling that you are. I hope one day you'll help me understand why."

Sadie's eyes follow her basketball, freely roaming across the court. We regard it affectionately, nostalgically, like a loved-up couple admiring the sun slip below the horizon in one of those movies Mum loves so much. Except we're on our bench, hands holding: so much more perfect for us than some cliched sunset.

Sadie rests her head on my shoulder and I lean my cheek against her outrageously messy hair.

"Sloopy?"

"Yeah?

"You want to hear something really crazy? I'm going to church next week."

I take in her words, contemplating my own. My free hand grips the edge of the bench and I press my fingers in five times.

"You want to hear something really crazy, too? I might test my luck and skip it next week. I'm not so sure I believe in all that stuff."

"My dad didn't either," she says quietly, but possibly just to herself.

The warm breeze gently propels Sadie's basketball towards us. It comes to a gentle stop, resting against our feet.

THE END